# TRAP GOD

# Troublesome

**Lock Down Publications and Ca$h Presents**

# Trap God

**A Novel by *Troublesome***

Troublesome

**Lock Down Publications**
P.O. Box 870494
Mesquite, Tx 75187

**Visit our website @**
www.lockdownpublications.com

Copyright 2019 Troublesome
Trap God

First Edition October 2019
Printed in the United States of America

**Lock Down Publications**
**Like our page on Facebook: Lock Down Publications @**
www.facebook.com/lockdownpublications.ldp
Cover design and layout by: **Dynasty Cover Me**
Book interior design by: **Shawn Walker**
Edited by: **Jill Alicea**

## Stay Connected with Us!

Text **LOCKDOWN** to 22828 to stay up-to-date with
new releases, sneak peaks, contests and more…
Thank you.

## Submission Guideline.

Submit the first three chapters of your completed manuscript to ldpsubmissions@gmail.com, subject line: Your book's title. The manuscript must be in a .doc file and sent as an attachment. Document should be in Times New Roman, double spaced and in size 12 font. Also, provide your synopsis and full contact information. If sending multiple submissions, they must each be in a separate email.

Have a story but no way to send it electronically? You can still submit to LDP/Ca$h Presents. Send in the first three chapters, written or typed, of your completed manuscript to:

LDP: Submissions Dept
Po Box 870494
Mesquite, Tx 75187

*DO NOT send original manuscript. Must be a duplicate.*

Provide your synopsis and a cover letter containing your full contact information.

Thanks for considering LDP and Ca$h Presents.

## DEDICATIONS

Dedicated to big bro, Seneca "A.B" Miller. I miss you. Sunrise: October 14th, 1984 - Sunset: November 11th, 2010.

# Troublesome

# Prologue

Raising the bottle of Ace of Spades to his mouth, Diamond took a drink of the champagne. Dressed in a cream-colored Armani vest suit that accentuated his frame with Mauri Gators and bedecked with enough diamonds to stock a jeweler's counter, he was the center of attention at the strip club, Red Velvet. It was hard to compete with a presence so large, not to mention one that was actually the owner of the club.

Tall and trim, with the posture of a ball player and the swagger of a big timer, Diamond could walk into a room and have it grow quiet. His walnut-shaded skin matched the hue of his eyes. He rocked a crisp hi-top fade, and a full, thick beard formed a pout that barely turned up at the corners, giving the impression that, even at his most serious, he was about to break into a grin.

Diamond was accompanied by two of his cohorts, his childhood homeboy named Gangsta, and his confidante named Toni. Seated in the VIP lounge, the table which Diamond n'em occupied was dressed with numerous stacks of cash and top-shelf bottles. Several strippers crowded them, and while Gangsta and Toni enjoyed their company, Diamond didn't show any of the strippers any interest. He peeped that most strippers were only sack-chasers, although Diamond did possess eyes for one stripper in particular named Surprise.

Surprise was tearing up the stage, wearing French-cut red see-through lingerie with a sexy-ass pair of Versace mirror stilettos. She performed to Cardi B's "Money", and ballers showered her with bills. Positioned on all fours, she made her phat ass clap while looking back at it.

*Damn, shorty knows how to do it to a nigga*, Diamond thought as his dick stiffened. All the while, he and Surprise eye-fucked one another during her performance. He bit down on his bottom lip and unobtrusively grabbed his crotch, and she sensually licked her full, cherry red lips. They both held lust in their eyes.

"Real shit, Diamond, this what we need," Gangsta was saying, breaking Diamond's concentration. He spoke just loud enough so that Diamond could hear him over the blaring music from club's subwoofers. "You should at least hear what the Rasta's have to offer. May even be a better offer than the Wop's."

"Maybe. But my connect wit' Balistrieri is all I need. I'll tell you what though, Gangsta. I won't guarantee that I'll accept, but I will hear out the Jamaicans' offer," Diamond told him.

"And you'll like what you hear," Gangsta added surely.

Toni poured Moet from its bottle into a few of the strippers' mouths. "Too bad the nigga Chase ain't here to pour up wit' us," she said. She turned the bottle up to her lips and then used her backhand to wipe away the champagne trekking down her chin.

"Nigga fiancée won't allow his ass to stay out late," Gangsta cracked, and the trio shared a laugh at the expense of Chase, who was their close homeboy.

Peeping at the Breitling on his arm, Diamond saw it was nearly two in the morning, and he figured he should head home himself. "I'm finna bounce. I'll catch y'all later," he said and then stood.

"Then we bouncin', too." Toni stood also.

"That ain't necessary. Y'all stay and enjoy yo'selves."

"Really, Diamond, we've enjoyed ourselves enough for one night."

"Speak for yo'self," Gangsta muttered. Apparently, he wasn't quite ready to leave. He enjoyed the company of the strippers, especially the one named Jade. Toni gave him a nudge. "A'ight, damn. But I'm takin' a bottle and one of these bitches wit' me."

Diamond waved over the head of his security, who went by Sarge. "I'm bouncin' for the night. Make sure you stay to close up the place," Diamond told him.

"Got it," Sarge assured him.

Out front of Red Velvet, where the trio had their whips parked curbside, Diamond gave his comrades some dap before parting ways. He headed towards his matte black Bentley coupe sitting on chrome 23-inch Rucci rims and egg-white custom seats.

Suddenly, a grey Caravan pulled to a screeching halt in the center of the street before the club. The van's side door quickly slid back open, and two hitters hopped out, gripping assault rifles with their aims on Diamond and the others.

Prrraaat! Prrraaat! Prrraaat!

Rrraaa! Rrraaa!

Once automatic gunfire erupted, Diamond instantly took cover beside a random vehicle. Toni dove onto the pavement; and Gangsta dropped the bottle of Ace, where it shattered on the ground, then he snatched up the stripper he had with him and used her as a human shield. It just so happened that Jade had declined Gangsta's offer to come along, or she would have been the one used as a shield.

Boom! Boom! Boom!

Boc! Boc! Boc! Boc! Boc!

Blam! Blam!

The trio drew their heaters and returned fire on the hitters. Patrons awaiting to be admitted into Red Velvet immediately broke out into a frenzy, all scattering every which way in hopes of avoiding stray bullets. Unfortunately for some bystanders, they were cut down by bullets that peppered the crowd - including the stripper Gangsta used to shield himself.

Urrrkkk!

Tires screeched as the Caravan peeled off. One of the hitters that was left behind was maimed from several bullets and sprawled in the street. With his diamond-encrusted .45-caliber in hand, Diamond stood over the helpless man, aimed on his dome, and stated, "I'm in power!"

Boom!

\*\*\*

"Bruh, we fucked up. The muthafuckas ain't even get a scratch on 'em!"

"Tell me somethin' I don't know," Banks retorted. He was growing more heated with each word he was hearing from the other end of the line. While sitting parked in his silver Infiniti G35 down the street from Red Velvet, he witnessed the failed hit go down.

"Can't believe y'all niggas couldn't do one simple fuckin' thing." Banks's hitter, Sticks was on the other end, afraid to say even a word.

"Banks, the niggas - "

"I'ont even wanna hear that bullshit!" Banks shouted into his iPhone and then heatedly slammed his clenched fist down onto the steering wheel. "Jus' fall the fuck back 'til I get at you." Click. He ended the call without warning as he pulled off down the street.

Lucifer, who was Banks's right-hand man, was seated on the passenger side. "Don't trip. I'ma burn them niggas," he swore.

Banks had plotted what was supposed to be a simple hit on Diamond, which turned out to be an epic fail. And now he needed to come up with another plot, and fast. Because he knew that eventually Diamond would retaliate.

***

Hearing the chime of his iPhone awoke Chase. He'd been in a sex-induced slumber after digging out his fiancée, Ashley. The digital clock glowing next to his phone on the nightstand at his bedside told him it was nearly three in the morning.

*Fuck textin' me at this time in the mornin'?* Chase mused. He grabbed the phone then checked its display and noticed the text message was from Gangsta. He touched the face of his iPhone, opening the message.

Gangsta// 2:41 a.m.
Get to the Theater ASAP.

Chase threw back the covers and hurried out of bed. He began gathering his clothes off the floor that Ashley had helped him out of earlier. Since it was dark in the room, he made more noise than he wanted to.

Stirring awake, Ashley clicked on the lamp positioned on the nightstand at her bedside. "Chase, where in the hell are you goin' so early in the damn mornin'?" she wanted to know, now sitting up in bed.

He stepped into his True Religion jeans and said, "It's Gangsta. He needs me."

"Gangsta can take care of himself. It's me and the twins who need you here at home with us," Ashley protested.

"Ash, I'ont have time for this shit right now." Jumping up and down on one foot, he pulled on his Air Jordan sneaker.

"But yo' ass always have time for the damn streets." Attitude. Chase was aware that Ashley didn't like that he lived the street life.

"Listen, bae." Chase stepped over to Ashley, "I'll be back for you and the twins as soon as I can." He went in to give her a peck on the lips and she turned her head, offering him her cheek instead.

Knowing that Ashley was upset, Chase had it in mind to make things right with her later. He collected his iPhone, keys, and Glock before heading out the door. Hopping into his white Audi A8, he stabbed off.

\*\*\*

The house was a handsome, traditional one that sat in the middle of the block. It was in a residential part of one of Milwaukee's wealthiest neighborhoods, and it was dubbed "the Theater," because there was a small theater room in the home. And it was a safe house for Diamond and his crew.

When Chase came rushing into the Theater, he found the others seated at the long, polished oak wood table. "Hell we gon' do 'bout this shit?" he wanted to know, apparently heated.

"Jus' chill, Chase," Toni suggested.

"Niggas try to off y'all and you expect for me to chill? Miss me wit' that shit, Toni," he retorted.

"All I'm sayin' is you bein' heated ain't gon' help us figure shit out," she told him firmly.

Gangsta piped in, "Ain't shit to figure out. We already know Banks sent those shooters. I say we move on that nigga tonight."

"Real shit," Chase echoed.

"We don't make a move 'til I say so," Diamond spoke up, making his position clear.

"Then what's yo' call? Bossman," Gangsta said, seething.

Diamond leaned back in his chair, which was positioned at the head of the table. "We wait for the right opportunity. 'Til then, let's focus on the operation."

Diamond was at the top of the drug empire. He hadn't been chosen as the head nigga in charge. He had the connect. But he had blossomed into the head position. Diamond was smart about his business, and a very respectable nigga. He was a real live gangsta, to boot.

Coming from poverty to power, Diamond gave his cohorts an opportunity extremely hard to come by. He was loyal like that. In the beginning, it had only been him and three others; his second in command, Gangsta, and Diamond's top-level managers, Toni and Chase. Diamond played the role of the magnanimous leader.

Eventually the crew grew to an abundance of men whom Diamond employed and indulged. He took care of them, lifted them up, behaved as their friend and benefactor. He felt protected by a crew that he believed would never turn on him. Perhaps he was more comfortable with the arrangement than he should have been. It was easy for him to forget that there were some things out of his control. And within their crew, consequences were hectic. To betray would earn one murder...

# Chapter 1

"I'm tellin' you, dawg, that mu'fucka tailed me."

Diamond and Gangsta observed the suspect navy blue Jaguar XJ from inside the Theater through slits in the window blinds. The Jag was parked near the corner, and due to its tinted windows, they couldn't see whom was inside, although Diamond was almost sure that whomever it was had been sent by Banks.

"Sure you ain't jus' on some 'noid shit?" Gangsta questioned, knowing how Diamond had been on edge since the futile hit at Red Velvet a few days back.

Diamond glanced at him, annoyed. "Nigga, course I'm sure. Been tailin' me ever since I left the damn club."

"And you thought it was a good idea to lead 'em here? If it is some of Banks's hitters, then now they know where to find us," Gangsta expounded.

"Then..." Diamond pulled his .45 from the small of his back. "Let's murk they ass."

Diamond headed for the back door, and Gangsta grabbed his Draco .50 off the mini-bar as he followed closely behind.

Gangsta's slick bald head, lazy eye that drifted off to the periphery, and rotund belly belied a lean cunning. Where niggas such as Diamond would kill to protect themselves, Gangsta went out of his way to murder. He thought it was the best way to get his point across.

In the dark night, the two slunk towards the Jag, and once they were up close, they gripped their guns, aimed and ready. Diamond held his fire while Gangsta squeezed the trig...

"Fall back!" Diamond demanded, noticing his girl, Tywanna, was in the passenger seat. Since the Jag belonged to Jade, he didn't recognize it. "It's only Ty."

Tywanna and Jade were both sitting in the Jag shook. One second they were tailing Diamond, and then the next second they had guns all in their faces. Another second too late, they would have been smoked.

Diamond stuffed his burner into the back waistband of his Balmain jeans. "Ty." He snatched open the passenger door. "Fuck you on tailin' a nigga and shit? You outta yo' damn mind? Coulda fucked around and got yo'self smoked like that." He was heated as hell at Tywanna's ass.

"Diamond, my-my bad!" she cried.

"Ain't as bad as it was finna be," Gangsta added.

Diamond gave him a stiff look. "I got this, a'ight?"

As Gangsta stepped away, he looked to Jade then placed a hand up to his ear as a make-believe phone and mouthed, "I'll call you later."

"Fuck's yo' problem, Tywanna, huh?" Diamond demanded to know.

"Uh, I-I, um..." Tywanna couldn't even explain her harebrained actions.

"Say somethin', dammit!" he pressed heatedly.

Tears began to form in the wells of Tywanna's eyes, but Diamond wasn't about to play all sympathetic toward her ass right now. She had some explaining to do. "Alright, damn," Tywanna gave way. "Jade had told me she heard some stripper bitch at the club talkin' about you, and - "

"Since when you did you start goin' off of what a punk hoe has to tell you 'bout a nigga/" he snapped, cutting her off.

Jade jumped offensively from the driver seat. "Nigga, uh uh, don't come for me." She snaked her neck.

"Punk-ass hoe, shut the fuck up. Maybe if you weren't so damn busy shakin' yo' funky ass at the club then you'd have yo' own nigga to stalk," Diamond retorted.

"Whatever, Diamond," was all Jade could say.

He returned his attention to Tywanna. "Check it: if you ain't confident in what we have, then don't be wit' me. A nigga out in these streets dodgin' cases and bullets so we can live good, and all that's on yo' damn mind is whether or not I'm fuckin' some other bitch. Ty, either you gon' let yo' homegirl tear us apart, or you gon' put yo' nigga first. The choice is yours."

"I'll never put you second to none, Diamond, and you know that."

"A'ight then. Bet' not pull no shit like this again," Diamond checked her. "Now take yo' ass to the crib, and be ready to get fucked whenever I get there," he added before swaggering away, giving her punk-ass homegirl more reason to be envious of her.

As Diamond approached the Bentley, Gangsta sat on its hood, shaking his head. "What, nigga?" Diamond wanted to know as he pulled open the driver door.

"Can't even handle yo' own damn girl. Ain't that some shit," Gangsta scoffed.

"Nigga, ain't shit I can't handle," he replied. "And get the fuck off of my whip 'fore you scratch the paint." Diamond stepped inside the whip and Gangsta followed. Diamond pushed the start button, the engine purred to life, and then he zipped down the street.

As they rode to their destination, the egg-white interior of the Bentley was filled with the tune of Gucci Mane's *Decapitated*. They were on their way to meet with the Jamaican Mega Don, Yul. Diamond didn't see a need for the meeting, but on the other hand, Gangsta saw it as an opportunity to make a power move.

The Bentley slid along the curb and parked before an abandoned-looking warehouse. The Rasta's had the warehouse heavily secured. There were men armed with assault-rifles standing on guard all around the building, and some on top of it. Security cameras were installed all over, from the inside out. The warehouse was impenetrable.

Diamond looked to Gangsta and told him, "I'll do the talkin'. You jus' be on point."

Gangsta nodded, though it didn't mean he actually agreed.

The two tucked their hardware on their person before exiting the whip, and then proceeded towards the building.

"Halt!" the dread-head ordered, whose name was Rasheym. He leveled his Israeli Uzi on them.

"Take it easy wit' that thing, rude boy," Gangsta warned. "We're here to see Yul."

A second Rasta named Siah spoke into his walkie-talkie. "De Yanks are here." His island accent was heavy. A second later the walkie-talkie crackled to life and a voice on the other end gave instructions to send them in. Before allowing them access, Rasheym went to frisk them, but Diamond refused to comply because he wasn't with having to be disarmed.

"Get on that damn radio and tell yo' boss that if there's an issue wit' us comin' in strapped, maybe we shouldn't come in at all," Diamond ordered. Siah delivered Diamond's message, and a moment later he received a reply to just leave Diamond and Gangsta be and let them in.

With Siah in lead and Rasheym in tow, Diamond and Gangsta were escorted inside and through a dimly-lit area of the warehouse. From the looks of the place, it was once a meat packaging company. Upon entering the back room, they came upon Yul, who was smoking a huge, stuffed blunt while seated on top of a large safe.

Yul didn't favor the typical Jamaican. He was moderately built, light-skinned with two different colored eyes, one green and the other blue, and wore his hair cut into a fro-hawk. Growing up in his native Kingston, Jamaica, he became an orphan at the age of thirteen when his parents were killed execution-style behind an unpaid drug debt. Due to hard times he endured, he relocated to the States, landing in Milwaukee. Nearly twenty years back, Yul began putting in work as a teenager, joining the Shower Posse - they earned their moniker because they showered bullets on their enemies. He climbed the ranks within the Posse. Then, when the head crime boss was convicted, Yul became the Mega Don.

"'Pologies if me Rasta's offended you outside. Dey only followin' me orders," Yul said, his island accent thick. He said something to Rasheym and Siah in Patois, and both stood off to the side. "Care for some ganja?" Yul held out the blunt of white ice.

"Keep it," Diamond declined.

"Actually, I'ont mind." Gangsta accepted the blunt and took a pull of it, not giving a fuck about the look Diamond shot him.

Yul hopped down from the safe. "Me respek a mon dat goes afta whut he wants," he said to Gangsta.

"If I want somethin', then I'll damn sure get it," Gangsta replied matter-of-factly.

"An' me don't doubt it, mon."

"I came here to talk business, nothin' else," Diamond cut in.

"Den let we discuss bidness," Yul responded.

"Let's."

"Me know 'bout who you are, Diamond, an' all ah de China white you are movin' through de streets."

"What's it to you?"

"Well, wit' me as you connect, not only will you be able to make mo' money dan you can even count, but you can also rule de streets. Me will provide you wit' a small army at you disposal, an' anyting else you shall need."

"And what's the catch?" Diamond inquired.

"De only ting me expect in turn is dat you purchase product from only me. An', as a consolation, me will lower de price ten grand less on each key dan you are currently payin'."

Yul knew that if one is offered the world then it is nearly impossible for a soul to refuse. But Diamond understood that a man is to profit nothing if he gain the whole world only to lose his own soul.

"Take it however you will, Yul, but I'ont need yo' connect." Diamond's soul wasn't up for sale. "And if you know about me, then you should know I already have money, an army, and the streets. That said, yo' offer ain't worth shit to me."

Yul didn't take the refusal unseemly, although he didn't approve of it. "Even a mon like you needs someone to watch you back at times," he stated indignant.

"Well, let me know when that time comes," he responded evenly. "Gangsta, let's bounce." Diamond turned for the exit.

Gangsta stood there discordant. He'd rarely seen Diamond so assertive. Shit, Diamond was his nigga and all, but to keep it a hunnid, he couldn't say whether it was the riches or what, but he felt Diamond was losing his edge. Fortunately, Diamond had him around to back him up.

"Didn't mean to waste yo' time, Yul. You know, bein' that time's money and all. Figured Diamond woulda been smart enough to accept yo' offer," Gangsta commented distastefully.

"No prollem, li'l one. Besides, me already have whole heap ah money. In fact..." He turned to the safe and placed his green eye to its retinal scan in order to disengage the lock. His was the only eye able to do so. Reaching inside the safe, Yul came out with a stack of hundreds and then tossed it to Gangsta. "Dere's mo' where dat comes from, yah dunno."

Gangsta stuffed the stack inside the pocket of his Robin jeans as he caught up with Diamond. The two made their way out of the warehouse.

Gripping his choppa, Rasheym approached Yul. "Me'll mummify de botty mon right now, eh?"

"Dat won't be necessary. At least not at de moment."

\*\*\*

Tywanna entered hers and Diamond's condominium and locked the door behind herself. As she stepped inside, she set her Michael Kors purse, her keys, and her iPhone on the end-table. She was still feeling harebrained about the entire thing with Diamond earlier. It was even worse that he was heated at her, and he had a right to be.

Noticing there was an unread text-message on her iPhone, she grabbed the phone, touched its screen, and read it. While reading the message, Tywanna cut on the walk-in shower, then gathered her shower essentials.

Hubby// 8:16 p.m.
Yo' ass bet' not pull no shit like that no
more. And be ready to fuck when a
nigga get home.

Tywanna couldn't help but smile at the photo on her iPhone displayed of Diamond. "Love you, bae!" she cooed to the photo.

In the shower, steaming water cascaded on Tywanna and she sulked in it. *Can't believe how I caused Diamond to accuse me of not trustin' him when, in fact, I trust him with my life*, she reflected. The couple had been together since they were teens -Tywanna fifteen and Diamond sixteen. A decade had gone by since then. She was Diamond's down bitch. She used to hold packs for him back when he was on the block, bag up dope with him, and stash his burners in her purse.

Tywanna could even remember all those years ago how Diamond had given his word that he'd get his cake up and move her out of the hood. And he kept good on his word. Now they lived in a condo near downtown, which was lavishly furnished. Not to mention the splurging, pampering trips, and expensive Lexus he cashed out on for her. She had it made in comparison to most girls that grew up poverty-stricken.

*Fuck that*, she thought to herself, *I ain't about to allow lack of trust to cause me to lose my man. Maybe he do have bitches he fucks, but I'm the bitch he loves.* And for her, it wasn't even about the money. She loved Diamond, whether he was paid or broke. Tywanna knew bitches just loved his style and his good looks, while she loved him for him. And she refused to let anyone tear then apart - friend or not. *Jade's ass probably just on some hatin' shit anyway*, she contemplated.

Following her shower, Tywanna padded barefoot into the adjacent master bedroom. As she passed by a mirror, she stopped and said, "Damn, I'm fine," to the reflection staring back at her. Tywanna was bright and attractive, curvy and petite - shorter than Diamond, even in heels. Her skin was mocha, her hair naturally long, and her big eyes light brown. She was a beautiful girl.

She sat on edge of the California-king bed and then lathered herself with cocoa butter lotion. Afterwards, she only dressed in a sheer black teddy without underwear so she could be ready to get fucked, like Diamond told her. Turning on the flat-screen mounted on the wall, she put on Jacquees's "You" music video. Then she poured herself a glass of Kim Crawford wine. Lying in bed on the satin sheets, she sipped at her glass, feeling the elation of the wine.

Visualizing how damn fine Diamond was made her pussy gooey. She loved her some Diamond: his swagger, his smooth voice, and his large dick. Damn, she loved his large dick so much. She even liked the paper thin scar that sliced through his right eyebrow, thought it exaggerated his thuggish style. She wondered which of Diamond's features their baby would have if they were to conceive one. As she thought about Diamond, she caressed her erect nipples.

\*\*\*

"Hell was that back there?" Gangsta was apparently heated.

"That was me tryna keep the peace," Diamond said as he swerved the Bentley around a vehicle in traffic. "Don't you get it, Gangsta? If I accept Yul's offer, then more than likely, it'll cause a war with Balistrieri."

"Fuck that spaghetti-brain muthafucka, I ain't afraid of his ass. See, that's yo' problem Diamond, you'd rather make peace than war. Well, there's a graveyard filled wit' niggas like you," he stated crudely.

"No, I'd rather the most unjust peace to the justest war!" Diamond retorted.

Gangsta shifted in his seat toward Diamond and then replied, "Ain't no fuckin' peace in these streets as it is. Think Banks's ass give a damn 'bout a fuckin' peace treaty? If shit was up to me, he'd be the first muthafucka I'd wage war on. And as for Balistrieri, he can choke to death on a damn meatball."

Diamond braked the whip to a stop at the stoplight on 27th and North Avenue. "Well, shit ain't up to you, Gangsta," he stated evenly.

"Damn right about that, 'cause shit would be a lot different." Gangsta thrust back into his seat.

If Diamond was the crew's noble mastermind, Gangsta was its warmonger, whose presence was slightly off-putting and discomforting. In matters of business, he was direct to the point of being blunt. The two were bonafide hustlers, and they each had a distinct style. Diamond was meticulous. Above all else, he wanted to protect the empire he built. Gangsta, on the other hand, wanted nothing more than to rule the streets by instilling fear and creating mayhem. Instead, Diamond assumed a more corporate model.

Out front of the Theater, Diamond halted the whip in the center of the street. "Gangsta, listen," he began, breaking the tense silence. "I know shit ain't been goin' how you'd prefer it to. But I need you to understand that I'm only doin' what's in our best interest. Droppin' bodies will only get in the way of us chasin' a check, 'cause once the body count begins to rise, then twelve becomes involved. And that ain't somethin' we need. That don't mean I won't unleash shooters if necessary. Feel me? Jus' lemme run this shit my way. Either you my nigga, or my opp."

"Nigga, get outta ya li'l chest, 'fore I give you some chest blows," Gangsta chuckled. "Know I been yo' nigga since we used to steal bikes and shit."

"Yeah, I know," Diamond smirked. They dapped before Gangsta stepped out of the whip, and then Diamond dispelled.

On the low, Gangsta was still heated. *Fuck what that nigga talkin' 'bout, his ass lettin' power go to his damn head. Should be mine any-fuckin'-way*, his conscience suggested.

Power, like a desolating pestilence, pollutes whatever it touches.

\*\*\*

Diamond slid from behind the steering wheel, shut the car door, and then beeped its alarm. He treaded through the condo's underground parking lot to the elevator and pressed the button to the floor his apartment was located. Inside the apartment, he didn't need light to show him the way to the bedroom. He found Tywanna lying in bed asleep wearing a teddy with no panties, her juicy, bare ass on display. He placed his iPhone and .45 on the nightstand then sat on the edge of the bed.

*Hell I continue to put my life in the line when I done already managed to make a better life for me and Ty?* he questioned himself introspectively. He wasn't rap star rich, although he was set. He owned a successful strip club, a lavish condo, and three luxurious whips: his Bentley GT Continental coupe, Porsche Cayenne, and Tywanna's Lexus IS. It was nothing for him to just relocate with Tywanna and start a family, and perhaps he would. At some point.

Tywanna stirred awake. "Wanna talk about what's on yo' mind?"

"I'm a'ight. Jus' go back to sleep."

"Diamond, you know that you can talk with me about whatever," Tywanna said consolingly. She moved near him and wrapped her arms around his neck from behind with her titties pressed against his back. "So, what is it?"

"It's all the shit takin' place in the streets. Everyone's out for one crown."

"Uneasy lies a head that wears a crown. And bein' that it's yo' crown everyone's out for, you can't trust no man. Not even those closest to you."

*Her ass always knows the right shit to say*, he thought gratefully. "Yeah, you right."

"Now," she kissed his neck, "lemme show you how much you can trust in me."

Their tongues prowled deep into each other's mouths as she tugged and pulled his clothes off and rolled onto the bed, unleashing passions, kissing, groping, and probing. He took her left titty into his mouth, and across it was a tatt engraved in fancy cursive which read "Diamonds Are Forever". It was a small reminder that she was indeed his.

Tywanna pushed his head away, begging, "Fuck me. I want you to fuck me good." She took hold of his large, hard dick and thrust him inside her wet-wet, clamping her legs around him. He took small, gentle bites of her lower lip, as he slid back and forth inside her snug, slippery pussy.

"You like that shit, love?" Diamond said as he pushed her legs back and dug her out.

Tywanna reached back over her head, gripping the satin sheets. "Ooh, baby, I like it like that," she groaned in pleasure.

Diamond enjoyed her fuck faces. The shit turned him on even more. He picked her up off the bed, holding her up by her ass while he stabbed in and out of her rapidly. She palmed the back of his skull and tossed her head back as she took the dick. Both were carried away by the insistence of passion.

"Diamond! Yesss, ummm!" She thrust her face against his shoulder, muting her screams as an orgasm racked her body. Her juices oozed, sliding down Diamond's inner thighs.

Feeling his own nut swelling in the tip of his dick, Diamond bent Tywanna over the bed and lunged deep in her twat from behind. Tywanna looked back at him over her shoulder while she perfectly arched her back and tooted her pretty ass in the air. He smacked her ass and fucked her hard.

"Damn, Ty, this pussy so good. Ahhhh shit!" Diamond released his seed deep inside her then fell on top of her panting. "A nigga luh yo' ass," he divulged.

"You better."

# Troublesome

## Chapter 2

"Ain't feelin' how them niggas got outta that jam. Got somethin' for they ass!" Sticks raved.

Banks cradled the phone between his shoulder and ear while he counted money. "Sticks, had yo' simple ass not fucked up, then Diamond n'em wouldn't be a problem. Shoulda jus' had Lucifer take care of the shit. Jus' lay low for now." He killed the call. Shit, he actually wanted to kill Sticks for fuckin' up.

For years Banks had toiled, small time, on the block, stackin' light cheese. Now at the age of twenty-seven, he was fast on the come-up in the streets. And over time, Banks formed his own outfit. A bronze-skinned, slim nigga with waves, he was a bonafide street nigga and refused to allow anyone to prevent him from seizing the streets.

"Banks, I'ont know why you put trust in niggas to do yo' dirty work," his bae, Lexi, expounded after overhearing Banks's end of the call. She fed a stack of bills into the money machine, and it made the frrraaap sound as it calculated the sum.

Banks collected the stack from the machine as he sniped, "I'ont trust Sticks, or no muthafucka."

Lexi held off feeding the machine and peered at him through slit eyes. "Not even me, Banks?" She sounded disgruntled.

"Lex, I didn't mean it that way," he vindicated. Reaching over the glass top dinette table, he grabbed her hand and comfortingly met her eyes. "You know a nigga trusts you. In fact, shorty, I trust you wit' my life. And you trust me too, right?"

"With all my heart."

"And I'll never break it," he promised. "Now let's get back to countin' this paper." They were in their plush, quiet apartment, adding up funds accumulated from his trap spots throughout the day.

Every step of the way, Lexi had been with Banks. She overlooked all of his cheating, pushed dope with him, and would put in gun work when necessary. She even took a gun charge for his ass before. Shorty was his ride or die.

Lexi was what one would consider a BBW. Her figure was similar to the plus-sized model Ashley Graham. She had a butterscotch hue, wore a buzz cut that accented her high cheekbones, full lips with soft brown eyes, and she rocked a bullring in her nose. She was the good girl type with a bad bitch attitude.

Frrraaap! The money machine instantly summed up the bills Lexi fed it, which amounted to a grand. Banks collected the stack, wrapped it with a rubber band before stacking it on the table with the others. Thus far they'd counted upwards to sixty racks, and still had a few more bags of money.

*\*\*\**

Toni sat parked in her red Mercedes-Benz CL600 awaiting her homeboy, Pelle. He emerged from the bando and headed for the Benz.

"What it do, Toni?" Pelle greeted as he stepped into the plush interior. He noticed the handle of her .10mm protruding from her Bottega Veneta handbag in the center console.

"Shit. A bitch out here chasin' a check."

"Dat's what's up." Pelle handed her a few stacks of cash, which she tossed into her handbag.

"Beneath the seat," she told him, and Pelle reached under the passenger seat, coming up with nine ounces of dog food compressed in cellophane.

Toni had been serving Pelle for the past eight months. He'd sought her out, in need of a plug. Having status in the street's drug trade, hustlers such as Pelle knew that to be plugged with Toni and her crew was valuable.

At just twenty-four, Toni was a bad bitch in the game. She was short, curvaceous, and light-skinned with dreadlocks dyed the color of red wine falling down to her small waist. Her born name was Tonisha, but everyone called her Toni instead because she was an epicene that acted like a bitch and thought like a nigga. And she wasn't the bitch to be fucked with.

Not quite a big cat in the game, Pelle was fast on the come-up. He was brown-skinned, chubby with long braids, and his voice was raspy. Pelle was about his money, and he'd kill for it if he had to.

"I notice you never count the cash." Pelle grinned, his chipped tooth showing. "A nine-piece is too much to trust anyone wit'."

Toni smirked before speaking. "You a good nigga, Pelle. You always come correct. But now that you mentioned it, should I count it?"

"Only if you don't trust me."

"If I didn't trust you, then I'da bodied you long ago," she responded in all seriousness. "In fact, I trust you enough to wanna introduce you to my nigga, Diamond."

"Cool. Jus' lemme know the time 'n place. I'll be in touch." Pelle stashed the dope on his person before stepping out of the Benz. *Jus' what I been waitin' for*, he contemplated as he returned to the bando.

\*\*\*

Gangsta could tell something invaded the space in Chase's mind. "What's wit'chu?"

"It's Ash. You know how she gets," Chase huffed. After having words with Ashley earlier, he needed a break from her ass, so he hopped in his whip and dipped to the Theater.

"Sounds like Ash been on yo' ass again." Gangsta was actually Ashley's older brother. More than anyone, he knew how in love Chase and Ashley were, and that they disagreed on the life Chase lived.

"She keeps pressin' a nigga to leave the game. And I'ont know what to do. The game is all I know," Chase vented.

Short, stocky, and boyishly handsome, Chase's appearance did little to reveal his sinister reputation. On the other hand, he was a family man. He took care of Ashley and their twins, Chance and Charity. Chase was good to his cohorts as well, down with them for whatever.

Gangsta rose from the brown leather sofa. "My nigg, apparently you can use a drink right about now." He stepped over to the mini-bar, grabbed two glasses and a partially filled bottle of Patron, then poured them both a generous amount of the tequila.

"Bruh, I love that girl and our twins more than myself. And I try to do my best by my family," he expressed.

"Yeah, I'm already knowin'." Gangsta returned to the sofa and handed Chase a glass, which he drained in one gulp.

"Anotha round," Chase requested, holding out his glass.

"Take it easy," Gangsta chuckled. He refilled the glass. "Li'l bruh, you need to see shit from Ash's view. Now you have more to live for." He took a swig of his Patron. "Maybe it is best that you get outta the game. 'Cause shit bound to get gangsta soon," he reasoned.

"I'm as gangsta as any nigga gets," Chase replied matter-of-factly.

"And I'ont doubt that. All I'm sayin' is... Hol' up." Gangsta's iPhone vibrated, indicating he had an incoming text. He fished the phone out from his jeans pocket and read the message.

Diamond // 9:17 p.m.
I'm outside.

"Check it, I have some business to tend to wit' Diamond. We'll have to resume this discussion anotha time. 'Til then, at least think on what I said 'bout gettin' outta the game," Gangsta told him. He polished off his drink before heading out.

Left alone with his thoughts and glass of Patron, Chase found himself harking back on the quarrel he had with Ashley earlier. *Ash is right. Bein' so damn tied up in the street life I somehow allowed it to matter more than my home life. Can't stand for her and the twins to have to visit me in prison. Or worse, a cemetery,* he thought considerately.

His family needed him, and he cared to be there for them. It wasn't like he didn't have more than enough money stashed away to go legit. *On the day of my weddin', I'm gettin' outta the game,* he vowed and then took a drink to it.

# Trap God

***

Diamond and Gangsta debarked from the Bentley. They showed up at the boat docks, where the transaction would take place. Since it was later in the night, the docks were scarcely populated.

A white male wearing an ill-fitting, off-the-rack suit approached, carrying a black leather briefcase. He was burly, wore a crewcut with a clean shave, and had frigid blue eyes. The sidearm and gold-plated shield both attached to his waistline made it lucid that he was, nonetheless, a lawman - DEA Special Agent Vincent Lynch. And like a lot of government representatives, he was in the pocket of the mob boss, Frank Balistrieri.

"How's things been going?" Lynch accosted Diamond. He offered Gangsta a look, and Gangsta returned a glare.

"Everything's good," Diamond responded evenly.

Lynch eyed him narrowly. "How about your little show outside of the nightclub a couple of weeks ago?"

"It's nothin' I can't handle."

"If need be, I can - "

"Told you I can handle it, Lynch. A'ight?" Diamond intervened in a temper.

"Then you be sure it gets handled, Diamond," he pressed.

Gangsta cut in, "Listen up, pig, I suggest you come correct."

"And I suggest you stand down." He rested his free hand on his sidearm. "Or…"

"What?" Gangsta clutched the handle of the banger protruding from his waistband.

The two had a stare down. Lynch's eyes were like daggers. In Gangsta's younger years, a bullet grazed his right eye during a shootout, and as a result, his eye drifted slightly, so that it often was fixed, discordantly, on whoever approached him on the right side.

"We're here to conduct business. So let's," Diamond firmly reminded them both.

Reluctantly, Lynch removed his hand from his weapon. He handed the briefcase over to Diamond. "Inside, there's fifteen kilos of smack. Now where's the cash from the previous front?"

"Gangsta, grab the bread," Diamond instructed.

Gangsta turned and retrieved a black duffle bag from the back seat of the Bentley. He tossed the bag at Lynch's feet.

"That's every cent. All $750,000 of it," Diamond assured him.

Lynch picked up the weighty bag. "If it isn't, Balistrieri won't be happy with you, Diamond. I'll be in touch." He shot Gangsta a final glare before turning for his unmarked black Dodge Durango and then departed.

"Can't believe you let that fuckin' pig come at you like that," Gangsta said disapprovingly. "And if he thinks you ain't capable of handlin' yo' business in the streets, then imagine what the streets thinkin'."

"Fuck what anyone else thinks, Gangsta. I'm measurin' every move," he retorted.

Gangsta stomped over to the whip and snatched open the passenger door. "Desperate times calls for desperate measures." He jumped inside and yanked the door shut with a thud.

With all that was on the line, Diamond had to maintain power over the streets. One thing he couldn't have was the appearance of weakness, because he understood that the appearance of power is equally important as the actual exercise of it. Therefore, to strengthen his power he must, in any circumstance, murder all enemies.

## Chapter 3

Upon entering the Cheesecake Factory, Tywanna scanned the place for her girlfriends. Ashley waved her over to the table she and the others had reserved.

"Heeey girl!" Ashley beamed. She pulled Ty in for a hug, and the two gave one another a double smooch on the cheeks.

"Girl, I see you lookin' all good." Tywanna admired her friend's beauty. Ashley had a pecan hue with a cute, petite frame, a chic short hairdo, and hazel eyes.

"Thanks. And you killin' it yo'self. Love those heels and that handbag."

"It's nothin' special. Just Alexander McQueen," she humble-bragged.

Jade piped in, "Both y'all bitches need to stop, 'cause neither of y'all ain't got shit on me." She remained seated while checking her glow in her pocket mirror. Jade was a redbone with an ass that couldn't go unnoticed, and shorty stayed on fleek.

"Whatever, Jade." Tywanna took a seat at the table. "Hoe, without all the damn makeup, wigs, and contacts, yo' ass cosmetically challenged. So fortunately for you, our bitch Ash here is a cosmetologist," she jeered, causing Ashley to snicker.

Jade just rolled her contact lens-gray eyes. After being sure her beat was on point, she put away the mirror in her oversized Christian Dior satchel.

Tywanna noticed the vacant chair at their table with a purse hanging by its shoulder strap. "Where's she, 'cause I'm ready to order."

"She stepped away to the li'l girls' room. Should be back here in a minute," Ashley said.

"Here I am." It was Lexi, and she took a seat. "Hey Ty. Didn't mean to keep y'all waitin', just had to take a call from Banks. The nigga stay keepin' tabs on this pussy."

"I know exactly what you mean girl, okaaaay!" Ashley gushed and held up her left hand, flaunting the three karat VVS diamond engagement ring.

Jade smacked her full lips. "That's you bitchs' problem, dependin' on a nigga and shit."

"At least we have niggas to depend on, unlike yo' thot ass," Tywanna half-joked.

"A well-paid thot at that," she admitted shamelessly.

"Get yo' schmoney hoe, aoow!" Lexi added, mimicking Cardi B.

"Anywho," Ashley intervened. "Shall we order?"

\*\*\*

"Money on the wood's all good, money outta sight causes fights," Toni bantered as the crowd of craps shooters formed in the neighborhood park. She shook the dice then rolled them, and they tumbled over the pavement until resting on winning numbers. "Nobody move, this a stickup." She smirked, collecting her winnings.

An unfamiliar nigga entered the park. He was promptly halted by a few thugs, who closed in on him with pistols drawn. "Nigga, fuck is you?" asked Major, who was one of Diamond's mid-level heroin distributors. He was down to push the nigga's shit back on the spot.

"Name's Pelle. Here to holla at her." He nodded at Toni, who was busy counting her winnings.

"Aye Toni," Major called, "you know this muthafucka?"

Toni stepped over to them. "Give 'im a pass, he's wit' me." She'd asked Pelle to stop by, expecting to acquaint him with Diamond and the others. "What's good, Pelle?" The two dapped.

Diamond steamed over towards the two, flanked by Gangsta and Chase. "Frisk him," he ordered Toni, and she eyed him, disconcerted. "I said frisk his ass. Now."

"Gon' ahead, Toni. I ain't got shit to hide." Pelle understood the measurements of security for a nigga with Diamond's power. He didn't falter while Toni patted him down. She relieved him of the heater he had on his waist.

The weapon was the least of Diamond's concerns. He just wanted to be sure the nigga wasn't wired. "This ain't the time nor place for a damn meet and greet. Get him the fuck up outta here. And if he try somethin', murk his ass," he told Toni.

Toni escorted Pelle towards the park's outlet with his own pistol jammed into his back. "Trust me, shit will work out when the time's right," she murmured to Pelle.

\*\*\*

Following by their luncheon date, the four girlfriends made their way to a bridal boutique. Ashley needed to pick out a wedding gown along with the bridesmaids dresses, and she cared to have her friends' input. Being the maid of honor, it was Tywanna's duty to support Ash every step of the way, and she didn't mind. The ceremony was scheduled in a few weeks, and Ashley wanted everything to be perfect, although she wasn't being a bridezilla about it.

"Ash, girl, you are so gorgeous in that gown!" Tywanna cooed.

"Really?" Ashley turned and viewed herself in the mirror for the first time wearing the gown. It was white, form-fitting, with a cutout back and plunging neck, designed by Norma Kamali. It was the fifth gown she'd tried on, and by far was the best one.

"Yes, girl. That gown is so you," Lexi commended.

"And once Chase sees you in it, trust, he'll fall in love with you all over again," Ty added.

"What you think, Jade?" Ashley cared to know.

"Uh huh, it's cute," Jade replied absentmindedly. She was too damn busy with her face in her iPhone while on Facebook to give her undivided attention.

Tywanna snatched the phone out of Jade's hand. "Tramp, what's so important you can't even look up at the damn gown?"

"Ty, if you don't gimme my damn phone back..." she complained. As she tried reaching for her phone, Tywanna held Jade back, denying her.

Seeing who Jade was socializing with on the 'book, Tywanna said, "Ugh! I can't see why in the hell you talk to his ass."

"Who is it, Ty?" Lexi probed.

"It's Gangsta."

Jade grabbed her phone back. "Bitch, I'm grown, so I can talk to whoever I please."

"I can't stand his ass," Tywanna said.

"Unh unh, Ty, don't do my brotha," Ashley piped in, defending Gangsta.

"I'm sorry, Ash, you my girl and all, but yo' brotha somethin' else." Tywanna felt like Gangsta was a bad influence on Diamond.

Jade stood and grabbed her satchel. "Say what you want. Gangsta treats a bitch good, and the dick is good."

"Eww! Jade, I did not need to hear that shit," Ashley scowled.

"Well, sweetie, you just did. And I'm finna go see what that D be like right now."

"Wait. You ain't gon' try on the bridesmaid dress before you go?"

"Girl, you ain't know? I can make anything look good. Even that hideous dress. Deuces bitches." Jade headed for the exit of the boutique.

"Bye, Felicia," Tywanna intoned, poking fun at Jade, who flipped her long inches over her shoulder on her way out.

Lexi shook her head. "That girl is a mess," she chortled.

"Enough about her," Ashley said. "Finish tellin' the bride-to-be how gorgeous I am."

*** 

While on the phone, Diamond stepped through the vestibule on his way to his and Tywanna's apartment. He was receiving some fucked-up news.

"The blue-goons jus' hit the trap. They snatched up T-Money and Savage," Major reported. "And get this: them bitches seized two blocks of boy and over a hunnid G's."

"Shut down the rest of the traps 'til further notice. And call up the lawyer, have him go see T-Money and Savage ASAP," Diamond instructed before ending the call. He wanted his boys to know they were in good hands. And the lawyer, Levin, held certain standards. Levin didn't defend government witnesses. If a client was snitchin', he'd drop the case.

Now Diamond had to make up for the loss, on top of having to deal with beef. Shit was getting heavy in the streets, and the weight seemed to fall on his shoulders.

He turned the corner and found Tywanna standing outside of the apartment. She fumbled with her keys in one hand while holding shopping bags in the other, struggling to unlock the door. *This girl wit' all her damn shoppin'*, he thought repugnantly.

"Hey, bae." Tywanna regarded him as he stepped up. "Will you gimme a hand with the door, please?"

"Maybe if yo' ass didn't have so many damn bags it wouldn't be such a problem for you openin' the door." He unlocked the door and then went inside the apartment without even bothering to help her with the numerous bags.

Tywanna noted his tone and concluded he was upset about something other than how many bags she had. She entered, closed the door behind herself, and sarcastically said, "Thanks anyway."

Diamond flounced down onto the plush leather sofa, and even though the leather was butter soft, it wasn't enough to curb him. After Tywanna placed her bags inside the closet, she clicked on the lamp, seeing that Diamond didn't seem to care to. The dim lighting was just enough to illuminate the stress on Diamond's face. Tywanna moved over to the sofa, kicked off her Jimmy Choo heels, and then sat on Diamond's lap.

"Ain't in the mood, Ty."

"And I ain't expectin' you to be," she made plain. "Diamond, baby, I ain't feelin' how the streets are takin' a toll on you. Believe me, I respect whatever you do and all, but you need a vacay from the street life."

Tywanna rarely ever badgered Diamond concerning his street affairs, because she knew and understood all that came with it, although she felt compelled to speak her piece. Diamond heard the concern in her voice, and admittedly, she had reason to be. Hearing her concern shifted his expression from rugged to balmy.

"You know what? You right. I do need a vacation," Diamond confirmed. "And we can go wherever you'd like."

"Diamond, I'ont mean an actual vacation."

"Well, I do. And we'll leave tonight." He pecked her on the lips.

***

Gangsta awoke in the morning with Jade lying in bed beside him. They were both ass naked. She'd come by his loft the day before, and they fucked 'til the wee hours of the morning.

He rolled out of bed and left Jade in a deep, sex-induced slumber while he took care of his whole nine and then got dressed in a white and tan Fendi jogger suit and tan Fendi sneakers. He grabbed the plate with remains of coke from the nightstand then snorted the powder, giving himself an adrenaline rush. He slapped Jade hard on her phat ass.

"Ow!" Jade jumped out of her sleep. "That shit hurts, Gangsta," she complained, rubbing her booty cheek.

"Didn't complain when a nigga was smackin' all that ass last night," he grinned, holding his crotch. "I'm 'bout to bounce, got some shit to do."

Jade stepped out of bed, her naked frame on display. "Well, I gotta get ready to go to get my nails done anyway. Mind if I take a shower?"

"Do yo' thang. And make sure you clean that twat for a nigga. Catch you later." Before leaving to bust his move, Gangsta grabbed his iPhone and pistol.

Jade knew Gangsta was hardcore, and she liked that about him. They weren't exclusively in a relationship; it was just sex. Although no matter how hard Gangsta was, she read that he was soft on her.

Since Diamond was out of town, Gangsta was left in charge, and today he'd do shit his way. Since all of the traps remained shut down, he had what he thought was a power move in mind.

While in his white Mercedes Benz G-Wagon en route, he phoned Chase via Bluetooth.

"What's da damn deal, G?" Chase answered over the speaker.

"On the way to scoop you up. Got some shit to handle."

"I'm wit' it."

The two ended their call, and ten minutes later, Gangsta was pulling to the curb in front of Chase's crib. It was a handsome home out in the suburbs. He texted Chase, letting him know he was outside. A moment later, Chase emerged from the house with Ashley trailing him, and she had the twins on either hip.

The twins waved at their uncle, and Gangsta waved back. He watched as Chase gave them all a peck before heading towards the ride. Gangsta could see that Chase had a life beyond the game, and he wanted Ashley to be happy. But he knew that walking away from the game wasn't easy.

"So, what's the move?" Chase asked as he stepped into the G-Wagon.

Gangsta pulled off. "Hit up West's line. Tell him to get them shooters on deck."

\*\*\*

Diamond sat on edge of the bed smoking a blunt, rocking only a pair of Ralph Lauren boxer briefs and socks and his diamond-encrusted pieces. Tywanna stood before him, bent over, making her ass bounce as she put on a private show for her man, wearing black and pink lace Victoria Secret lingerie with a pair of pink patent leather fuck-me pumps that made her smooth, sexy-ass legs look more shapely. The couple was checked into a honeymoon suite at the Marina Inn out in Myrtle Beach, South Carolina.

"Bring that ass here." Diamond pulled her onto his lap.

Tywanna gave him a seductive lap dance. "You like that, zaddy?" she purred.

"Fa sho," he commended thuggishly, and then he took a pull of the blunt. "We needed some quality time alone together. Wit' me busy runnin' the game, there ain't much time for us to enjoy each other's company."

"And I cherish the time you spend with me more than the money you spend on me. 'Cause time is personal, and splurgin' on me is too easy," Ty added.

"Neva thought about it that way." He hit the blunt, then put its remains in the ashtray.

"Well, I think about it all the time," she admitted. Tywanna pushed him back in bed then straddled him, and he palmed her booty. She toyed with the diamond-studded necklace around his neck.

"Diamonds are forever, you know," he quipped with that smirk which Tywanna couldn't resist.

"Then you mine forever." She pulled him close by the necklace and kissed him, and their tongues danced around with one another.

Diamond pushed Ty onto her back then rolled on top of her, trading places. He planted a course of kisses down her neck. The feel of his soft lips was sensational on her flesh, causing her back to slightly arch. Gently, he bit her shoulder, and she enjoyed the mild pain. His kisses trailed downward over her fine skin.

He took a mouthful of her perky titty, carefully sucking and nibbling on her hard nipple as he reached and pulled off her ruffled panties. Then he stuck his fingers into her gooey pussy, causing her to set free a moan. He continued to suck her nipples as he moved his fingers around inside her. Then he pulled them out and licked off her juices.

Diamond gazed into Tywanna's eyes and said, "A nigga don't ever wanna have to be without you, I'm beggin' you to always hold me down."

"I love when you beg. Get on yo' knees," she instructed him provocatively with a smirk.

Diamond knelt in between her wide open legs. He buried his face in that juicy pussy, sucking and licking and rolling his tongue all over her clit.

"Oooh, Diamond, do it! I love it, nigga, make me cum!" Tywanna cried. She went wild, grinding her pussy in his face.

"Mmm, tastes so damn good," Diamond told her. He had pussy all over his face and beard. The taste and scent of her was driving him crazy! He sucked her clit into his mouth, flicking her clit with his tongue. Tywanna's body tensed. He stuck his tongue deep into her pussy, and she trembled with pleasure as she came in his mouth. Then he held her until the trembling stopped.

After their fuck session, in the bar of the Marina, Diamond and Tywanna occupied a table for two. They wanted to enjoy as much of Myrtle Beach as they could. They'd do more suckin' and fuckin' later on.

Once they ate their meals, they planned to hit the town on a shopping spree, and then it was off to the spa for a couple's massage. This was Diamond's moment to chill with Tywanna, and he wanted to enjoy every moment of it, although he was aware of the bloodshed and money woes that awaited him back home in the streets.

Tywanna forked at her Chef's salad. She noticed Diamond had been absentminded for the better part of their meal. "You know, Diamond, you'll have more than enough time to worry about whatever's goin' on in streets once we're back home. For at least the moment, it'd be nice if you focus on just us," she told his ass.

"My bad, love. Jus' so much shit on a nigga mind."

"Which is the idea of us bein' on this vacation right now. So you can unwind," she reminded him.

Diamond reached across the table and grabbed her small, manicured hand in his. "You right. For the time bein', I need to put the streets outta my mind." He raised her hand to his lips and gently gave it a kiss.

"Diamond, I'm…" Tywanna let her words trail off.

"What is it, Ty?" He was curious.

She wanted to tell him how their lives were about to change, but she didn't want to put too much on him in that moment. So instead she said, "I…I love you."

Diamond's love belonged to none other than Tywanna. He couldn't get enough of her smile, pretty brown eyes, mocha skin, and cute ass. It made his dick hard just looking at her. "And I love you, Ty. That'll never change," he promised.

For the time being it was all about her and him, so the streets would have to wait.

# Troublesome

***

West pulled his Suburban around the corner onto the side street. He'd been tailing Banks's Infiniti, looking for an opening to make a move. He observed Lucifer step out from the passenger side of the Infiniti and make his way inside the liquor store. West and the two others riding along with him all jumped out of the SUV with cannons in hand, and the trio ran up on the limo-tinted Infiniti.

Rrraaa! Rrraaa!

Blam! Blam! Blam! Blam!

Prrraaat! Prrraaat! Prrraaat!

The three shooters aired out the Infiniti, causing it to suffer shattered windows, flat tires and numerous bullet holes. Once they ceased fire, West stepped up and took a look inside the vehicle, finding a bullet-riddled corpse slumped in the driver's seat. Only it wasn't Banks.

"Shit." West was highly disappointed.

Blocka! Blocka! Blocka! Blocka!

Lucifer rushed out from the liquor store, lettin' off on West n'em. West fled to his ride while the two others dumped back. Lucifer smoked one of the two, and the other retreated to the Suburban behind West. Lucifer opened up on the SUV as it sped away. Then he hurried over to the Swiss-cheesed Infiniti to check on his boy. It was Sticks, and unfortunately he was DOA.

***

"Niggas thought they caught me slackin'." Banks chuckled after ending the call with Lucifer about what had just went down. He'd let Lucifer and Sticks use his whip to catch some plays, and fortunately, he chose not to ride along.

"I'ont know why you makin' light of the shit, Banks," Lexi commented. She stood before the mirror wrapped in a towel, applying her beat.

"'Cause it's light work to me," he replied arrogantly.

She turned, facing him. "All I'm sayin' is maybe you need to take the shit a li'l more serious."

Banks sat up in bed, grabbed the remainder of the blunt from the ashtray on the dresser, then fired it up. "Lex, believe me, I'm dead serious."

"I just don't want nothin' bad to happen to you, Banks." She returned to fixing her face in the mirror.

"And nothin' will." He stepped out the bed in a wife-beater and boxers, then stepped up behind her. "Hell yo' ass finna go?"

"To get a mani-pedi with Jade."

"Don't know why you even hang wit' her ass," he scoffed.

"And what's so wrong with me hangin' with her?"

"I got my reasons," was all he offered.

"Well, she and I have been friends for years, and I trust her," Lexi expressed. "Anyway, I need my nails done. You know a bitch gotta stay lookin' good."

"Right now you lookin' good enough to eat!" He cupped her titty with his free hand, massaging her hardened nipple between his fingers. And before Lexi knew it, she was rubbing her ass against his stiff dick.

"Mmm... Banks, stop before you make me late to my appointment," Lexi uttered.

"Jus' make sure you bring yo' ass back right afterwards so I can tear that pussy up," he said into her ear.

Lexi kissed him before stepping away.

While smoking on the purple to ease his mind, Banks began to form how he'd retaliate on Diamond. Unbeknownst to him, the gunners were actually sent on behalf of Gangsta. He thought about Sticks catching slugs in place of him. *Shit, had Sticks not fucked up the hit on Diamond, then maybe his ass wouldn't have fucked around and got smoked*, he thought. Now, for his own sake, he had to dispose of Diamond.

\*\*\*

"Fuck you mean it wasn't Banks?!" Gangsta had rushed to see West. They were sitting in West's Suburban, parked in the alley. It was as though Gangsta needed to hear again what had taken place in person just to be sure it wasn't actually a fuckin' joke, and West wasn't laughing.

"It was some other nigga pushin' his whip. Thought it was him," West uttered.

"Nigga, leave the thinkin' to me. 'Cause obviously you thought wrong!" Gangsta raged. Not giving West the chance to speak another word, Gangsta drew his pistol.

Boc!

Gangsta domed West, splattering his fuckin' noodles all over the windshield. Then he casually stepped out from the Suburban, leaving West's body slumped over the steering wheel, causing the horn to sound off. He hopped into his G-Wagon, where Chase was awaiting in the passenger seat.

"Fuck was that about?" Chase asked.

"Nigga fucked up in a major way," Gangsta told him.

"Damn. And I liked the li'l nigga." Chase shook his damn head. "But that's jus' part of the game."

"The game is cold, but it's fair," Gangsta added, giving Chase something to think on. He push-started the G-Wagon and then departed down the alley.

Gangsta realized the bind he was now in, and he realized it could potentially cause a falling out between him and Diamond if Diamond was to figure out what he'd attempted to do without his consent. So Gangsta had to come up with a solution somehow, and faster than a speeding bullet.

## Chapter 4

Following their vacation, Diamond and Tywanna were returning home from Mitchell airport after flying in. Diamond turned the Porsche truck into the condo's underground parking lot and then parked beside Tywanna's Lexus. He offed the engine, rested his head back against the headrest, and let out a deep breath. Back to life, back to reality.

During the ride home, Diamond thought about the odds he was up against. Maybe Gangsta was right. Diamond didn't want to end up in a grave due to wanting to be spared war, as though the absence of war was the same as peace.

"Everything alright, baby? You haven't spoken a word since we left the airport," Tywanna pointed out. She noticed he seemed taxed.

"Listen, Ty, I gotta go handle some shit. I'll be back as soon as I can," he told her.

"But we just got back. Besides, it's late, Diamond," she protested.

"And I'm aware of that, so don't wait up for me."

Ty vehemently pushed opened the passenger door and jumped out the ride. "If you gonna go and do somethin' stupid, then you might as well stay here with me," she tried to persuade him.

"Do I look stupid to you?"

Tywanna hit him with a stale-face and said, "Sometimes." She slammed the door shut before steaming away.

Diamond would straighten shit out with Ty later. He pulled into to traffic en route to Red Velvet. During the trip he tried phoning Gangsta, and he got no answer. Since landing from his flight earlier he'd attempted to call Gangsta, and thus far his ass had yet to call back. Diamond hoped to find him at the club so they could discuss how they'd move on Banks, and he knew Gangsta would be all for that. If only he knew that Gangsta had gone behind his back with a failed attempt to body Banks.

Out front of Red Velvet, Diamond parked the Porsche truck at the curb. He retrieved his .45 from the trap compartment, then stuffed it at the small of his back before stepping out and making his way inside the club. As Diamond walked through, he dapped up Sarge and a few others.

"Welcome back," Sarge said.

"Fa sho'. Maybe we can have a drink later."

"Only after the club closes," Sarge added. He was a short, buff-ass nigga, dark-skinned with a crewcut. He'd served as a sergeant in the army over in Iraq before an honorable discharge after losing his leg up to the knee from a landmine explosion. And Sarge moved in a militant way.

As Diamond moved along, Jade approached him wearing next to nothing in just some pink sheer boy-shorts and white leather hoe-boots with her nipples covered in pasties. "Hey, Diamond! Glad you back," she greeted him excitedly.

Diamond rejected her attempt to hug him. "We ain't cool like that, Jade," he spurned her. "Shouldn't you be up in one of these niggas' faces right now, shakin' yo' ass and poppin' yo' pussy or somethin'? Make yo'self useful and go make some damn money." He banished Jade and went about his business.

With her ego bruised, Jade headed for the back dressing room to grab her cell. *Nigga think he all that. Well, I got somethin' for his ass,* she thought seethingly.

Diamond stepped over to the bar, where Toni was seated on a barstool. He noticed she had Pelle in her company. He dapped up Toni and disregarded Pelle.

"Gangsta 'round here somewhere?" Diamond wanted to know.

"Ain't seen him," Toni said.

*Where in the hell is that nigga?* Diamond wondered. "I'll be in the office. If Gangsta shows up, then send him to me." Diamond stepped away.

\*\*\*

"Ohhh, yeeesss! Fuck me...hit this pussy, Baaanks!"

Banks had Lexi bent over the edge of the bed while he beat the pussy up from behind. "Who dat nigga, huh?" he grunted.

"You are, baby," Lexi panted, gripping the sheets. "Ummm, right there...that's my spot!"

Banks's iPhone rang and, without halting his thrusts, he grabbed the phone from the nightstand. "This better be 'bout somethin' as good as pussy," he answered, sounding disturbed.

"That depends on whose pussy. ' Cause trust, ain't nothin' as good as mine," Jade insinuated on the other end of the line.

Banks ignored her comment. "What is it?"

"Um, the nigga Diamond here at the club right now," she informed, keeping her voice low so no one else could overhear her.

The mere mention of Diamond seemed to always demand Banks's undivided attention. He pulled his dick out of Lexi's wetshot, leaving her face down, ass up. "Say no mo'. I got it from here."

"Just make sure you run me my coins ASAP, Banks," Jade told him. He'd promised her five bands if she called him the moment Diamond showed up at the club. She'd actually set up the first hit. She owed Diamond no loyalty, so she had no problem taking Banks up on his offer. Yeah, Ty was her girl and all, but what she didn't know wouldn't hurt her. Jade was just a selfish hoe like that.

"Don't trip. I got'chu."

After ending the call, Banks immediately hit up Lucifer. It was time to seek revenge on Diamond. Revenge was the sweetest joy next to getting pussy.

\*\*\*

Alone in his office, Diamond removed his .45 from his person and set it on top his desk. He pulled out his iPhone then tried Gangsta once again. He impatiently waited while the line rang, on the fifth ring Gangsta finally answered.

"Gangsta, I been tryna get in touch wit' you. Yo' ass coulda got back at me," Diamond fumed.

"Recognize who you talkin' to. I ain't yo' bitch," Gangsta replied curtly. "Now what's up?"

Diamond thought better against checkin' his ass. "Jus' get to the club ASAP. We need to discuss how we gon' move on Banks."

In that moment, Gangsta felt repentant about going behind Diamond's back in his attempt to have Banks offed. Maybe it'd be best if he just came out and told Diamond? But he decided not to.

"'Bout time you decidin' to make a power move," Gangsta said.

"Power is measured in enemies," Diamond stated.

Meanwhile, Lucifer parked behind the club. He and three others hopped out of the ride, each strapped. He wanted to get inside undetected, so he texted Jade to come let them in through the rear fire exit.

"Where that nigga at?" Lucifer eagerly asked once Jade opened the door.

"Stepped into his office down the hallway." Jade prudently peeped the surrounding to be sure no one witnessed the role she played in whatever was about to go down. "Hol' the fuck up. Gimme my money," she requested, placing her hand on Lucifer's broad chest to stop him as he began to make his way inside.

Lucifer fished a bankroll out of his pocket and handed it to Jade. Once Jade was paid, she scurried out of sight. Flanked by his boys, Lucifer inconspicuously went in search of Diamond. Just so happened Sarge and his security staff were dealing with a drunk and disorderly patron.

"And why all of a sudden do you wanna get at the nigga Banks?" Gangsta questioned Diamond on the other end of the line.

"'Cause it's either him or me. And I know he won't spare me if he had the chance."

"Good you finally see shit the way I do."

"Gangsta," Diamond started tranquilly, "I know you and I haven't been havin' mutual feelings lately, but I have undyin' love for you. And - "

Kaboom!

Diamond's phone conversation with Gangsta was interrupted once the office door was abruptly kicked open. And to Diamond's dismay, Lucifer stood in the doorway wearing a mug and leveling a pistol on him.

"Yo, Diamond, you still there?" Gangsta called out, not understanding why Diamond suddenly went silent on the other end.

In that moment, Diamond briefly weighed his options: do or die. He dropped his phone and reached for his own weapon.

Blocka! Blocka! Blocka! Blocka! Blocka!

Lucifer let off, not giving Diamond a chance to grab his .45 off the desk. The impact of the slugs Diamond took to the torso caused him to crumple onto the floor.

"See you in hell, bitch-ass nigga," Lucifer declared before hurrying on his way out.

Hearing the shots erupt, Toni realized they'd come from the back area where Diamond was. "Diamond!" she yelled out as she and Pelle rushed towards the back of the club with their bangers drawn.

Boc! Boc! Boc! Boc!

Blocka! Blocka!

Toni and Pelle came across Lucifer and his boys, and both sides exchanged shots. One of Lucifer's boys was dropped from a bullet to the head, and Lucifer and the others continued bustin' as they backed their way out of the fire exit.

Toni ran into the office with Pelle in tow, finding Diamond on the floor, bleeding profusely. "I got you, Diamond, jus' stay wit' me," she urged in distress.

"We need to get him to a fuckin' hospital in a hurry," Pelle told her.

The two carried Diamond out to Pelle's navy blue Yukon Denali and placed him in the rear seat. Toni sat in the rear seat also, holding Diamond's head in her lap. Pelle stormed towards the hospital.

Gangsta had overheard everything that went down over the phone. Guilt consumed him, because had it not been for him shit wouldn't have come to this. Then again, had Diamond had the heart to get at Banks in the first place, it would be Banks with a bullet in his ass instead. At least, that's how Gangsta tried justifying it. But what if Diamond was to die? Even though they weren't seeing shit the same way, Diamond was still his boy, and Gangsta didn't have reason to wish death upon him.

\*\*\*

Tywanna rushed to Froedert hospital after receiving the call that Diamond had been shot. She couldn't control her wave of emotions. The thought of losing Diamond was more than she could bear. How could she live without him? He was the love of her life, and without him, her life would be incomplete.

She was surrounded by loved ones consoling her - including Jade. For over an hour, they'd been anxiously awaiting while Diamond was in surgery, and the surgery performed on him was to remove two slugs from his chest. Tywanna's stomach was in knots not knowing his condition. She could only hope that he'd be fine.

The surgeon treaded over the linoleum floor towards Tywanna and the others. "Please. Simmer down," the surgeon requested as she was bombarded with questions of concerns. Once everyone quieted down, she gave them the news. "You'll be happy to know that Mr. Miller's surgery was successful. Aside from some scars, he'll be just fine."

The news went over well with everyone except Jade, who did her all to remain composed.

"Doctor, can I see him?" Ty asked.

"Yes. But only for a short while. He'll need his rest." The surgeon showed Tywanna to Diamond's room.

Guilt was so thick on Gangsta that he needed to get the hell away. "Give Diamond my regards for me," he told Toni.

"Gangsta, now's not the time to jus' bounce. Diamond needs us now more than ever," Toni said.

"Jus' give him my regards, will you?"

"Be best if you stick around to show ya boy some respect," Pelle interjected.

Gangsta eyed him dreadfully. "Fuck is you to question my respect for anyone? I have respect for those who have respect for me." He respected Diamond, not only for himself, but for his character, for his integrity and judgement and iron will. But he had respect for him most for the enemies he made, because a nigga couldn't be too careful in his choice of enemies.

"A nigga will do many things to get himself respected; he'll do all things to get himself envied," Pelle stated.

Gangsta stepped into Pelle's personal space. "I burn niggas like you, homey," he spat.

"Was thinkin' the same 'bout you," Pelle retorted, not backing down.

"Yo, that's enough," Toni intervened, stepping between the two.

Gangsta mugged Pelle before turning for the exit.

Having feelings of guilt of her own, Jade decided to take the opportunity to leave with Gangsta. "I'm gonna go with him to make sure he's alright," she decided. "Tell Ty to call if she needs me." She caught up with Gangsta and together they walked out.

Tywanna quietly shut the door behind herself. She slowly approached Diamond, who was lying sound asleep in the bed. He was hooked up to machines that beeped and blinked for one reason or another. She'd always seen him as impregnable, so it was painful for her to see him in such condition. Tears sailed down her cheeks.

She couldn't bear the thought of losing Diamond to the streets. She'd never really thought about it up until now. She knew the streets had made him, therefore, she understood the streets could destroy him. Her hope was to have a future, a life and a family with Diamond. But if he continued to run the streets then she feared they stood no chance of fulfilling her hopes together.

She would never even consider telling him to choose between her and the streets, for she understood he loved them both for different reasons. But unlike the streets, she was able to offer him things that mattered, such as love, devotion, a child. That being so, the streets couldn't compare to her, and she hoped Diamond realized that. So it was a choice he'd have to be willing to make on his own.

"Hey bae," Tywanna spoke in close to a whisper. With the backside of her hand, she faintly brushed Diamond's cheek. "I love you so, so much. It's not easy for me to see you like this. I know you wouldn't want me in here cryin' and shit." She let out a small laugh.

"Diamond," she went on, "I was afraid we'd lose you too soon. We need you more than you know. We won't be complete without you, because you are a part of us." Tywanna grabbed Diamond's hand and placed it on her stomach.

The door shut just loud enough to gain Tywanna's attention. Looking back over her shoulder, she found her mother, Sandra. Tywanna prudently removed Diamond's hand and held it in her own.

Sandra stepped over to the bedside and stood next to Tywanna. "How far along are you?" she cared to know.

"Four weeks." Ty was actually excited about her pregnancy, and she was joyful about starting a family with Diamond.

"Does he know?" she inquired, her eyes on Diamond. This was the very first she was even learning about her daughter being with child.

"No. At this time he doesn't," she responded ruefully.

"And why doesn't he, Ty? It's best he knows soon," Sandra said keenly, her eyes now fixed on Tywanna. "Perhaps if he does then he may give up the street life."

Tywanna felt a faint squeeze from Diamond's hand and found him peering up at her through restless eyes. "Baby, I'm so glad you're awake!" she cried.

"Shit," Diamond winced in pain as he attempted to sit up in bed.

"Take it easy, baby." Tywanna helped him sit up. "How you feelin'?"

"Besides bein' hooked up to all these damn machines, I'm fine." He did his all to try concealing his pain.

"Good to see you're okay, Diamond," Sandra said sincerely. "Well, I'll leave you two alone. I'm sure there's somethin' Ty would like to say to you in private." She gave Tywanna a look before making her way out.

"Somethin' you wanna say to me?" Diamond inquired.

"Diamond, I was so damn scared I'd lose you."

He grabbed Ty at the waist and pulled her close. "I'm here for you."

"Diamond?" Tywanna called out in a whisper.

"Yeah, love."

She drew back from his hold and met his inquisitive eyes. "I'm…I'm havin' yo' child," she divulged.

Astounded, Diamond didn't know exactly what to say. Indeed he was proud, in spite of not being sure if he'd even live long enough to see his unborn child due to his lifestyle. Nonetheless, he wanted nothing more than to have a family with no one other than Tywanna.

"Ty, why didn't you tell me sooner?"

She hung her head. "I just didn't wanna add to yo' stress."

He palmed her chin, lifted her eyes to his, and said, "Listen, there's nothin' you could do or say to stress a nigga. I'm here for you no matter what."

"Diamond, I just want us to be a family," she uttered.

"Ty, from now on, every day I'll live for you 'n my seed. Everything I do I'll do it for both of y'all. See, my life ain't promised, but it's sure gettin' better. I have nothin' but love for you, and all I want is for my unborn child to have a better life than I did," Diamond expressed. He wondered, in case he didn't make, if his child would get to feel his love. He placed his hand on Ty's stomach and, to his unborn, he said, "Remember, Daddy loves you."

"Diamond, I love you, and there's nothin' I wouldn't do for you."

"Ty, true love is doin'. Not jus' words and feelings. And what you willin' to do shouldn't be said, it should be done," Diamond divulged, and the two shared a deep kiss.

# Troublesome

## Chapter 5

"Take a seat, Gangsta," Diamond directed firmly.

In the Theater, Diamond was seated at the head of the table while the others were seated on either side of it - including Pelle, who occupied the seat at Diamond's side, which was normally Gangsta's.

Gangsta took a seat in an available chair, the whole while muggin' Pelle. "Hell's dis nigga doin' here? He ain't part of the crew," he stated rashly.

"I asked him here, 'cause he has a right to be," Diamond said.

"And what gives him the right at all? You hardly even know dis nigga."

"All I need to know is he was down to ride for me, and I respect him for it. Does that answer yo' question enough?"

"Diamond, I been ridin' for you since we jumped off the porch!" he said emphatically, and underlined it further by striking the table. "Don't tell me you believe dis nigga willin' to die for you, too. 'Cause, without a doubt, I will."

Diamond maintained his composer. "And I'ont doubt you'll ride or die for me, Gangsta. But lately you haven't been so steadfast."

"What'chu tryna say, you don't trust me or somethin', Diamond?"

"You made it difficult for me to," Diamond replied. He leaned forward in his seat. "Mind tellin' me what the hell went on while I was outta town? 'Cause word in the streets is I attempted to body Banks. I'm sure you played a part in it somehow, Gangsta, so don't gimme no lies."

Gangsta casually sat back in his chair. "It's like this: I sent some niggas to off Banks and obviously it didn't go as planned. Now here we are," he explained quite frankly.

"Nigga, the fact that you didn't let me know a damn thing nearly cost me my life," Diamond fumed. Now anger could be detected in his usually placid voice.

"Thought I'd do what you seem to lack the heart to, and that'd be the end of it," he replied intractably.

Diamond eyed him sharply. "That's what you thought, huh?" he huffed. "Well, leave the thinkin' to me, 'cause obviously you thought wrong."

Those words were like a slug to Gangsta's head, for he had used those exact words on West before putting a slug into his. "I'ont need no muthafucka to think for me," he raged and jumped to his feet, knocking over his chair. "In fact, I think I should be the nigga in charge 'round dis bitch any-fuckin'-way!"

"I leave you in charge for a few days, and now you think you should be the nigga in charge of shit? There's a reason why I'm in charge."

"You in charge 'cause we let you be in charge, Diamond."

"So we agree that I'm in charge. Now, pick up that damn chair, sit yo' ass back in it, and be humble," Diamond ordered sternly.

"Think it's best that I leave," Gangsta declared obstinately. "Chase, if you wit' me, then let's get the hell outta here." He turned for the door.

"Gangsta, come back," Diamond told him.

He halted in his tracks. "Are you tellin' me as my friend, or the one in charge?" Diamond paused. "Damn shame you have to think about that," Gangsta said, then proceeded on his way out.

Chase stood up. "Look, I'ma go wit' him to keep him level-headed," he rationalized. "Diamond, you and him need to figure this shit out ASAP. I'd hate to have to take sides." He made his way out the stash house.

Diamond slammed his clenched fist down onto the table out of frustration. He winced in pain.

"You a'ight, Diamond?" Toni wanted to know.

"Maybe I took shit too far and allowed anger to get the better of me."

"Fuck that, Diamond, ain't yo' fault," Pelle piped in. "Gangsta shouldn't have went behind yo' back, 'cause it damn near got you smoked."

"Yeah, but you and Gangsta been down for each other too long for you not to reconcile wit' him, Diamond," Toni added.

"Toni's right," Diamond admitted. "No matter how I feel about Gangsta at the moment, it doesn't change all the shit he and I been through. I'll talk wit' him when the time's right. But for the time bein', I gotta put shit wit' Gangsta outta my mind and focus on these streets." He knew that the power struggle over the streets caused him to exude strength being that his enemies was coming seeking weakness, and he would let them find nothing but defiance, destruction, and, God willing, death.

***

Gripping the .9 Glock fitted with a thirty-shot pole lying across his lap, Banks perpetually checked his surroundings, as he and Lucifer moved through traffic. Lucifer pushed his red Acura TSX sitting on 26-inch rims while Banks rode shotgun. They were on their way to meet the plug.

The two were actually cousins, and Lucifer was the trusted underboss to Banks. Lucifer, with a build reminiscent of a brick wall and a villain-styled widow's peak, was often found at Banks's side, a literal right-hand man who watched the operation like a hawk and could be counted on to handle the dirty work.

After having Diamond clapped up just days ago, Banks knew to be prepared for retaliation. He'd been informed by Jade that Diamond managed to survive, and Banks was discontent about it.

"So the li'l redbone was ridin' my face, right, while the thick-ass snow bunny straight deep-throated a nigga joint!" Lucifer was going on and on about the threesome he had experienced with two bad bitches last night. "Then I had 'em both bent over and - "

"Yo, would you shut da fuck up? And turn this damn music down, got it blastin' all loud and shit," Banks said rigidly, and then he turned the music completely off. "All of the damn talkin' and music is a distraction." The belief of a cautious nigga. He checked the rearview mirror, making sure they wasn't being tailed.

Lucifer glanced over at Banks, shaking his head. "Actin' like that pussy-ass nigga Diamond got'chu scared or some shit," he huffed.

"Nigga, I ain't neva scared," Banks rebutted angrily. "Ain't stupid neither. I'm smart enough to know that at some point, the nigga gon' clap back. Which is exactly why..." He held up the .9. "You see this bitch right here."

"Then let's put his ass in the dirt beforehand." He peeped the sideways look Banks was giving him and said, "Hell you lookin' at me like that for?"

"Shoulda did that shit when you had the damn chance. It ain't gon' be easy gettin' that close to Diamond again, so it's best we stay ready for his ass." Banks knew that Diamond would stay scheming, tryna get at him.

***

"Would ya look at what the cat drug in?"

Upon entering the mansion, Lynch was met by two well-dressed Italian men, Little and Alphonse, both of whom looked dapper in their tailor-made suits. But make no mistakes, they were armed and dangerous.

Little was short, stout, and balding with a little-man complex. For him murder came easy. Alphonse was a good-looking guy, who, unlike most Italians, didn't speak as much. He was well-tempered, yet merciless.

"How's it hangin', Lynch?" Little said.

"Hangin' in there," Lynch responded.

Alphonse frisked Lynch, and after confiscating his sidearm and, most importantly, not discovering any wires on him, he stepped aside. "He's clean."

"Care for a drink? Al, get Lynch here a drink, will ya. What'll it be?" Little offered.

"I'll pass on the offer, thanks anyway. I'm here to see Frank."

"No prob'. Just need to check and see if he's available. Follow me, eh." Little led Lynch while Alphonse tailed.

They stepped into the massive dining room. There was polished marble flooring, handcrafted Italian leather furniture, an antique grand piano, expensive-looking paintings on the walls, and a great crystal chandelier draped from the high-rise ceiling. It was apparent the place was decorated by someone with very rich taste.

Frank Balistrieri, who was wrapped in a silk Versace robe with Versace loafers on his feet, was seated in one of the handcrafted chairs, enjoying a Cuban cigar. He was the head gangster of Milwaukee, also known as the Crazy Bomber because he often used homemade exploding devices. a method that made many of his enemies buy remote controls for their cars, used to start the engine.

An educated man with a lot of rich taste, Frank had business with the bosses of the Las Vegas casinos who were giving part of the profit to the Chicago Mafia. Frank was tall, slickly attractive, at ease, and slightly less traditional than his colleagues. His gilded hair curled towards his shoulders and his smile was a quick nova flash of charm and power.

Lynch had been summoned to see Frank. He mainly worked for Frank due to being blackmailed by him, and Lynch couldn't just arrest him, because he knew Frank had more than enough on him to put him away for the rest of his natural life. Thing is, Frank dangled over his head the bodies of two undercover cops, whom Lynch had knocked off for Frank for a generous fee during his earlier years on the force. Since then he'd been forced to be a gangster's gofer: Frank's.

Being under Frank's thumb, Lynch was made to rip-off seized narcotics from the police evidence department in order to distribute it to Diamond and other top-level drug associates on Frank's payroll. Lynch knew that he was in over his head and needed to find a way out. He'd been plotting a long time to free himself of Frank's power.

Little approached Frank. "Boss, are you available? Because if not, then I'll have to tell Lynch here to come back another time," he said.

Frank simply gestured for Little to allow Lynch to see him, and Little followed his orders. "Aw, c'mon Lynch, don't gimme that look like you wanna bust my chops. Just doin' my gig, you know," he said after noticing Lynch eye him narrowly. He and Alphonse left the two men alone.

"Have a seat, Agent," Frank instructed evenly, puffing his cigar. With no objections, Lynch sat on the sofa across from him. "I'm aware of the hornet's nest our mutual friend has on his hands. Diamond's an investment of mine, Agent, and I can't have anyone getting in the way of my venture. I have a lot riding on Diamond, so I need him to be able to be profitable, which means, however, you must shield him."

"I've been on top of it, Frank."

He fixed Lynch with hard eyes. "Then why haven't you done a damn thing about it?" he asked austerely. "I want it dealt with pronto, Agent. Whoever the fuck is giving Diamond trouble, find out whom he's connected to, and then see to the connect."

"You mean you want me to hit him where his pockets hurt?" Lynch inquired.

"No, no, no. That's not enough." Frank dumped ashes from the cigar into the crystal ashtray, taking from under the sleeve of his robe the smooth, thin gold of a $1.5 million Vacheron Constantine timepiece. "I want 'im whacked, Agent," he clarified. "You see, the idea is to eradicate the connect, then have Diamond recruit his clientele. That way there will be less turf wars getting in the way of making money, as long as everyone's on the same side. It's a simple conquest." He puffed the cigar.

"Enough said, Frank. It's done," Lynch assured.

"And I expect it to be done faster than you can say fettuccini. Capisce?" He exhaled smoke in Lynch's face. "Now get outta 'ere."

\*\*\*

The four girlfriends were gathered at Ashley's place. They sat at the dinette table, having wine and helping with wedding invitations. In just a few weeks, Ashley and Chase were set to exchange vows, and it couldn't seem to come soon enough for her.

Lexi licked shut one of the invitations and then placed it on top of the stack of others on the table. "So, where's the hubby-to-be?" she asked.

"His ass out runnin' the damn streets," Ashley said. "Let him tell it, he's out puttin' food on the table. Don't get me wrong, I respect that he's man enough to do what he have to so he can provide for his family, but it stresses me the hell out always worryin' about him, you know. I just want him safely home with me and the twins."

"Trust, I feel you, girl," Tywanna chimed in. "It never really bothered me before what happened to Diamond, but now I can't help but feel the same."

"How's he doin', by the way?" Ashley asked.

"Better. Nigga too damn stubborn to let a coupla bullets slow his ass down," she made light of it. "What I'ont get is how the hell did those niggas get inside the club with guns and how was they able to get so close to him."

"Simple' It had to be a set-up," Lexi suggested. "And more than likely it was someone he least expects. Maybe one of the girls who work for him at the club."

"You think?" Tywanna inquired. By sheer happenstance, she had never mentioned the name of Lexi's lover to her man, which kept him from connecting the dots. But beside her, someone else was getting nervous as hell.

Jade accidentally on purpose knocked over her glass of wine on the table, hoping to shift the topic. "My bad, Ash." She jumped to her feet. "I'll get it." She grabbed paper towels from the countertop.

Tywanna hurriedly picked up the invitations before the spilt wine could ruin them. "Are you okay, Jade? 'Cause lately you been actin' kinda strange," she pointed out.

"Girl, I'm good," she said with a counterfeit smile. Her conscience was eating away at her, knowing she had played a role in having Diamond set up, so she didn't feel comfortable around her girls. So lately she'd been keeping her distance from them, especially from Tywanna.

"Slut prolly just need some dick," Lexi cracked.

"Whateva, Lex. I can get some dick from yo' nigga if I want."

"Jade, please. Banks wouldn't even fuck you with another nigga's dick." Lexi was certain of that.

The twins could be heard crying over the baby monitor, and Ashley went to check in on them. A moment later she returned with the twins on each hip. Tywanna took one of them off her hands. Ty wondered about the gender of her own baby she was carrying. Thus far none of her girls was even aware that she was pregnant.

"Do y'all realize how long it has been since we been out together?" Lexi said, breaking Tywanna's thoughts. "I have an idea. How 'bout we all go on a date together with our men this weekend."

"You mean like a group date?" Ashley asked.

"Yeah, it'll be fun."

"I'm down," Tywanna agreed.

"Well, I'ont know if I'll be able to get a babysitter so soon," Ashley stressed. "But I'll see."

Lexi looked over to Jade. "How 'bout you, are you down with us?"

"Sorry girl, I'ma have to pass. Got some shit to do this weekend. But y'all bitches have fun," Jade responded casually. *Ain't no way in hell am I finna put my ass in a position to have to be around Diamond and Banks at the same damn time*, she added introspectively.

"Guess that leaves just the two of us." Lexi smiled at Tywanna. "We'll have fun," she assured.

"And I'm sure Diamond and Banks will enjoy each other's company," Jade added with a feigned smile.

Neither Tywanna nor Lexi was privy to the hatred their lovers possessed for each other, which, to their dismay, could actually turn their date-night into a date with death.

\*\*\*

While Toni pushed the Benz, Diamond occupied its rear seat with Pelle alongside of him. They rode through the north side of the city where the crime rate was consistently on the rise, poverty was a way of life, drug infestations were affluent, and murder seemed to be a daily ritual.

"You know," Diamond looked over to Pelle, "things I do ain't jus' about the money. Believe it or not, I care to make a difference in the hood. Mainly for the young ones unfortunately growin' up the way I did wit' nothin'."

"I feel you, dawg." Pelle didn't expect Diamond to be so sympathetic, since most people in positions of power were usually self-centered.

Toni weighed in from the driver's seat. "Diamond's kinda a gentle gangsta for the drug economy."

To Diamond, the ends justified the means. It was a warped version of the American dream, a Robin Hood mentality tailored to the drug trade, a belief that if you worked hard and beat the system, then funneled some of your cash back into the community, at least some of the system's casualties would benefit from your enterprise.

"So this is jus' a temporary hustle for you then, right?" Pelle wanted to know.

"Only a hustle, not a career. And one of these days, I'll be done wit' it," Diamond swore. "Listen here, Pelle, I think you a real nigga. And I want you to know that I ']preciate you practically savin' a nigga's life. If there's anything I could do for you, jus' let me know."

"Diamond, yo' appreciation is more than enough," Pelle said humbly.

Once alone with Toni after they dropped off Pelle, Diamond casually said to her, "Toni, I decided to take Pelle in. But under one condition: if he doesn't turn out to be who he claims to be, I'ma murk his ass. And, I'ma murk you."

She understood Diamond meant that.

***

"Wah gwan, bredhren? Me expected you'd be back." Yul wasn't surprised that Gangsta requested to have a conclave with him. They met at an intimate Jamaican eatery.

"Yeah, well here I am," Gangsta said as he sat across the table from Yul. He peeped Rasheym and Siah lurking in the shadows, not too far away from their leader.

Yul was enjoying a plate of curried goat. Not least of Jamaica's offerings - not to him, anyway - was the country's food. The spicy dishes were adapted from African, Chinese, and East Indian dishes, but somehow uniquely Jamaican. "Back on de Island in me hometown of Tivoli Garden, me mudda used to cook us meals fit for a king. Plantains, barbecued tofu, jerked chicken. But nuddin was betta dan her curried goat," Yul reminisced. He looked up from his plate and fixed his piercing, colored eyes on Gangsta. "Dat was until de messenger ah death came for her."

"Condolences," was all Gangsta could find fit to say.

"No need, becuz me understands wid de pleasure of livin' comes de obligation of death - which is why me don't fear anyding. An' me see de same in you, Gangsta," Yul told him. "Now, me understand dat you'd like to take me up on me earlier offer."

"Let's not forget, I ain't the one who refused."

"And whut about you partner, Diamond?"

"Who gives a fuck about 'im? Not me." Gangsta made his feelings clear. After his contention with Diamond, Gangsta thought it was time that he be in charge of his own outfit, so he decided to affiliate with the Jamaicans. This way he'd have a powerful backing.

Yul smirked. "Dat's why me like you, rude boi. You don't give a fuck 'bout no one but you damn self." He did realize that Gangsta could be his own worst enemy, and the enemy from within is unpredictable to oneself.

"If I'ont do for myself, then no one else will. Certainly not Diamond."

"Me'll make you a richer mon dan Diamond ever could," Yul assured.

"Let's not downplay the power he holds. The nigga might be silent, but he's deadly," Gangsta acknowledged.

"So we disrupt his operations. A mon can't go to war widout funds to back him. Mon will pay millions for defense, but not one cent for tribute."

"Trust me, Diamond's not the easiest enemy to go up against."

Yul leaned in close towards Gangsta like he had a secret to tell, and then, in close to a whisper, he said, "Before me left de Island, me went to de obeah-womon to grant me great power, an' put a curse on all ah me enemies."

***

Rising steam fogged the entire bathroom, as hot water cascaded down on Banks while he stood inside the walk-in shower. With his eyes shut, he just allowed the water to massage away his strains.

His beef with Diamond weighed heavily on him. He knew it wouldn't be over until one of them was dead and gone, which was exactly why he needed to dead Diamond sooner rather than later. He didn't have shit personal against Diamond; to him it was business. Perhaps in part it was personal, he had to admit. But...

Banks's thoughts were interrupted upon hearing someone at the front door of the apartment. He cut the water and hurried out of the shower, wrapping himself in a towel, then grabbed his .9 off the lid of the toilet and insidiously made his way into the dark front room. The door opened, then the entrant stepped inside, and before the door could be shut, Banks pressed the muzzle of the .9 to the unsuspecting entrants dome - finger on the trigger.

"Don't make me blow yo' fuckin' head off," Banks hissed.

"Banks, it's only me." It was Lexi. She clicked on the light. "Now get that damn thing away from head," she insisted in a rather composed manner.

Banks withdrew the weapon, letting it hang at his side. "My bad, babe. Shit jus' been so hectic lately, and I can't afford to take any chances," he stressed.

She could see the anguish on his face. "Baby, them streets are stressin' you. Maybe I can help you get the streets off yo' mind. I set up a double-date with one of my girlfriends, I hope you don't mind."

"I'ont know 'bout that, Lex."

"Pleeease," she cooed as she stepped close to him. She pulled the towel from around his waist and it fell onto the floor at his bare feet, leaving him in his birthday suit, and then she kindly handled his dick.

"A'ight, I'll go. But only 'cause you said please."

"I'm sure we'll have a nice time." She kissed Banks's lips and then said, "Luckily you didn't blow off a bitch's head, or I wouldn't be able to do this."

She began to plant a trail of soft kisses down Banks neck. Her lips felt pleasant on him. She gently bit the flesh of his shoulder, and Banks enjoyed it. She kissed her way down to his fat, hard dick, then licked up and down its shaft before she deep-throated him.

"Damn, boo, yo' head game da shit!" Banks commended her. The remarkable feeling of Lexi's warm mouth and gentle lips caused him to bust a nut. And he loved his nasty bitch who swallowed what was on the menu.

## Chapter 6

"Shit gon' go my way 'round dis bitch from now on!"

Gangsta stood on the rooftop of his G-Wagon with his Draco in hand. He commanded the attention of the crowd before him. Major was among the crowd. Gangsta declared himself taking over yet another part of Diamond's turf. He'd already recruited numerous of Diamond's low-level distributors, flooding them with the dope Yul was giving him on front.

"You'll push packs for me, take orders from me, and make payments to none other than me. And if anybody got a problem wit' it, then I suggest you learn to deal wit' it," Gangsta ruled.

One of the niggas among the crowd had enough balls to step forward and ask the question that everybody was thinking. "But, what about Diamond - "

Boc! Boc!

Gangsta popped the ballsy nigga in his chest and neck, fading him on the spot, and making it a point to affirm with the rest that he was dead serious. He sharply eyed the entire crowd, seeing that he'd gotten his point across, judging by the distressed looks painted on their faces. His method was reckless, but effective.

"That's what I think about Diamond, in case anyone else wanna know," Gangsta rendered. He realized that it would become a power struggle over the streets, and to be triumphant, he was fully prepared to use firepower.

\*\*\*

Diamond was heated as hell after ending the call with Major, who informed him about Gangsta's latest antic. Diamond didn't know what the fuck had gotten into Gangsta, who'd all of a sudden chosen to commit treachery. He wanted to know Gangsta's incentive, but whatever it was, murder was the only consequence apt for his violation. He phoned Gangsta.

"Make it quick, I'm busy takin' over the streets," Gangsta answered hostilely, aware that it was Diamond on the other end.

"Gangsta, what the hell are you doin'?" he asked heatedly.

"Doin' what I shoulda a long ago, and ain't a damn thang you can do about it."

"I'm the one wit' the connect, or did you forget? You have no product without me."

Gangsta chuckled indifferently. "Diamond, fuck you and that spaghetti-snapper connect of yours. Have my own connection now. I'm fuckin' wit' the Rasta's, and if you was smart, you woulda done the same."

Diamond huffed. "It don't astound me that you connected wit' Yul behind my back. Who needs enemies wit' friends like you?" he stated with malice before terminating the call.

Not only did Diamond have to deal with Banks attempting to move in on his territory, but now also Gangsta. He couldn't say which of the two posed more of a threat to him, but he understood they both had to be eliminated due to the threats they posed respectively. He foresaw their beef meeting a dead end with a barrage of bullets.

***

Wrapping a belt tightly around her brittle arm in a desperate search for a valid vein, the dope fiend anxiously prepped herself to get a fix. Her arm suffered countless track marks due to being constantly penetrated by a syringe. After finally finding a proper vein and then injecting herself full of boy, she was heavily sedated.

Banks observed the fiend as the dope caused her to nod in and out of consciousness. *Can't understand how anyone can allow a substance to control their damn life*, he thought in disgust.

It mainly bothered him because he could vividly remember witnessing his mother OD right before his eyes when he was only nine years old; and now he was supplying the very drug which had taken his mother away from him. The irony. He wondered if the fiend had any shorties of her own she should have been home caring for, instead of being out chasing a fuckin' high.

Not being able to deal with the guilt, Banks just needed to get away in order to clear his head. He made his way out of the bando, and on the front porch, Lucifer came after him.

"You a'ight, fam'?" Lucifer noticed that Banks seemed peeved.

"Jus' need to take a ride alone. You know, so a nigga can get his mind right."

"Banks, the nigga Diamond got shooters out here lurkin' in these streets, so I think it's best I ride wit'chu," Lucifer suggested.

Banks raised his shirt only enough to reveal the thirty-shot stick protruding from the .9mm stuffed in the waist of his skinny-jeans. "Think I'll be straight." He let his shirt down and said, "I know you right and all, cuz, but my .9 is gonna ride wit' me."

Lucifer began to protest, but then decided maybe it was best to leave it be. "Cool then. Jus' hit my line if you need me, and I'll - what the fuck!"

Blocka! Blocka! Blocka! Blocka!

Boc! Boc! Boc!

Two gunmen had suddenly appeared from the side of the bando, where they had lurked in the dark gangway awaiting their target, and then opened fire. Fortunately, Banks and Lucifer were quick with drawing their weapons and returning shots. Once the gunfire on either side subsided, both gunmen were left on the lawn stretched out like the Air Jordan logo.

"See what the hell I mean?" Lucifer said heatedly. "Diamond ain't gon' stop 'til either you or he's on a damn T-shirt."

"And better him than me," Banks stated. He heard sirens wailing in the distance. "Shut down the trap. Twelve gon' be tapin' off the area soon."

\*\*\*

"So what exactly is it you wanna talk with me about?" Lexi inquired. She didn't get why Jade insisted on talking with her alone. They were in Lexi's crib, seated on the sofa in the front room, sharing a blunt while Rihanna crooned from the speakers in the background.

"Lex, you been my girl for a while. Don't get it twisted, Ty and Ash are my girls, too. But this has to stay between me and you," Jade told her.

Lexi eyed her warily. "Girl, you know we don't do secrets and lies. As far as I know, we have always kept it real with one other about everything," She took a pull of the blunt.

"Well, this'll have to be exceptional, 'cause it'll ruin my friendship with the others. And maybe you, too," she vexed.

"Jade. Don't sit here and tell me yo' ass been creepin' with one of our niggas. If so, then you done crossed the damn line, 'cause you know we don't get down like that. And it bet not be Banks, or -"

"No, Lex, that ain't it," Jade interfered, sounding agitated.

"Oh. My bad," she said with relief. "Then, what is it Jade?" She inquisitively eyed her. Tears began to slide down Jade's cheeks, and Lexi scooted closer towards her, comforting her with a hug. "Must be somethin' terrible 'cause you ain't the cryin' type of bitch." She handed Jade the blunt, along with a Kleenex from the end table.

Jade took a puff of the loud, allowing smoke to fill her lungs before exhaling. She used the Kleenex to dab away her tears, and then took a deep breath, collecting her composure. "It was me, Lex," she uttered.

"It was you what?" Lexi was thrown.

"Who had set up Diamond," she contritely confessed, needing to tell someone.

Lexi didn't expect for that to be the matter. "Bitch, I can't believe yo' ass right now. You s'posed to be Tywanna's girl, but you sit here and tell my ass you was the one who set up her man? And you expect for me to just keep that shit between us, bitch, you got me fucked up." She was livid.

"For yo' info, I set his ass up for Banks!" Jade admitted.

"What?" Lexi jumped to her feet, never expecting to hear that.

"Yeah, that's right, bitch. Yo' man paid me to have Tywanna's man set up. So you won't tell the others, especially Ty. 'Cause if you do it'll come between y'all's friendship."

Abruptly, Banks hurried into the loft with his .9 in hand and locked the door behind himself. During his entire drive home, paranoia caused him to perpetually check his mirrors for any sign of a tail while gripping the pistol in his lap. He also circled the block four times before deeming it safe enough to park. He was still on edge from the shootout back at the bando.

"Banks!" Lexi fretted as she hurried over to him. "Everything alright?

"Aside from nearly gettin' bodied, I'm good," Banks said afflicted. To his surprise, he noticed Jade seated on the sofa. "Didn't mean to interrupt whateva this is." He set the pistol on the coffee table.

"It's nothin' important, just girl chat," Lexi deflected.

Jade stood and said, "I was just leavin' anyway. Lex, we'll finish our chat some other time." She hit the blunt once more before passing it to Banks. "Seems you really need it." She departed the loft.

Banks observed Jade from the window. *Hope the hoe ain't mention shit to Lex*, he thought. He took a pull of the blunt as he observed Jade step into her Jag and then dispel.

"Baby, are you sure you're okay? Maybe you should sit," Lexi suggested.

"Tol' you I'm good, Lex, damn." He came off annoyed.

"Here I am all worried 'bout yo' ass-n-shit, and you gettin' heated. Well s'cuse me for even carin'," Lexi stressed, full of attitude. She turned for the kitchen.

Banks followed her. "You right, babe, I'm trippin'," he admitted. "Actually, if it makes you feel better, I 'preciate when yo' li'l sexy ass worry 'bout a nigga." He put on that grin she couldn't seem to resist.

For Lexi, the thought of her losing Banks or Tywanna losing Diamond due to one another's lovers was unbearable. She wouldn't be able to look at Tywanna the same either way. She didn't want to have to choose between her lover and her friend, although if she had to, then she would choose to stand with her love. And she was sure Tywanna would do the same. For love trumps all.

Shaking her dreadful thoughts away, she pulled his plate of food out of the microwave, then said, "Ready for dinner? Made yo' favorite: lasagna."

"Thanks." He grabbed the plate, then set it aside on the countertop. "But I'd rather have dessert first." He pulled her close to him, lowered his mouth onto hers, kissing her passionately. In that moment, he felt a desire for her. Maybe it was because she, of all people, made him feel secure. He loved her ass. She meant a lot to him.

He swept everything off the breakfast bar onto the floor, lifted Lexi up by her ass and sat her on top of it, then pulled off her boy shorts. Banks dug into the fridge. He came out with a bottle of chocolate syrup.

"Boy, what the hell is that for?" she asked, interested.

"Dessert," Banks grinned. He drizzled chocolate on her crotch, and she spread her legs wide and palmed his skull while he was on his knees with his mouth on her sweet pussy.

"Oooh…umm, yes, Banks. Taste this shit, boy," she moaned as she watched him flick his tongue over her pearl-tongue, and he gazed up into her eyes. Lexi closed her eyes and let her head fall back as she came.

Banks rose to his feet, undid his YSL belt, and let his jeans fall down around his YSL sneakers. He then slid his fat, hard dick inside her. She felt so damn good to him as he jabbed in and out of her wetness. "Damn, Lex, dis wet-wet got a nigga ready to bust and shit," he grunted.

"You got it wet, but baby, you can get it wetter," she motivated him seductively. As Banks dug deeper inside her, she wrapped her arms around him, digging her nails into his back.

"Aww shit, boo." Banks released his juices.

"Banks," Lexi began in a whisper, "just know that I worry 'cause I love you. And I'ont wanna lose you, even if you do get on my damn nerves at time." She pecked his lips, getting chocolate on her face.

"Don't worry so much about losin' me, 'cause you won't," he solemnly swore.

\*\*\*

The waiter dexterously filled the four flute glasses with Moet before stepping away from the table. Diamond and Tywanna were along with Lexi and Banks on their double date. They occupied a table at an upscale restaurant, Fox & Hounds, located in downtown. They were all dressed to the nines.

Banks raised his glass. "Toast: to a night to remember."

"Cheers." They all clinked glasses, followed by a drink of the champagne.

Banks set his drink on the table. "Long time no see, Diamond," he said casually.

Diamond looked over the rim of his glass at Banks as he sipped the champagne. "Yeah, damn shame we haven't been able to catch up in a while." He could hardly maintain his cool. But he got satisfaction that Banks seen him still breathing after being hit up, even if he was still in some pain.

"C'mon, Lex," Tywanna said and she rose in her Christian Dior heels. "Let's go to the powder room and freshen up." She grabbed up her clutch purse.

Lexi had mixed feelings about leaving the two men alone unsupervised, since she was quietly aware of their animosity. She leaned in and pecked Banks on the lips. "Play nice," she advised. Once collecting her handbag, she went along with Tywanna to the ladies room.

"Had I known you'd be here I wouldn't have come," Diamond admitted, eyeing Banks.

"Feelin' is mutual."

"Apparently we both came to appease our girls, so let's keep things civil for them tonight."

"How 'bout this." Banks leaned forward, resting his elbows atop the table. "Outta respect for our girls, we keep 'em outta our beef," he proposed.

"Agreed." It was obvious to Diamond that Banks loved Lexi as much as he loved Tywanna. Even though he had a dislike for Banks, he had nothing against the nigga's girl. And on the strength that they both loved their girls as much as they did, he wouldn't want Tywanna or Lexi to become casualties of war due to him and Banks, although he understood that all is fair in love and war.

Meanwhile, in the restroom, Tywanna looked herself over in the mirror. She noticed the slight baby bump and wondered if the others did as well. Peering through the mirror at Lexi, who stood beside her, Tywanna peeped how Lexi seem distracted.

"Lex, is everything okay? Yo' ass been absentminded all evenin'." Tywanna could see that something was on Lexi's mind other than the date.

"Sure, I'm okay," Lexi responded unconvincingly.

"Girl..." Tywanna placed a hand on her shoulder. "Now you know of all people you can tell sis what's on your mind."

"It's Banks and Diamond..." Her words trailed off.

"What about 'em? They seem fine, so don't worry," Tywanna said, naïve to the facts. "Listen, let's just enjoy the remainder of the evenin' with each other and our men, 'kay?"

Lexi mustered a miniature smile. "You're truly a good friend, Ty."

"I know, right!" Tywanna giggled. "Seriously though, I don't know what I'd do without any of my girls."

*Let's just hope you'll never have to find out*, Lexi thought introspectively. She hated to admit that Jade had a point. If Tywanna learned about Banks and Diamond being enemies, then it could potentially ruin her and Ty's friendship. She didn't even understand why Jade decided to reveal such information to her to begin with, although she felt that, at least for the moment, it was better Tywanna not know. Or maybe...

"Sis." Tywanna spoke in a soft tone, breaking Lexi's thoughts. "You're gonna be an aunty," she revealed.

Lexi gasped, hands covering her mouth. "Girl, I'm so happy for you and Diamond." She pulled Tywanna in for a hug. In that moment, her mind shifted to the possibility of Tywanna and her unborn losing Diamond. "Ty." she grabbed her hands and met her eyes. "Just promise to be a strong mother now matter what."

Tywanna heard the sincerity in her friend's voice, as well as saw it in her eyes. "Promise."

\*\*\*

Gangsta fucked Jade doggy-style and pulled on her long weave. "Damn, bitch, dis shit got a nigga 'bout to bust a nut," he grunted.

"Bust, nigga! Bust all on my ass!" Jade enjoyed being treated roughly during sex. Gangsta grasped her ass as he dug deep inside her, and she threw it back, meeting his every thrust, taking the pipe. "Ohhh shit, Gangsta! Gimme dat big-ass dick!"

"Take this pipe, bitch. Yeah, jus' like that." On the verge of nutting, he pulled his piece out from Jade's wet-shot and then skeeted on her ass.

After smashing, the two remained ass naked and chilled in bed. They were at Gangsta's crib.

Jade straddled Gangsta. He snorted a line of coke from a small glass mirror and then held it out for Jade's indulgence also.

"Noticed you ain't been at Red Velvet lately. Guess it's true you had a fallin' out with Diamond, after all," Jade probed.

"Fuck Diamond. Nigga think the world's his. Well, I'ma fuck up his whole world," he vented.

She detected resentment in Gangsta. Telling him she'd played a part in setting up Diamond crossed her mind, but she figured it was best to keep it to herself, at least for now.

Gangsta laid back in bed. "Don't chu have someplace else to be tonight?"

Jade smacked her lips. "If you want a bitch to bounce, then nigga, just say the word."

"Shorty, it ain't even like that, so lose the damn 'tude."

"Mm hmm, I can't tell." She rolled her contact-lens-blue eyes.

"Jus' thought maybe you had to be at the club, or wanted to chill with yo' girls, or somethin'." He snorted another line.

"Well, FYI, I'ont have to work the club tonight. And as for my girls, Ash is at home with Chase, and both Ty and Lex are out on a double date with Diamond and Banks. So no, Gangsta, I'ont have someplace else to be," she illustrated. Relieving him of the mirror, she tooted a line of the coke.

*Hell Diamond and Banks doin' out together? I'm sure they're schemin' on me*, he contemplated. He sat up, "Where'd yo' girls say they were goin' on their date?"

"Why you worryin' 'bout them when you right here with me," Jade carped.

"Hoe…" He vise gripped her by the throat with one hand, causing her to drop the mirror. "If yo' ass know what's good for you. then you'll tell me what I wanna know. Now!" he demanded angrily.

"Lexi mentioned they were goin' to Fox & Hounds," she told him out of fear. "Now lemme the fuck go, Gangsta." She was short of breath.

Wasting no time, Gangsta jumped out of bed and hurriedly dressed. He collected his keys, iPhone, and .40-caliber as he rushed out of the loft headed for his ride.

Jade remained in bed, catching her breath. She was aware that Gangsta was on his way to catch two bodies with one gun on Diamond and Banks. She just hoped Tywanna and/or Lexi didn't become casualties in the process.

\*\*\*

Banks casually sat back in his chair, sipping his glass of Moet. "Word on da street is you and Gangsta are no longer allies."

"Guess word travels fast," Diamond affirmed.

"Now you gotta worry 'bout he and I both comin' after you," he smirked.

"Let's get one thing straight, Banks:  I ain't worried 'bout nothin'. And don't you realize Gangsta's gonna come after you before he will me?"

"Let 'im come." He turned the fingers of his free hand into a make believe pistol. "I won't be slackin'. By the way, that goes for you, too. Feel me?" He sipped his drink.

"I'ont take threats lightly."

"Then take it as a warnin'." He placed his glass on the table. "Ever considered you and I bein' business partners? Ain't a bad idea, you know," Banks half-joked.

"I'ont need partnership wit' you or Gangsta. Rather wipe out the competition."

"C'mon, Diamond, don't be that way," he lightly chuckled.

"And between the three of us…in the end, I'll be the last nigga standin'."

Banks locked eyes with him. "Over my dead body."

Diamond leaned forward, rested his folded arms atop the table. "I can have that arranged," he warranted.

The girls approached the table, walking arm-in-arm, and then took their seats. "You two enjoy each other's company while we were in the powder room?" Tywanna asked.

"Of course," Banks answered with a feigned smile.

"Was jus' talkin' man-to-man," Diamond said.

Lexi observed the looks the men exchanged. *If looks could kill*, she mused. Hoping to reduce the tension, she said, "How 'bout we place our orders?"

"Sounds good to me," Tywanna said, and then waved over their waiter.

\*\*\*

Following dinner, Banks and Lexi stood outside of the restaurant, awaiting the valet's return with the vehicle. Diamond and Tywanna had already gone on their way. Banks didn't expect for the evening with Diamond would be so temperate. Only due to their girls did they remain civil. But he knew once he crossed Diamond in the streets, then it was war.

Banks's iPhone rang. He checked its display and noticed it was another call from Jade, and once again he pressed "ignore", sending her ass directly to voicemail. It was the fourth time she'd called within an hour. Banks didn't care to be bothered with Jade's shit. He just cared to spend the rest of the night with Lexi without being disturbed. He couldn't wait to get her fine ass home and make love to her nice and slow.

"Who in the hell's blowin' up yo' phone? Lemme find out it's some thot, Banks," she half-joked.

He slid the phone back into his inside breast pocket of his Tom Ford suit jacket and said, "Jus' an associate. Sure it can wait. Tonight's all about you."

"How about you?" She intertwined her arm in his. "Did you enjoy the date?"

"Actually, it wasn't bad."

"Handled yourself better than I expected," she admitted.

"What's that s'posed to mean?" he wanted to know.

Her eyes locked with his. "Means Jade told me everything, Banks." She released her arm free of his.

"Lex, I can explain." He didn't even know where to begin.

"Why didn't you tell me what the hell was goin' on?" Lexi asked, upset.

"'Cause I didn't wanna put you in the mix of this shit, a'ight?"

"Regardless I'm in the mix of it. So is Tywanna. Banks, I'ont want her gettin' hurt in all of this," Lexi stressed.

"Don't worry, I'll do my all to keep her outta harm's way." The agreement he made with Diamond to spare Lexi and Tywanna he planned to keep, so as long as Diamond kept his end of the agreement.

"And what am I to tell her? It's hard on me to keep somethin' so acute from Ty. You seen the way she was all over Diamond tonight. The girl truly loves him. It'll break her heart if somethin' happens to him; especially by the hands of one of her bestie's man," Lexi expressed.

"I'm sure it ain't easy for you to keep what's goin' on from Tywanna, but it's better you do. I'ont even understand why in the hell Jade's ass ran her mouth to you," he added.

"And what if she decides to tell everything to Ty? Then once she learns I knew and kept it from her, it'll ruin our friendship."

"Believe me, she won't be tellin' Tywanna a damn thing. She knows if she tells Ty, then it'll get back to Diamond, and if he finds out she had anything to wit' his life nearly bein' taken, he'll more than likely body her ass," Banks expounded. "Listen, I get that Ty's yo' friend and all, but Diamond's my enemy. And it's better him than me."

That was a harsh reality for Lexi. She realized the beef between Banks and Diamond would cause her or Tywanna to lose one of their men. In the end, it would be a lose-lose situation.

"Banks," Lexi began hesitantly, "Ty's carryin' Diamond's un-born child. This is why I'ont want anything happenin' to her. I won't be able to live with that."

"And nothin' will happen to her on my behalf," he promised. "Maybe we should try for another shorty of our own."

"I'd love that," she smiled. Lexi had miscarried their baby be-fore, and though it had devastated them, it also brought them close.

Banks pulled her close to him, "I luh yo' ass, baby girl," he thuggishly conceded. The couple affectionately shared a kiss.

Valet pulled up before them in Banks's pecan-colored Ashton Martin DB9. Banks tipped the valet driver, then pulled opened the passenger door for Lexi to enter the whip.

"Banks, behind you!" Lexi warned.

Blocka! Blocka! Blocka! Blocka! Blocka!

A second too late, over Banks's shoulder, Lexi caught sight of a hooded gunman creeping up from behind. The gunman hit Banks with two slugs in the shoulder blade, which sent him down to the pavement. Lexi promptly came out of her handbag with her Glock .17. She held her own during a shootout with the gunman, forcing him to retreat.

Lexi fell down to the ground onto her knees beside Banks. "You alright?" she cared to know.

Banks sat back up against the whip. "I'll be fine, thanks to you savin' my life," he said appreciatively.

She offered him a faint smile. "I'm yo' ride or die, right?" She grunted in pain and clutched her abdomen.

"Lex, what's wrong?" Concern was painted on his face.

He removed her hand and saw she'd been shot. Their eyes slowly met, hers filled with tears and his with sorrow. Lexi went faint. He grabbed her and eased her back on the pavement as she fought to catch her breath.

"B-Banks...I-I..." She struggled to speak as blood filled her lungs.

"Shhh, jus' focus on breathin', baby." He looked around at the onlookers and shouted, "Someone get me some fuckin' help!" Banks couldn't believe what the hell had just taken place. He never meant to put Lexi in harm's way. She coughed up blood and her breaths gradually abated. "Lex, baby, don't die on a nigga. I need you," he pled quietly.

Sadly, a moment later Lexi took her final breath and Banks held her lifeless body firmly wrapped in his arms. "Never meant for it to end this way. So sorry, Lexi," he spoke in a whisper.

Lexi was Banks's heart, so for him to be without her meant that he was left heartless.

## Chapter 7

In his gloomy, still apartment, Banks sat depressed on the sofa, drowning his sorrows in a bottle of Remy. Thoughts of Lexi swam through his mind: the way she knew him better than anyone else; how she was able to make him laugh even when he was heated; the tenderness of her body in his arms. The more he thought about her, the more the reality of her being shot to death pained him.

The two bullet wounds he suffered turned out to be superficial; both pierced through and through. Had it not been for Lexi, he would have been gunned down. He wished it was him instead of her.

Abruptly he hurled the bottle across the room. It crashed against the wall and shattered to pieces. Guilt over Lexi losing her precious life because of him was too much for him to bear. He'd rather be dead than to live with a guilty conscience. He grabbed the .9 from his lap, pressed its muzzle to his temple…

Knock, knock, knock.

The knock at the door spared him. He wasn't expecting anyone. He wanted to be left the hell alone. With his pistol in hand, he ripped open the front door and leveled it on the uninvited guest. Banks was perturbed by who was standing at his door step. "Jade," he uttered. She grazed past him on her way inside the apartment.

*** 

As Diamond pushed the Porsche truck through traffic, Tywanna looked over at him. His features were softened by the shadow, but even in the dark she could see the paper thin scar that sliced through his right brow. A few years back, Diamond walked into the butt of pistol and he would probably walk into another. Maybe even more bullets. Not a comforting thought for Tywanna, nor was his street life comforting.

It began to rain. Dribbles spattered on the windshield and Diamond activated the wipers. He bent the whip into a gas station lot and then pulled beside a gas pump. "Want anything?" he asked as he retrieved his .45 from the trap compartment, which he concealed on his person.

"Just a pack of Skittles." She smiled, displaying the tiny gap in between her teeth that Diamond found so cute. He leaned over and kissed her lips before stepping out. Ty's iPhone rang, and she answered knowing who the caller was by the ringtone. "Hey Ashley!"

Diamond stepped inside the station, where he paid for some petrol and purchased a pack of Skittles. Back outside, he stood back up against the truck while the pump worked on automatic. Off in the distance, thunder clapped, the draft from the brewing rainstorm caused him to flip up the fur hood of his Montclair jacket. It was a fall night.

He thought about how it'd be best that he and Gangsta had a meeting of the minds, not necessarily to attempt changing Gangsta's mind, but to learn exactly what was on it - whether it was money or murder. Whichever, he knew Gangsta had his mind set.

After pumping the gas, Diamond returned to the whip. "Here." He held out the pack of Skittles, which Tywanna left hanging. Glancing over at her, he noticed tears sailing down her cheeks, causing her mascara to run. "Baby, what's wrong?" he asked, concerned.

"It's Lexi. She's...she's dead," Tywanna wept. "Ashley told me that Lex was murdered last night."

"Baby, I'm sorry," he said and pulled Tywanna tightly close to him. He knew that in that moment, she really needed him to comfort her. And he couldn't help but wonder what Banks had to be going through. Diamond didn't even want to imagine how it'd affect him to lose Ty. He felt the need to reach out to Banks and offer his condolences. But for the moment, he only cared to hold Tywanna tight.

It pained Tywanna deeply to lose one of her besties. She was close to Lexi, so much so that, before the others, she had opened up to Lexi about her pregnancy. And she'd keep good on her promise to Lexi to be a strong mother no matter what.

\*\*\*

"Hell are you doin' here, Jade?" Banks inquired as he shut the door behind her.

"Thought you could use some company," Jade replied, and he didn't object. "Why is it so damn dark in here?" She clicked on the light. Banks had been sitting in the dark so long, his eyes needed a second to adjust.

Notably, every picture frame with photos of Lexi were faced down. Jade saw the liquor bottle that'd been smashed against the wall. And Banks looked as though he hadn't been asleep. Jade understood he was emotionally hurt.

"Sorry 'bout Lex," she spoke quietly.

"She's dead. And it's my own fuckin' fault."

Jade stepped closer to him and said, "It ain't yo' fault, Banks. And Lex wouldn't want you to feel like that." More than anyone, it was Jade's fault for putting them in grave danger. "Banks, I-I…"

"What is it, Jade?"

Jade hesitated. She'd come over to tell him all about informing Gangsta of their whereabouts, but couldn't bring herself to do so. "I'm sure this is hard on you," she said instead.

"Can't get Lexi off of my damn mind," he uttered.

"Maybe I can change yo' mind for you." Jade palmed the back of his head and pulled his mouth onto hers. Banks didn't resist. He went along with it and reached behind her, palming all of that ass in his free hand. She prudently grabbed the pistol from him and set it on the coffee table, wanting both of his strong hands to caress her fond frame.

They sucked each other's tongues. Banks's dick was hard and Jade's pussy was wet. He lifted her off her feet by her ass, and she wrapped her legs around his waist as he carried her to the bedroom.

Followed by helping each other out of their wears, they were ass naked in bed while Banks hit Jade from the back aggressively, pounding out his frustrations on her. It sounded similar to a round of applause as their flesh met. He was balls deep in her guts as he pulled her hair and dug her out. She stuffed her face in the pillow and gripped the sheets.

"Yaaaas, Banks! It hurts sooo good," Jade groaned in pleasure. She got off on being fucked rough, and the feeling of balls slapping against her pussy always seemed to make her cum.

They both understood that them having sex with one another was morally wrong, and Lexi damn sure wouldn't approve of the shit. But, for at least the moment, Banks just needed to clear his head, and Jade just wanted to feel needed. He beat the pussy up until he felt a nut swell in the tip of his dick, and he busted.

Speechless, the two lay in bed, Banks contrite about what had just happened while Jade was content with it. They'd betrayed Lexi, someone who'd always been nothing to them but loyal.

Banks abruptly hopped out of bed, picked up Jade's bra from the floor, then threw it at her. "Get dressed, then bounce," he ordered flatly.

"Banks, I'ont know why you actin' all like that. We didn't do nothin' you didn't wanna do," Jade commented, putting on her bra.

"Listen here and listen clear, punk-hoe." He lost his temper and charged over to Jade, where she was still in bed. "Don't get shit fucked up. Ain't a damn thing between us," he stated as he poked her forehead with his index finger. "It only makes shit more complicated knowin' you s'posed to be Lexi's friend."

Jade stepped out of bed and slid into her thong. "Believe me or not, I love Lexi as much as you do."

"Jade, you don't know how to love!" he spat, cutting her off. His iPhone rang and took his attention, he grabbed it from the dresser and answered. "Talk."

"Heard about yo' girl, Banks, and I jus' wanna offer my condolence." It was Diamond.

Hearing his voice enraged Banks. "Nigga, fuck you callin' me for after what you did? Thought we had an agreement, Diamond?"

"Hell are you talkin' 'bout?" Diamond was perplexed.

"You disregarded the fuckin' agreement we had, now Lexi's dead!" he raged, under the impression that Diamond had sent the shooter at him last night.

"It wasn't me, Banks."

"If not you then, who?" Banks inquired.

There was a brief moment of silence as they pondered it.

Both of them said, "Gangsta."

It was clear to them both that Gangsta was playing for keeps. And Diamond and Banks understood it was the only way when a nigga played the streets.

"Gangsta mos' def' gonna get his," Banks asserted.

"Understood. I jus' wanna know, will you continue to honor yo' end of our agreement?"

"I no longer have a reason to, right? And by the way, congrats on the baby." Part of Banks was bitter that he'd never get to conceive a child with Lexi.

Diamond was taken by surprise. "How'd you know?" he asked curiously.

"Was the last thing I heard from Lexi."

"Once again, my condolences," Diamond offered.

"Keep it, Diamond." Click. Banks ended the call without warning.

As she dressed, Jade eavesdropped, and from what she gathered, Banks figured Gangsta had something to do with Lexi being murdered. If only he knew she had a part in it, then she had no doubt Banks wouldn't think twice about putting a fuckin' slug in her top. She hoped he never found out. But the biggest surprise for her was that Tywanna was apparently pregnant.

Her conniving-ass figured that right then would be a better moment than any to use Banks to her advantage. "Sounds like you got a problem on yo' hands," she commented.

"Hoe, didn't I tell yo' ass to bounce?"

"Just sayin', I might be able to help you out," she baited him as she headed out of the bedroom.

Banks had to admit that he could use Jade, even though he resented her ass. He caught her as she was finna step out the front door, pushed the door shut and said, "How can you help me?"

"I got'chu. Just leave shit to me." She knew he wouldn't refuse. Taking in his nakedness, she found his dick with a hard on. "I take it you prefer me to stay."

\*\*\*

Tate moved a black pawn forward on the chess board. Funny thing was, he wasn't playing with anyone else, just against himself. It was the way he stayed ahead of the game. He viewed the game from every position. He played every side. Tate had to know what every man was thinking all the way down to the smallest muthafucka like the pawn.

Where most were quick to surrender or disregard the pawn, he was too clever for that. The pawns were his hitters. If he surrounded himself with steadfast hitters, involve them all in the game, then they keep his territory strong and solid.

A man of prestige, slim with hard eyes, and a bald-fade, Tate had plans to rule Milwaukee's crime world. He headed his own outfit, for which he supplied with product and artillery as needed. Actually, Banks was one of his drug lieutenants. Tate was an OG in the game. He was very precise and meticulous with his every move, understanding that, like a game of chess, he needed to make his next move his best move.

Tate looked up from the board to Lynch, who sat at the table opposite of him. They were meeting at Tate's barbershop, Magic Clippers. The shop served as a front, preventing the IRS from snooping in his business. It was his way of maintaining a low profile. They were in the backroom of the shop, where drug deals, loan sharking and gambling took place. That was just another day in Magic Clippers.

"You come to me lookin' to have Balistrieri touched. Why should I even consider helpin' you out, cop?" Tate said.

"Because…" Lynch took it upon himself to make a move on the board using a white rook. "I'm not your problem. Just a businessman. And, not only will it benefit your operation, but I'm sure you'll need a favor in return one of these days." His ploy was to get rid of Frank in order to seize control of his operation, and double-crossing him was the only way Lynch could get free of Frank's powerful grip. So aligning with Tate was in his best interest, because they both needed the mob boss dead.

"A man can never be too careful about his decisions," Tate advised. He moved a black knight on the board. "If he makes the wrong one, he loses. He loses because he never understood the game. The game is cold, but fair. I'll take good care of Balistrieri." He knocked over the white king on the chess board. "Checkmate."

***

The female OBGYN applied lubricant to Tywanna's baby bump while she lay back on the clinic bed, and Diamond sat beside her, holding her hand. They were at the clinic for a check up on the baby. The gynecologist rubbed the wand over Tywanna's belly, performing an ultrasound.

"There's your precious baby," the gynecologist said, pointing at an image on the sonogram. "And the baby appears to be as healthy as can be. Since you're a little past fifteen weeks, we can determine the baby's gender. Would you two care to know the sex?"

"We'd love to," Tywanna said.

The gynecologist shifted the wand on Tywanna's belly for a different angle of the baby's image. "I'm glad to inform that it's a girl," she smiled.

Seeing the image of their daughter growing inside of Tywanna humbled Diamond. "So I'ma be the proud father of a baby girl."

"And I'm sure she'll be Daddy's li'l girl," Tywanna said.

"If she looks anything like her mother, she'll be the prettiest thing in the world," he told her.

Tywanna slightly squeezed his hand. "She'll change our lives."

"For the better," Diamond added. As a man he wanted to be there for his child and his love, so he knew he couldn't continue to live the way he did for much longer.

***

"Neva trusted dis nigga any-fuckin'-way, but Diamond always says allow a nigga to reveal his true nature," Toni commented.

Pelle switched lanes in his Denali. "In this line of business, you should neva trust anyone. How you gonna trust someone when everyone's criminals?" he explained.

Pelle kept a distance as he and Toni unobtrusively shadowed the Chevy Impala in traffic that was a few vehicles ahead. The driver was Savage. Over the past few hours, they'd been on Savage's tail, ever since Diamond had him bonded out. Diamond learned from Levin that once Savage and T-Money had gotten jammed up in the raid, then Savage mentioned Diamond's name, and that was a major violation to the code of the game.

At the stoplight on 27th and Burleigh Street, Savage braked the Impala. His ass actually felt like shit for snitchin'. But he was too much of a fuck-nigga to just accept the time he faced in prison. He was willing to do any-fuckin'-thing to please the courts in hopes of a time cut, even if that meant droppin' a dime on the nigga who treated him like family. It was niggas like Savage who fucked up the game, because they had the game fucked up.

Pelle peeped Toni checking her banger and told her, "Put that away, I got dis nigga." At the stoplight, Pelle slowed alongside of the Impala. The Denali's driver window rolled down. Pelle took aim with a .40-caliber Glock.

Blam! Blam! Blam! Blam! Blam!

In a flash, Savage's Impala was sprayed with bullets. He was killed instantly.

"Snitch-ass nigga got what was good for him," Diamond stated merciless. He was seated at the head of the table in the Theater before his top-level crew members. He poured himself a shot of Henny, downed the shot, then poured himself another. "The bigger issue is not knowin' how much info he provided the blue-goons. I'm sure they'll be watchin', so, from now on, we gon' shake shit up some."

"What'chu got in mind?" Pelle delved.

"For starters, I want the bread and product picked up and dropped off at different times, days, and places."

"Smart," Toni piped in. "That way, whatever the snitch-nigga informed them, we'll throw 'em off by doin' otherwise."

"Always good to be smart enough to outthink the feds," Diamond stated. He leaned back in his chair, then downed his second shot of liquor. Now not only was he involved in beef, but also a possible indictment. Shit was getting more and more real in the streets. Being in beef was one thing, but being indicted was another. Either way, he'd go down bustin'.

*** 

Lexi looked like an angel. Her hair was laced, her beat was perfect, and her manicure was fresh. She was dressed in a white Donna Karan dress. Even in death, Lexi brought life into the room.

Tears slid down Tywanna's cheeks as she stood before the white and gold casket. Seeing Lexi brought back many memorable moments. *Girl, you may be gone, but you will never be forgotten*, she thought.

Ashley held Jade's hand in support. They stood beside Tywanna. Jade couldn't even bear to look at Lexi. She felt nauseated and faint mainly due to feeling horrible and guilty. Not being able to bear it any further, Jade ran out on the funeral. Tywanna and Ashley went after her.

Ashley placed a hand on Jade's shoulder from behind causing her to startle. "It's just me. You're fine," Ashley said soothingly. "You okay, girl?"

She slowly nodded. "Just needed some fresh air, that's all."

"Jade, are you sure that's all?" Tywanna searched, sounding concerned. "You just haven't been yourself lately."

Jade took a deep breath. "Shit just been real crazy for me lately, okay? And on top of that, one of my besties is in there lyin' in a damn casket. I'm just goin' through some shit right now."

"Lexi was our best friend too, Jade, so we understand that much. But whatever else you're goin' through, you need to tell us and we can try to help you through it," Tywanna said.

"Trust me, there's nothin' either of you could possibly do to help my situation." Jade knew that for the most part, she was on her own. She couldn't tell them what her situation was, or they would turn on her for sure.

"Jade, just let us try helpin' you," Ashley insisted.

"Never mind it; I can handle myself!" she snapped. After collecting her composure, she said, "Look, I'ont mean to get outta character. Y'all are my girls, and I'ont want anything to change that. Just leave me be, and I'll be fine."

"Alright, girl, if that's what you want. But we're always here for you if you decide you care for our help," Tywanna said.

"Group hug," Ashley insisted.

The trio embraced, and in that moment, Jade felt terrible knowing what they didn't. Tywanna and Ashley didn't realize what she was capable of.

"You ladies okay?" Banks inquired as he came walking up. "I noticed when the three of you ran out on the funeral, and I decided to come check on you all."

"We're fine, thank you. Jade here just needed a moment," Ashley answered.

"Anything I can do to help you, Jade?" he asked.

"I'm good. My girls got me." She felt strange in his presence, and at Lexi's funeral of all places, especially after what happened between them. She couldn't even imagine how Tywanna and Ashley would react if they found out.

"Well, I 'preciate y'all for comin' today," Banks told them.

"Lex was one of our best friends, and we wouldn't have missed this day for nothin' in the world," Tywanna spoke.

"Yeah, Lexi always spoke highly of y'all."

"It's sad what happened to her. We're sorry for yo' loss," Ashley piped in.

"It's y'all loss as much as it mine," he responded.

"If you don't mind my askin'," Tywanna began, "how was she
_ "

"Murdered?" he completed her words. "Let's jus' say she went out a ride or die bitch. Now, are y'all ready to get back inside and pay Lexi her respects? How 'bout you, Jade?"

"Don't worry, Jade, me and Tywanna are here with you," Ashley assured.

"And so am I," Banks added.

They all went back into the funeral home. Ironically, Jade was the one who felt dead on the inside.

# Troublesome

## Chapter 8

"Damn nigga, pass da gas," Gangsta said to Chase, who hit the blunt once more before passing it. They were in Gangsta's G-Wagon, halted at a stoplight. "How's my li'l sis?"

"She's takin' the loss of Lexi hard. The funeral was a coupla days ago, and ever since, Ash ass been an emotional wreck. Fucks me up seein' her cry, knowin' you're the one who smoked her homegirl."

He glanced over at him. "Didn't say shit to her 'bout it, did you?"

"Course not. That'll jus' be too much for her to deal wit'."

"Bitch got smoked for interferin' in shit," he stated unremorsefully. "Didn't get the chance to finish off Banks 'cause fuckin' Lexi spared the pussy-ass nigga. Was tryna catch him and Diamond together and leave 'em both stretched. Coulda sent a coupla shooters at 'em, but I want both of them niggas personally. Didn't mean to smoke shorty, but Ash will get over it. Ain't like she lost someone like you. Feel me?" He puffed the blunt.

Just the thought of leaving Ashley and the twins in the cold world made Chase understand why it was very necessary he put his family first. "G, I reflected on what you and I discussed before, and I decided it's best that I get outta the game. The day I marry Ash, I'm out for good. Can't leave her and the twins out here to fend for themselves, so, more than anything, I'm doin' this for my family," he expressed.

"Can't do shit but respect you for puttin' yo' family first. And I'm lookin' forward to officially welcomin' you into the fam', bruh. Speakin' of the weddin', as yo' best man, I'm mos' def' gon' make sure yo' bachelor's party's lit." Gangsta smirked, and pulled off in traffic.

After being out catching plays with Gangsta, Chase returned home late at night - or rather, early in the morning. He entered the house and quietly shut the door behind himself, not wanting to awake Ashley or either of the twins. But he wasn't surprised to find Ashley sitting on the sofa awaiting his ass, like she did most nights.

"Why do yo' ass choose to run the streets day and night, Chase, when you have a whole family here at home? You texted me, I'ont know how long ago, sayin' you'd be home soon, and now here it is one-somethin' in the mornin'," Ashley complained out of concern.

Chase removed his Marc Buchanan jacket and hung it up on the coat rack near the front door. "I done tol' yo' ass before that you don't have to wait up for me, Ash. Can't help that puttin' food on the table keeps a nigga out longer than I intend to be at times."

Ashley jumped to her feet and got in his face. "Chase, I'm tired of sittin' alone in this house with the twins while you out in the streets doin' you."

"Doin' me? Shorty, I'm doin' what I gotta do for us." He brushed by her on his way to check in on the twins.

Ashley muffed his head and said, "I can't stand you."

Chase instantly turned and entered her personal space causing her to startle. "You can't stand me?" he repeated, agitated.

"Yeah, that's right, nigga. I can't stand yo' ass," she replied spitefully. As Chase headed towards the front door, she ran over to the door, blocking him from leaving. "Where you goin', Chase?"

"Move, Ash!" he snapped and pushed her.

Tears rimmed her eyes. "Baby, please don't go," she begged.

Chase never meant to make her cry. He grabbed her at the waist and pulled her into his arms, then kissed her passionately and bit her bottom lip. They continued to kiss as Chase walked her backwards to the sofa. He dropped his jeans around his ankles and sat down on the sofa and Ashley straddled him, sliding down on his dick until her pussy met its base. She tossed her head back while he gripped her ass and bounced her up and down on his lap. His dick was hard and her pussy was slippery.

"Ummm...yes, baby. Dis dick feels so damn amazin'," Ashley moaned faintly.

"You like dat shit. Huh?" He gently bit on her jugular vein.

"Ooohh... hell yeah. Yeeess, Chase, yeeess." On the verge of orgasm, Ashley's body began to quiver uncontrollably. Her soft moans always did a thing to Chase. He got off knowing he satisfied her. He sucked on her titties and flicked his tongue over her erect nipples as he slammed her down on his dick. The combination of both pleasing feelings caused Ashley to cum, her juices oozing onto his balls. She continued to grind and wind her hips on his lap until Chase busted a nut.

Following their makeup sex, they lied back on the sofa. Chase held Ashley in his arms, while she rested her head on his chest.

"Chase," she started tranquilly, "when I say I can't stand you, what I mean to say is I love you. But babe, you gotta give up the streets for yo' family. I be goin' crazy thinkin' about somethin' happenin' to you out there."

Chase was lying back with his eyes shut. "Shhh, I'm tryna get some Z's. Besides, girl, I know you love a nigga, and I love yo' ass, too. I get why you don't like me out there in those streets, and I be afraid of the thought of a nigga murkin' me one of these days also."

"Chase, don't even think that." That wasn't a comforting thought for her.

"Fa real doe. Didn't think I'd live this long," he divulged.

Ashley peered up at him. "But if somethin' happens to you, what about me 'n the twins?"

"Y'all will be straight. Now let's get some sleep."

Being without Chase was something Ashley didn't even want to think about. She couldn't stand the realization that due to his lifestyle, more than likely the outcome for him was inevitably prison, or worse, death. But quiet as kept, she didn't know that he'd vow to get out of the life on the very day of their wedding.

\*\*\*

Gangsta held out a bottle of Merlot. "Why don't chu celebrate wit' us, Diamond," he offered.

The celebration was Chase's bachelor's party, and Gangsta thought it would be clever to throw it at Red Velvet. They occupied the all-red room in the VIP section with several of their crew members. Gangsta knew that Diamond wouldn't care for him to be there, but he didn't give a fuck about Diamond's feelings towards him.

"Gangsta, you got some nuts showin' up here," Diamond stated sternly.

Gangsta leaned back on the sofa and turned up the bottle to his lips. "No nuts, no glory." Jade was bent over shaking her ass in his face.

"It's cool, Diamond," Chase intervened. "We jus' here to celebrate before my big day tomorrow. I was hopin' you 'n Toni would join us. Y'all wit' it?" He looked from Diamond to Toni, who stood beside him. Sarge stood intensely behind them. After Diamond was shot up inside the club, the security was tight.

"Damn, Chase, I'm surprise Ash let yo' ass out for the night," Toni half-joked.

"Only 'cause she's out wit' her girls turnin' up at her bachelorette party," he chuckled.

"A'ight, we'll join y'all," Diamond said, not wanting to offend Chase, since he still had love for the nigga. "Bottles on the house." He and Toni took a seat on the red velvet wraparound sofa. Diamond purposely sat beside Gangsta, with the understanding to keep his friends close and his enemies closer.

As the night prevailed, it seemed normal: bottle service flowed, strippers bounced their ass, ballers made it rain. While the others partied like the good ol' days, Diamond couldn't seem to relax in Gangsta's presence. Diamond didn't know where Gangsta's mind was at, and he figured now was a better time than any for them to have a meeting of the minds.

Diamond leaned towards Gangsta and said to him, "I know you had somethin' to do wit' Banks's bitch gettin' bodied."

Unwavering, Gangsta eyed him. "Am I s'posed to feel bad or some shit?"

"You could at least have some fuckin' remorse. Lexi was innocent!" he hissed.

"Remorse is for the weak. See, that's the difference between me and you, Diamond." Jade now straddled him and wound her hips.

"The difference is, I'd rather do shit mindfully," he remarked. "Tell me somethin', Gangsta, what the hell are you after?"

"Power. And I'll gun down any muthafucka who's in my way in order to get it," he warranted.

Diamond knew right then and there that Gangsta had his mind set on murder. "Gangsta, a gun will get you power, but it won't keep you in power."

"Depends on the nigga wit' the gun," he replied, his mind made up.

As Pelle approached, he peeped Gangsta muggin' him. "Yo, Diamond, there's some suit here askin' to see you," he informed, pointing towards the bar, where Lynch was seated. "What'chu want me to do wit' 'im?"

"Send 'im to my office. I'll be there directly," Diamond instructed.

Once Pelle went on his way, Gangsta said, "See, you took dat nigga in. Jus' remember, if you take in a starvin' dog, he won't bite you. That's the principle difference between a dog and a man."

Chase staggered to his feet. He was wasted. "Let's hit it. Got a long day tomorrow," he slurred. "Diamond, you'll be there, right?"

"Fa sho'." Diamond knew Tywanna was going to drag him along anyhow.

"Hoe, get up off of me." Gangsta pushed Jade aside, ending her lap dance. Unbeknownst to him or Diamond, the entire time she was ear hustling. Gangsta signaled for his crew to make an exit. "As for Lynch, I advise you to leave that pig alone. It ain't healthy for you," he told Diamond before stepping off.

Toni stood beside Diamond. "Hell Gangsta think he is?"

"That's jus' Gangsta showin' his true nature. Find out who allowed him in the club, and fire his ass ASAP," Diamond ordered as he eyed Gangsta all the way out of the club. He knew it was only a matter of time until he and Gangsta had it out.

Lynch was waiting in Diamond's office, seated behind the desk with his feet propped up on the desktop like he owned the damn place. "I like the new addition to your crew much better than that Gangsta," he commented, speaking about Pelle.

"Hell are you here about, Lynch?" Diamond cut to the chase. Toni and Pelle stood on either side of him.

"Very persistent, I see. Here's the deal, Diamond." Lynch planted his feet on the floor, rested his elbows on the desktop. "From now on, I'm gonna need thirty-five percent of all your earnings from drug trafficking."

Diamond was perplexed. "Hol' up, what about the percentage Balistrieri's already collectin'?"

"Frank won't even matter pretty soon," he insinuated. "Besides, your business with him has nothing to do with your business with me."

"This ain't business; it's robbery."

"Call it what you will. But I advise you to get on board."

"Lynch, why the change all of a sudden? Because if this is about the cash Balistrieri - "

"There'll be a lot of changes soon enough, including Frank," he said, cutting Diamond off. "This is only the beginning. I'm sure you can afford it. I mean, judging by your tailored suits, luxury vehicles, condo's and all."

"I can't agree to this," Diamond stated.

Lynch stood and then stepped from behind the desk. "Either you will, or you'll regret it. I'll give you a week to think on it." He exited the office.

Toni slammed the door shut. "We can't jus' allow him to play us," she insisted.

Diamond sat on edge of the desk. "Nobody's gettin' played."

"Then what are you gonna do about this?" Pelle wanted to know.

"I'll figure it out," he replied. "Damn. I need a drink. I'll be at the bar if either of you need me."

At the bar, Diamond ordered himself a glass of Henny. *Lynch has another thing comin' if he believes he can jus' get over on me*, he thought to himself. He took a drink of the liquor.

During her floor rounds, wearing white lace boy-shorts and bra with yellow six-inch Christian Louboutin stilettos, Surprise made her way over to Diamond. "Why the long face?" she probed.

Diamond put back his drink and slammed the empty glass on the bar with a thud. "Rather not talk about it," he told her.

"Then we don't have to talk at all." Surprise grabbed him by his silk tie, pulling him towards a private room in the back.

Usually Diamond didn't indulge in strippers, but he was feelin' Surprise. She had a creamy caramel tone, wore her hair shaved on either side with long hair down the middle like a horse's mane, was thick in all the right places, and covered in numerous tats.

When they made it to the room, she wasted no time as she slowly unbuckled his Ferragamo slacks. She pushed him back on the sofa, knelt, and took his large, hard dick into her warm, wet mouth. Diamond hypnotically gazed into her eyes as she slowly sucked and licked on the tip of his joint.

"Damn, shorty...you doin' dat!" Diamond groaned his commendation.

Surprise lifted her head and said, "Shhh. No talkin', remember?" She went back to topping him off, and he palmed the back of Surprise's head, encouraging her to deep-throat him. She sucked him so damn good his toes curled.

*** 

The wedding was everything Ashley could imagine. It was held at a small, intimate church with only their close family and friends. Ashley and Chase had stood before the pastor and professed their love for one another. The twins were so cute as the flower girl and ring bearer. The bridesmaids were elegant and the groomsmen were dapper, everyone dressed in white. The entire setting made for a wonderful wedding ceremony. And the best part of it all for Ashley was when Chase vowed to be nothing more than a family man from this day forward.

Subsequent to the ceremony, the assembly were gathered outside of the church. Everyone took a moment to congratulate the newlyweds before seeing them off to their honeymoon.

Tywanna could see that Ashley was the happiest she'd ever been, and she was happy for her. "Ash, girl, I can only hope to be as happy as you are one day," she smiled.

"I believe you already are, knowin' how happy Diamond makes you," Ashley replied.

"Aww, that's sweet," Tywanna cooed.

Jade smacked her lips. "Enjoy it while it lasts," she commented, sounding like a hater.

"Jade, have several seats," Tywanna told her. "Any who. I'm glad yo' day was perfect, Ash."

For the first time all day, Ashley frowned. "Well, almost perfect. It woulda been if Lexi could be here with us."

"Girl, don't cry, you gonna mess up yo' makeup. And if you cry, then you're gonna make me cry." Tywanna used her hand to fan dry tears rimming her eyes.

"And I'm sure Lex was here with us in spirit," Jade input with her snake ass.

"Thank y'all for bein' here with me on my special day," Ashley said.

"You know we got'chu, girl," Tywanna assured.

Jade didn't even care to be there. She only showed up because she knew it would be strange on her part had she not. "The weddin' was nice and all, but girl, I apologize for havin' to leave in a rush." She smooched both girls on the cheek. "And bitch, enjoy yo' honeymoon," she added as she went on her way.

*Her ass been actin' new lately*, Tywanna thought.

Meantime, Diamond left Toni and Pelle standing near the ride, he approached Gangsta and Chase. "Fellas," he greeted them.

"Chase, I'll be over here if you need me," Gangsta said. He gave Diamond a cold stare before walking off.

"Don't mind him," Chase advised. "Listen, Diamond. I know shit been difficult wit' Gangsta lately, but don't allow these streets to cause yo' best friend to become yo' worst enemy. I can see that y'all still have some love for each other."

"Well, it's a thin line between love and hate," Diamond stressed. "Enough about that. Best wishes to you."

"Thanks."

"Now that you're outta of the game, what's the plan?" he cared to know.

Chase watched the twins playing with each other. "Start myself a legit business and devote my life to my family."

"Sounds like the good life."

The girls made their way over to Diamond and Chase. Tywanna wrapped her arms around Diamond's torso and kissed his cheek. The twins scurried up to Chase and he scooped them both up in his arms, their tiny, dirty hands ruining his white tuxedo. Ashley couldn't be happier standing beside her husband in that moment, for all she wanted was for him to devote himself to his family.

"It's a beautiful thing seein' you wit' yo' wife and kids," Diamond said.

"The day you have a fam' of yo' own, then you'll come to understand that their lives means more than yo' own," Chase told him.

Diamond gently caressed Tywanna's belly, and replied, "I'm sure."

"You mean to tell me - "

"Yeah, that's right. Ty's pregnant," he proudly confirmed. A family of his own was something Diamond desired, and Tywanna hoped that carrying his child would eventually change his lifestyle.

"C'mere girl." Ashley pulled Tywanna in for a firm hug. She grabbed one of the twins from Chase. "Diamond, you be sure to protect yo' family with yo' life if you have to."

"Without a doubt," Diamond swore.

Chase shook Diamond's hand and said, "Welcome to fatherhood."

"Let's not make this day about us. It's yo' day; we're jus' here to show our love," Diamond spoke humbly.

"And we 'preciate the love, my nigga."

An all-white Hummer HZ stretch limousine pulled to a halt before the church. It was there to whisk the newlyweds off to their honeymoon - or so they thought. Unexpectedly, the Hummer's tinted windows slid down, then out came barrels of submachine guns, and Lucifer rose up out of its sunroof aiming a Mac-90.

Prrraaat! Prrraaat! Prrraaat!

The fusillade of bullets peppered the assembly. Screams of horror broke out and, in a panic, people attempted to avoid possibly being shot and killed.

Instantly, Diamond hit the pavement, taking Tywanna down with him. While shielding Tywanna and his unborn, he drew his .45 from the small of his back then opened fire on the Hummer.

Toni and Pelle took cover beside the huge bronze statue in front of the church as they returned fire. Bullets attacking the Hummer caused Lucifer to duck inside. As the Hummer sped off, Gangsta filled it with bullet holes. He stepped in the center of the street behind the Hummer, continuing to squeeze until it erratically bent the corner. The results of the shootout left several gunshot victims.

Ashley wailed in aguish. "Chase, baby, please be okay," she begged. Chase had taken a few slugs while shielding her and the twins once the shots erupted. He was sprawled out on the pavement, and Ashley was on her knees applying pressure to his wounds as he bled profusely. "You're gonna be okay, Chase. I'm here for you, baby," she wept.

The twins cried at the top of their lungs seeing their daddy lay on the ground hurt and covered in blood.

Diamond helped Tywanna up from the ground. "You a'ight?"

"I'm fine," she assured him before hurrying over to aide Ashley.

Gangsta rushed over to Chase. He stood above him, staring into his lifeless eyes. He squatted and used his hand to shut Chase's eyes permanently. "He's gone," he spoke in a whisper.

In solace, Diamond placed a hand on Gangsta's shoulder. "My apologies. Chase was a good friend," he said sincerely.

"Fuck offa me!" Gangsta pushed Diamond's hand away and rose facing him, pointing his pistol in Diamond's face. "You have somethin' to do wit' dis shit, huh, nigga?"

Noticing Toni and Pelle ready to make a move, Diamond held up a hand directing them to stand down. He narrowly eyed Gangsta and said, "If you really believe I'd do some shit like this, Gangsta, then apparently you don't know me as well as I thought."

"Then how da hell did Banks know where to find us?" he quizzed furiously.

"Gangsta, yo' guess is as good as mine!" Diamond replied riled.

"Maybe you told him the night you and him was together."

"I woulda never did that jus' to get at you, no matter what."

"And why should I believe yo' ass?"

Ashley intervened, making Gangsta lower his weapon. "Diamond wouldn't do somethin' like this." Her eyes shifted to Diamond's. "Would you?"

"Chase was a friend of mine, and I would never do anything to bring harm to his family," he swore. "I apologize for what happened here." He turned for his ride with Ty at his side, and Toni and Pelle close behind.

Tywanna looked back over her shoulder at Ashley, who had her face buried in Gangsta's chest, bawling. Sadly, Ash lost the love of her life the very day they vowed to be together until death do them part.

# Troublesome

## Chapter 9

Dope fiends made their way by the drove to cop a fix from the dope boys posted out on the block during the early morning rush. It wasn't shit for the D-boys to reel in two or three racks individually on a good day. And this was a key reason as to why this specific block, which was located in Banks's turf, was considered valuable. The majority of all the serves made there were at least a hundred bucks or better.

While the D-boys were preoccupied serving fiends, an old-school candy-red Monte Carlo sitting on 28-inch chrome Forgiato rims yielded before them. "Aye, who da fuck is dat?" One of the D-boys took notice of the conspicuous M.C. and nudged another beside him, then nodded his head towards it. Neither of them had seen the M.C. before. The passenger tossed up its Lambo door and then partially exited the whip, one of his Prada sneakers planted on the pavement while leveling his Draco at the D-boys.

"Tell Banks I'm lookin' for 'im."

"What da fu--"

Boc! Boc! Boc! Boc! Boc!

The nigga fanned out the D-boys, leaving some maimed and others murked, including a fiend. He pulled down the door as the M.C. sped down the street.

\*\*\*

Several D-boys posted in the neighborhood park they frequented and served fiends. The particular park was a trap spot in Banks's turf and produced lots of cash. Kids barely played there due to its consistency of drug deals, drug busts, and drug wars. None of that prevented the D-boys from continuing to trap there.

"I'ma cop me a Benz," one of the D-boys said to the others.

"A Benz? Nigga, I'm tryna cop me a Bugatti!"

"Fuck outta here, not wit' the li'l bread you makin'!" The crowd of D-boys busted out laughing.

"Watch, y'all gon' see."

As the D-boys talked shit amongst each other, they weren't aware of the nigga toting his Draco in approach. The sound of him cocking the weapon instantly commanded all of their undivided attention. "Let Banks know I'm out here lookin' for 'im," he said coolly.

Boc! Boc! Boc! Boc! Boc!

After leaving the D-boys hit up, the nigga casually walked off like it wasn't shit.

***

It was one of Banks's main trap-houses. The locks could be heard being disengaged from the inside before coming open. To the D-boy's dismay, it wasn't a fiend. Instead, he was greeted with the muzzle of a Draco and a mean mug.

Boc! Boc!

Slugs tore through the D-boy's face, and before either of the two inside seated on the worn out sofa could reach their straps, the nigga sprayed them as he stepped into the house lettin' off. He stood over the one D-boy who managed to survive, aiming the Draco in his face.

"Look m-man, don't k-kill me," the D-boy pled. "Jus' take all the money and w-work, it's - "

The nigga jammed the barrel into the D-boy's mouth, causing him to gag. "Shut da fuck up! Now listen close. Only gon' spare you so you can tell the nigga Banks I won't stop lookin' for his ass." He withdrew the Draco and placed it barrel upward against his shoulder. "Da name's Gangsta."

***

"What we gon' do 'bout dis nigga Gangsta? Can't keep lettin' 'im shut down the traps. Already lost out on too much damn bread 'cause of his ass," Lucifer stressed. He spoke through the Bluetooth connected to Banks's Ashton.

"Fuck the money; it's nothin' to make up for. But I ain't gon' jus' let da nigga make my crew look weak in these streets. Gangsta got another fuckin' thing comin' if he thinks I'm duckin' action," Banks said heatedly.

"I'll send some shooters at da nigga tonight."

"Nah. He'd be expectin' some shit like that. Give it time. 'Til then, we lay low and focus on gettin' those traps back functionin'."

Banks disconnected his Bluetooth and the call. He was heated as hell. Over the past few days, Gangsta had aired out some of his top trap spots, shutting them down and sending him a message. He knew that Gangsta was out to avenge Chase's death, just as much as he himself was out for revenge of Lexi's death. Instead of grievance, they each sought vengeance.

He was headed to meet with his connect, Tate, who he'd known since he was a shorty. Actually, Tate used to run shit with Banks's father until he was murked, and he looked out for Banks after his mother OD'ed a few years later. Tate was something like an uncle to Banks.

Banks pulled the whip to the curb before Magic Clippers, which was closed for the night. Inside, the two were alone while Banks was seated in a barber hair and Tate shaved his face with a straight-razor.

"You know, shavin' is jus' like hustlin'. When you go wit' the grain, then it's smooth. But if you go against the grain, there's the possibility of gettin' cut," Tate philosophized.

"I hear you, O.G." Banks assured.

"Got somethin' big lined up, and I'm puttin' you in charge of it. In other words, I'm puttin' my trust in you, Banks. And if you ever try me…" He pressed the blade to Banks's throat. "I'll slice yo' throat from ear to ear." The blade went just deep enough that it caused Banks to bleed a bit. "Understood?"

"Trust. You don't have to worry 'bout that."

"Good." Tate handed him a towel to wipe away the blood with. "Listen, I need you to dead someone for me. The sooner the better."

"Jus' name 'im."

"Frank Balistrieri."

"The mob boss? Shit bigger than I thought." Banks, like most, was well aware that Frank was the boss of bosses in the city of Milwaukee. What he wasn't aware of was the fact that he was also Diamond's connect.

One of Tate's men named Ant stepped in from the back. "He's here," he informed Tate.

"Okay, Ant, send 'im in," Tate instructed. He'd been expecting his newfound business associate.

Once Lynch entered, Banks immediately took notice of the service weapon and shield attached to his hip. *Hell's goin' on here?* he thought to himself, perplexed.

"Had I known you still had a customer, I woulda given you time to finish up here," Lynch said as he took a seat in the next barber's chair.

"Actually, he's one of my lieutenants. Lynch, Banks. Banks, Lynch."

"Now that the introductions are out of the way, let's get down to business." Lynch cut to the chase. "When can I expect you to fulfill your end of the bargain?"

"Whenever an opportunity presents itself, then Banks here will take out Balistrieri. But you and I both know he ain't the easiest to touch. In between time, what about the product?"

"Great question. For the time being, all product I supply you with, I'll be expecting forty percent of the proceeds. Once Frank's out of the picture, then we can renegotiate the terms."

"Forty's a li'l steep, don't you think?" Tate stressed.

"Yeah, well, if Frank finds out I'm dealing with you on the side, then he'll blow me to smithereens. And I wouldn't want that. So forty is as low as I'll go. The sooner you get rid of him, the sooner you take his place," Lynch expounded.

*Dis muthafucka's crooked*, Banks figured. He understood just how powerful Balistrieri was, although apparently he was being supplied by Lynch. Therefore, to eradicate Balistrieri would mean he could have the resources to supply the streets. Not to mention a fed on his side. And there wouldn't be anything Diamond nor Gangsta could do to stop him.

Banks held out a hand and said, "Jus' leave Balistrieri to me."
Lynch shook his hand. "Fortune favors the bold."

\*\*\*

Upon stepping into the kitchen, Diamond expected to find Tywanna cooking breakfast. But he knew something was off when he didn't smell any aroma while in the bathroom taking care of his nine. It was unusual for her not to have breakfast prepped for him. In fact, he'd noticed that she wasn't her usual self over the past few days. He didn't know what had gotten into her, but whatever it was obviously bothered her.

*Her ass coulda at least made a nigga some toast*, he mused in frustration as he looked inside the fridge. He grabbed a nearly empty carton of orange juice, then shut the fridge door.

Tywanna entered the kitchen, already dressed and ready to leave.

"Mornin'," Diamond greeted. "No breakfast?" He turned up the carton of juice to his lips.

"Why don't you make yourself a bowl of cereal," she suggested indifferently as she placed a cup into the dishwasher.

"You expect for me to make some damn cereal?" he complained.

"Not unless you care to eat."

Diamond set down the carton on the marble counter, which he stood leaned back up against. "What's been botherin' you lately?" he pried.

"Nothin', Diamond," she replied flatly. As she tried bypassing him, Diamond grabbed her arm, halting her.

"I'm talkin' to yo' ass, Tywanna. Clearly it's somethin', so let's talk about it," he pressed.

She folded her arms beneath her breasts, shifted her weight to one side, and studied him for a moment. She had contemplated how Gangsta reacted towards Diamond at the church. Evidently there was some beef among them involving Banks, from what she had gathered.

It brought her to reflect back to the evening of Lexi's death, remembering Lexi had concerns about their men, which led her to believe Lexi was privy to the beef. She wondered why Lexi didn't just tell her. Perhaps if she had, then she could have saved Lexi's life. More than anything, it upset her that Diamond didn't tell her a damn thing.

"Okay, then let's talk about it," Tywanna finally said. "How dare you, Banks, and Gangsta put everyone in grave danger due to whatever beef there is between the three of you?"

"Tywanna..." He looked away. "It ain't even s'posed to be this way," he uttered.

"Well, it's too late for that, because now Lexi and Chase are dead!" she shouted as tears trekked down her cheeks, causing her foundation to run.

Diamond pulled her into an embrace. "Sorry for how shit is, but it's this way for now."

"It seems none of you took a moment to consider how y'all beef would affect others. And Diamond, I'm carrying yo' child. You're the one who promised to live every day for us." She cried while in his arms.

"Girl, I love you and my unborn more than myself, and I'm willin' to do my all so I can live for the both of you." He lifted her head at the chin meeting her eyes; the light that laid in her pretty browns was his hearts' undoing. "This'll all be over soon," he assured and wiped away her tears.

"Hopefully for the best." She didn't know exactly what he meant. She just hoped no one else would have to lose their life. "Look, I have to go right now. Ash needs my help with organizin' funeral arrangements."

"Gotta bounce, too. Business in the streets to tend to."

"As usual," she quipped.

"I'll get at you when I'm on my way home."

"You do that." She headed towards the bathroom to redo her face.

Diamond went into the bedroom and tossed on a green and red Gucci sweatshirt with black jeans and red leather Gucci boots. He then collected his iPhone, keys, and .45 before he bounced.

\*\*\*

"That's six-hunnid G's, cash-money." Major had dumped out stacks of cash wrapped with rubber bands from a Nike bag on top of the table in front of Diamond. They were in the Theater along with Toni and Pelle.

After Major tallied up the profits he'd collected from Diamond's trap spots, there wasn't as much as there normally would be due to parts of Diamond's turf being intruded by some of Banks's and Gangsta's perspective crew members. Diamond had to fix that, and fast.

"Pelle, put this bread in the safe wit' the rest of it. I'll need you to take it to have it cleaned. Know a bitch name Keisha who runs a check-cashing joint. She'll trade the dirty bills for clean ones she gets off the money truck." The night before the first and fifteenth of every month when everyone would cash their welfare checks, he'd send someone to exchange the dirty bills. Of course, within a week, many customers of the check-cashing place would bring their county money to his trap spots and he'd take that money right back to Keisha.

Pelle used a hand to sweep the stacks from the table back into the bag. He headed for the safe, which was located in the bathroom and designed to covertly sit beneath the floor panel, making it invincible to the naked eye.

Diamond moved over to the mini bar, poured himself a glass of Henny, and then took a swig. "Yo, Major, I dig how you been handlin' yo' business for a nigga. How'd you like to be in charge of yo' own crew under me?"

"I'd be honored," Major replied humbly.

"Good, because I believe in death before dishonor," Diamond stated. He'd always taken notice to Major's capabilities, thought the young nigga reminded him of himself.

Major was humble, and he was far from arrogant. He was comfortable and confident. Dark-skinned with a low cut, and good-looking, Major was a paper chasin', and pistol toting nigga. He was gentle, yet somehow threatening.

Diamond returned to his seat at the head of the table. "I'm puttin' you in charge of any territory of mine that's been infiltrated. Once you eliminate all intruders by any means, then I'll supply you wit' the product you'll need to keep up wit' the demand. You jus' wipe out the soldiers. I'll focus on their captains."

*I'd be better off runnin' my own fuckin' crew than Major*, Toni thought seething.

Pelle returned from locking away the money and took a seat at the table. For the most part, he'd replaced Gangsta, and Diamond trusted him with his life.

Peering into the friendly faces of those seated before him, Diamond understood he who has one enemy shall see him everywhere. "One night," he began slowly, "I prayed to the Man Above, I asked him could he please remove the enemies from my life. Before I knew it, I started losin' friends. And I'ont expect to lose anymore." He threw back the remains of his Henny.

***

Tywanna and Ashley were seated at a small table for two in Starbucks. After making some arrangements, they decided on taking a break.

"Girl, somethin' troublin' you?" Ashley probed, observing how Ty hadn't been herself for the better part. "Don't tell me Diamond's ass done did somethin'.."

"Uh, no. Well, yeah…" The discussion she had with Diamond earlier was thick on her mind. "You know what? I'm sorry. Ash. Here I am trippin' over my li'l problem when instead, I should be here for you."

The busgirl arrived at their table with their drinks: Tywanna's mocha latte and Ashley's cappuccino. After placing the drinks on the table, she bustled away, on to fulfill her next customer's orders.

"How's things been goin'?" Tywanna asked.

"Truthfully, it's been hard," Ashley admitted. "I hardly been able to eat or sleep. And I'ont know what the hell to tell the twins whenever they ask where's their daddy. Ty, I just don't know what to do." Tears welled up in her eyes. It was clear that losing Chase had taken a toll on her.

"I'm sure things ain't easy without Chase. But do you think he'd want you to just give up? He loved you 'n the twins, and you shouldn't give up on the strength of his love."

Ashley used a napkin to dab the tears from her eye wells. "Thanks for bein' here for me, Ty."

"Always." She reached across the table and grabbed her hand. "What are friends for?"

"Just wish Jade was here, too."

Tywanna waved off the thought of Jade. "Don't even worry about that hoe. More than likely her ass was too damn preoccupied with some nigga's dick in her mouth to talk on the phone when we called," she half-joked.

"Uh uh, girl, you need to stop," Ashley halfheartedly defended Jade, while at the same time laughing at her expense.

Little did they know, Jade was deliberately avoiding their calls, texts, and social media sites. Some friend she was.

As Tywanna took a sip of her latte, her iPhone chimed, indicating she received a text. She retrieved the phone from her Chanel bag. *Hell does he want?* she mused, seeing the text was from Diamond. She touched the screen, opening the text.

> Hubby // 1:42 p.m.
> Love, hopefully ur day has gotten
> better. Tonight I'll make it up to u.
> =). And tell Ash I hope she's fine.

> Wifey // 1:44 p.m.
> Don't wait up. Stayin' by Ash's place
> tonight to make sure she good. TTYL.

Before putting her phone away, her reply text was sure to let Diamond know that tonight wasn't his night. She was still upset with Diamond's ass. Nigga got shit twisted if he thought he'd be gettin' some na-na tonight, she reflected.

"How 'bout I spend the night with you by yo' place? We can just chill, watch movies and eat junk food," Tywanna suggested.

"Sounds good to me." Ash smiled.

*** 

Upon entering the condo, Diamond shut the door behind himself. Since it was nightfall, the place was dark. As he stepped inside, suddenly a lamp was clicked on, illuminating the living room.

Knowing that Tywanna wouldn't be home for the night, Diamond instinctively drew his .45 from the small of his back, taking aim at the intruder. To his dismay, it was Lynch casually seated on the leather sofa, legs folded.

"Take it easy, will ya?" Lynch suggested.

*Must be outta his fuckin' mind comin' into my shit without permission*, Diamond considered.

"No need to worry, Diamond. I'm alone." Lynch noticed him scanning the place for others. He shifted uncomfortably in his seat. "I'd appreciate it if you put that thing away. Gangsters with guns makes me nervous."

"Hell are you even doin' here?" Diamond allowed the .45 to hang with its barrel downward at his side.

"Got tired of waiting outside in my car for you, so I decided to let myself in. Hope you don't mind."

"Actually, I do," Diamond retorted. "What the hell is it?"

"Well, Frank wants to have a chat with you. Apparently your operation hasn't been as lucrative lately."

"What can I say? Business is slow at the moment," he reasoned.

"That won't be a good enough reason for Frank. So I suggest you take my offer, if you care for me to put an end to your money problems."

"I'd rather take my chances."

"Suit yourself." Lynch stood and added, "He'll be expecting you. I'll contact you with the meeting arrangements as provided." He headed past Diamond for the door.

"Lynch," Diamond called over his shoulder. "If you ever enter my shit without my permission again, I'll shoot without askin' any fuckin' questions."

Lynch chuckled. "Next time I'll be sure to have a warrant. By the way, I like what you've done with the place." He exited, pulling the door closed behind himself.

Diamond knew it was only a matter of time until he had to not only deal with Gangsta and Banks, but also Lynch if he wanted to keep power over the streets.

# Troublesome

## Chapter 10

"These will look good on you," the salesgirl said with a smile, holding up the latest Air Force Ones sneaker that had just hit PlayMakers.

"Gimme two pair!" Lucifer requested.

"Be back in a moment." She headed for the back of the outlet to grab the sneakers. Knowing he'd be checking out her ass, she switched her hips more than usual for added affect as she strutted away. She was a redbone with a figure eight frame.

*Damn, shorty know she bad*, Lucifer reflected.

The entrance door of the outlet opened and three random niggas stepped inside, laughing and talkin' shit amongst themselves. Lucifer peeped how Banks was on edge, knowing that Gangsta had it out for him.

"Banks, you been watchin' that damn door since we got here," Lucifer pointed out.

"Can't afford to be caught slackin', may cost me my life," Banks replied in his defense. "So while you watchin' the pretty li'l salesgirl's ass, I'll be watchin' my own ass."

"On what, she ain't got a phatty doe!" Lucifer playfully nudged Banks with an elbow. Seeing that his attempt to lighten the mood failed, he tried a different approach. "Look all around us right now, we got shooters on deck. And I'm confident none of 'em will hesitate to bust. Besides, we're both strapped. Jus' chill and cash out on whatever you like. Here." He grabbed an Air Jordan sneaker off the wall of sneakers and handed it to Banks. "Deze on me."

It was hard for Banks to relax, knowing that shit could pop off at any moment. He had no doubt that Lucifer was down for whatever, although he needed Lucifer to be ready for whatever. Because shit was bound to pop off whether a nigga was ready or not.

Banks's iPhone buzzed, breaking his thoughts. Pulling out his phone, he saw it was a text from Jade.

> Jade // 2:16 p.m.
> I need some of that dick.
> Stop by my spot for a

quickie. =)

Banks // 2:17 p.m.
Yo' ass cray. BYKT.
In a min.

The two had been continuing to smash over time, and admittedly, Banks had taken more of a liking to Jade than he'd expected to.

Returning with two shoeboxes, the salesgirl handed them to Lucifer. "Just for you," she smiled, showing interest in him.

"Good lookin', um…Nina." He read her name tag.

"No biggie. And yo' name?"

"Lucifer," he grinned, displaying his gold teeth.

"Anything else I can do for you, Lucifer?"

"How 'bout you let a nigga take you out sometime, wherever you'd like."

*Dis nigga fine as hell, and he got a bag. I'ma give 'im a shot,* she considered. "Well, there's a concert at the Rave this weekend I'd like to attend."

"Then we'll be in dat bitch VIP status," he assured her and handed her his iPhone to log in her digits.

Banks stepped over to two of the hitters, Ice and Big Man. "Pull the whips out front," he directed. Once Banks and Lucifer hopped into the Ashton, Banks said to him, "I ain't feelin' the idea of steppin' out to some damn concert while all this beef and shit goin' on, Lucifer."

"Cuz, look at like this: whether we go to the concert or not, we're still gon' have beef. Ain't no need for it to prevent us from livin'," he expounded.

Even though Banks got his point, he still didn't like the idea.

The Ashton pulled out in traffic with those hitters behind them.

\*\*\*

"Oh, hell no!" Tywanna exclaimed, not liking what she was witnessing. "This hoe got some explainin' to do." She and Ashley observed from the Lexus as Jade showed Banks out of her apartment complex.

After giving Banks a quick shot of pussy, Jade stood in the doorway wearing boy-shorts and a fitted baby-T-shirt as she watched Banks step into the Ashton. Once the whip dispelled she went inside, closing the door behind herself. The entire time she wasn't aware that she had eyes on her.

Tywanna and Ashley had stopped by Jade's crib unannounced to see what was up with her, since she'd hardly been around them for several days. But what they didn't expect to see was Jade with Banks.

Tywanna pushed open the door of her Lexus then hopped out, and Ashley followed suit. "Jade, open up the damn door!" Tywanna beat on the apartment door furious.

"Calm down, Ty. We don't even know what's goin' on," Ashley suggested.

"Well. we're about to find out." She beat on the door some more.

Jade ripped open the door. "Bitch, hell's yo' problem beatin' on my damn door like you payin' the lease? Gon' have my neighbors complainin' and shit," she spoke with attitude. She turned and walked over to the sofa, taking a seat.

"My problem is you, Jade," Tywanna stated as she stepped inside the apartment with Ashley close behind.

"And why am I not surprised?" Jade remarked sarcastically.

"Mind tellin' me what the hell you was doin' with Banks?"

The question took Jade by surprise. She didn't realize they'd seen Banks leaving her place. "Do it matter?" she asked quite frankly.

"Course it matters, Jade, because Lexi was our friend. And we don't mess with our friends' men," Ashley piped in.

"Lex was our friend and all, but Banks is his own man."

"Don't tell me you was fuckin' him behind Lexi's back," Tywanna pressed.

"I wouldn't have done her like that."

"And now makes it any better? You's a thirsty-ass trash box," Tywanna spewed.

Jade jumped to her feet and remarked, "You know what, Ty? I'm tired of yo' ass always havin' somethin' to say 'bout my damn life!"

"Well in case you haven't noticed, boo-boo, yo' life ain't shit."

"Like yo' life's all dat. Bitch, bye!"

"At least I ain't the one fuckin' someone else's man," Tywanna spat.

"Like the bitch who's fuckin' yours?" Jade retorted.

Ashley stepped in between them and intervened. "Enough, you two. Ever since Lexi's been gone, our friendship has been different. She wouldn't want this of us at all. And Jade, Tywanna has the right to be upset. It's wrong of you to mess with Banks. Think about how Lex would feel. And what about my brotha, Jade? Gangsta really feelin' yo' ass."

"Ash, I'm sorry, but I'ma do me. Lexi ain't here to feel no type of way," she replied heartlessly. "And I'm sure Gangsta ain't the kinda nigga to have feelings for no bitch."

"You're too damn selfish to think about anyone but Jade!" Ashley was trembling with anger.

Tywanna wrapped her arm around Ash for comfort. "Jade, I can't believe it took all of this for me to realize you ain't a true friend," she spoke evenly.

"It is what it is," Jade told her, standing with her arms folded beneath her breasts.

"No, Jade. It is what you made it," Tywanna responded. "Hoes like you make it hard for us good women."

"Ain't nobody got time for that, Ty. You just need to worry 'bout keepin' yo' baby's daddy in check." She peeped how Tywanna looked at her surprised. "Yeah, that's right. I know all about you bein' pregnant. And you wasn't even gon' tell me. Some friend you are," Jade scoffed.

"Jade, the way I see it, you didn't deserve to know." Tywanna stated matter-of-factly.

"Go on, get the hell outta my house!" Jade spat as Tywanna guided Ashley out of the apartment.

Needing to escape the reality of shit, Jade pulled out a sack of coke. Lately the coke seemed to be the only friend she needed.

\*\*\*

A Rolls Royce with darkened windows drew up before Diamond, where he stood in front of Fiserv Forum arena downtown. Little emerged from its passenger side, purposely holding his suit jacket ajar to reveal his pistol. He looked up at Diamond, and questioned, "You packin'?"

"That a trick question?" Diamond grinned. He handed over both his guns - one from his front waistband and the other from the small of his back. Ever since bodies began to fall, he decided to stay double-breasted.

"Twin diamond-encrusted .45-caliber gold-plated handguns. Nice," Little commented, admiring the hardware. He pulled open the rear suicide door, inviting Diamond to enter.

Diamond peered into the interior and saw Balistrieri sitting in the corner, staring out the window. He was dressed in an immaculately tailored grey suit, soft white shirt, and black tie and shoes, all designed by Yves Saint Laurent. He looked like money.

Diamond got in, and the door closed behind him with a thud. He found himself in the surprisingly quiet interior, observing the mob boss huddled in the corner, ignoring him. The Rolls smoothly glided off.

Looking out the window at the passing scene of trash whirling along the streets and gutters, clogged traffic, hawking peddlers arrayed along the street, and drunkard windshield cleaners staggering through traffic with filthy squeegees, Frank thought, *Life in this town really sucks.* Turning away from the window, he relaxed back against the soft leather seat, his eyes fixed on Diamond.

"You know," Frank began casually, "I don't like how business has been on your part as of late. It's one thing when your money is short. It's another when it begins to affect mine." He reached into the inside pocket of his jacket, fished out a gold cigar case, and removed from it a Cuban cigar. "Stogie?"

"Thanks, but no thanks," Diamond respectfully declined, as Frank held out the cigar in offering.

"Damn things are no good for you, anyway." He replaced the case in situ and then set flame to the cigar using a gold lighter. "It seems you haven't been able to move much product lately, and it's unacceptable. We had an agreement, Diamond, and you're not holding up on your part. And we both know, a loyal man sticks to his agreements. He doesn't make excuses for why he cannot do the job correctly," he expounded and then puffed the cigar.

"Mr. Balistrieri, I assure you our agreement still stands, as much as my loyalty. By any means, I'll see to it you receive every penny of yo' money. I know how much it means to you."

"Do you really know how much my money means to me? I don't think so," he stated assertively, interrupting Diamond. "As a dirt poor kid working odd jobs for wise guys, I swore I would be rich one day. Made my first million when I was around your age and never stopped to count the rest. Now I own a vast amount of real estate, shopping centers, and oil fields, and have one of the world's largest collections of primitive art.

"During my lifetime, I have collected three ex-wives, a dozen mistresses - including two actresses - and several champion race horses, but the only thing that really means something to me is my money." He eyed Diamond sharply. "I suggest you do whatever's necessary in moving more product and getting me my money, or I'm afraid I'll have to cut you off, Diamond…at the head."

Diamond knew he was serious. A connect like Frank Balistrieri was an opportunity that was extremely hard to come by. Therefore, Diamond was loyal to him. "I'll be sure to keep our agreement, Mr. Balistrieri," he assured him.

"Perfecto." Frank exhaled a cloud of smoke.

The Rolls pulled to a halt at a stoplight. A moment later, the grey Caravan yielded beside the luxurious vehicle.

While in the mob boss's presence, Diamond figured now would be a better time than any to mention the proposition Lynch offered under the table. "I'd like to discuss another matter wit' you, if I may."

Frank took a pull of the cigar, then said, "Shoot."

As if on cue, abruptly the side door of the van slid back, and a gunman was leveling a submachine-gun on the Rolls.

Prrraaat! Prrraaat! Prrraaat! Prrraaat!

The hail of gunfire caused Diamond to instinctively duck while Frank never even flinched, as though he was untouchable. What neither Diamond nor the gunman ever expected was that the Rolls would be bulletproof, causing bullets to ricochet.

Once realizing the bullets had no effect on the vehicle, Diamond hesitantly rose in his seat. And he thought he'd seen that Caravan before, he just couldn't place it.

Little laughed at the gunman, finding his attempt a joke. Frank casually rapped on the partition between the front and back seats. Little looked up into the rearview mirror at Frank, who offhandedly motioned towards the Caravan, which had dispelled. Little said something to Alphonse, who was chauffeuring, and they took off after the van.

Seeing that they couldn't shake the Rolls, the Caravan yielded, then the gunman hopped out. He stood in the center of the street, firing at the Rolls', windshield as it sped towards him. His attempt to scare off the Rolls was to no avail, as Alphonse pressed down on the accelerator, going nearly 100 mph. He mowed down the gunman, sending him flying before a crash landing. The Caravan took off again without chase.

Little exited the Rolls with his snub nose .357 Smith & Wesson in hand as he stepped up on the critically injured man. "Who sent ya? I want a name," he insisted.

"Y-you'll…n-neva get a name outta m-me, so…do w-what you gotta d-do," the man urged.

Little leveled on the man's head and said, "It's your funeral, kid."

Bang!

With no further questions, Little put a bullet into the gunman's cranium, splattering his noodles on the pavement. He reentered the Rolls and then Alphonse pulled off.

\*\*\*

Diamond parked his Bentley beside Tywanna's Lexus. He stepped out and headed towards the underground parking lot's elevator as he observed his surroundings. He knew that if someone was bold enough to come after Balistrieri, then he had to be vigilant.

*Who the fuck else has enough resources and power to go up against a mob boss?* he asked himself. The more he turned over the inquiry in his mind, the more Lynch seemed capable. And he didn't even get the chance to discuss the matter concerning Lynch with Balistrieri after the escapade. But he'd definitely keep it in mind.

Inside the condo, Diamond called for Ty, getting no response. *Her ass should be here 'cause her whip's downstairs*, he reflected. Then the thought of Lynch sitting on the sofa crossed his mind, causing him to draw his .45s. Most of the overhead lights had been cut off, bathing the place in a strange ballet of dancing shadows. The vertical blinds were open, revealing the incandescent sprawl of the city. Treading lightly through the pad, he found Tywanna standing out on the balcony drinking in the view, her arms rested on the rail.

Tywanna was collecting her thoughts. Shit with Jade earlier had her thoughts everywhere. One thing in particular was Jade's claim that some bitch was fuckin' Diamond. She tried not to allow it to bother her, but admittedly, it did. She loved Diamond and trusted him, although she knew that no matter how good a bitch treats her nigga, he'd still fuck another bitch if he wanted to. *Should I even bring it up to his ass?* she pondered.

Diamond laid both of his weapons on the counter before stepping out onto the balcony. "Ty, didn't yo' ass hear a nigga callin' you?" he fumed.

"If so, I woulda answered."

"Maybe if you didn't have the damn door closed then you woulda."

She shook her damn head. "Diamond, the door wasn't even closed all the way. So just chill."

"Told you a thousand times you gotta be on point."

She came out of the pocket of her silk robe gripping a .380 ACP with a pearl handle Diamond had bought her for personal security. "See?" she said and then placed the gun back inside her pocket.

Changing the topic, he told her, "You goin' to stay at yo' mama's for a minute."

"And why I gotta go stay at Mama's?"

"'Cause. I'ont need you around wit' all this shit goin' on in the streets."

She stood with her weight shifted to one side, arms folded beneath her breasts. "So I'm s'posed to just put a hold on my life?"

"Listen, Tywanna, I'ont wanna hear it. So have yo' shit packed and ready to go by tomorrow," he insisted.

Tywanna turned back to the view, looking out at the darkness draped over the city. She couldn't stand it whenever Diamond became stubborn with her. On the other hand, Diamond needed her to understand that he only cared to get her and their unborn out of danger. His love for them made him feel the need to provide protection and security.

"Bae," he began tranquilly as he stepped up behind Tywanna and wrapped his arms around her torso and planted his hands on her baby bump. "I'm only doin' this for the safety of you and our li'l one. I can't deal wit' the thought of y'all bein' placed in danger on my account. Jus' know I'm doin' this because of my love," he expressed.

Diamond kissed and sucked her neck, and Tywanna pressed her soft ass back against his hardness. He undid his Hermès slacks and let them fall down around his Mauri Gators. Tywanna grabbed his dick, pushed her panties to the side, and then guided him into her wetness. As he gripped her at the waist and stroked her deeply, she slightly moaned and braced herself by holding on to the rail. He bit down on his bottom lip while pounding away at her box, and she looked back over her shoulder into his eyes.

"Girl, you luh me?" Diamond wanted to know as he dug her out.

Tywanna arched her back just right, allowing him to hit her spot. "Mm hmm, yes Diamond, I love you so fuckin' much, baby!" she groaned.

"And, bae, a nigga luh the shit outta yo' ass, too."

Whatever thoughts they had before were replaced by the pleasure of their sex. Although they understood that sex ain't better than love.

## Chapter 11

In the dark night, the cemetery was a ghost town. Diamond stood before Chase's gravesite. It was painful for him to be there. He hadn't attended the funeral because he just couldn't bring himself to, even after much deliberation. Looking down at the headstone, the reality of Chase's death hit Diamond hard.

"Ain't s'posed to end like this for you, Chase," he thought aloud. "You had a wife and kids - a family. And now they have to find a way to live without you. All 'cause of me and Gangsta. Damn…" He shook his fuckin' head, thinking back to Chase telling him not to allow the streets to come between him and Gangsta. "Rest in peace."

So lost in the moment, Diamond wasn't aware of his surroundings as Gangsta stepped up behind him undetected and confiscated the .45 from the small of Diamond's back. "Expected you'd have it there, as usual," Gangsta said, leveling the weapon on Diamond's back.

Swiftly, Diamond spun and simultaneously drew the twin .45 from his front waistband, leveling it on Gangsta's chest. "Yeah well, now I walk wit' two of 'em," he replied sternly. "Are we gon' talk it out, or shoot it out?"

"Go ahead, talk. But I'd rather shoot it out, and see who lives to tell the story later." He readjusted his fingers, getting a firmer grip on the weapon.

"Well, I called you so we can talk civilly. I'ont understand, Gangsta. What the hell turned you into enemy to me?"

"Diamond, it was never about us bein' enemies. It's about bein' in power. Somethin' you kept me from," Gangsta expounded.

"Then why not facilitate yo' own operation? Why invade my turf and recruit some of my men?"

"Don't take it personal, I did the same to Banks. In the end it won't even matter, 'cause both y'all niggas will be dead," he implied firmly.

Diamond held Gangsta's eyes. "That's how you see shit comin' to an end? How 'bout I shoot you, right here right now?"

"Shoot me, and I'll shoot you," Gangsta warned.

"And what about Banks, huh? Are we s'posed to jus' shoot each other to death and leave him be? Why don't we come together and take him out. And once Banks is six feet deep, you can make his turf and men yours then leave mine the hell alone," Diamond suggested.

Gangsta had to admit it wasn't a bad suggestion. "I'll need time to consider it."

"Jus' keep in mind there's not much time to waste."

Changing subjects, Gangsta said, "Tell me, Diamond, why didn't you show up to the funeral? Thought you was Chase's friend." He'd been the one to choose the particular location as their meeting grounds solely to move Diamond.

In that moment, Diamond couldn't even look him in the eyes. "I...I felt responsible for his death," he divulged.

"Feelin' is mutual," Gangsta admitted.

While the two stood before Chase's gravesite holding one another at gunpoint, it was obvious they didn't like the idea of being enemies, although it could be no other way, since they were vying for power over the same streets.

Diamond lowered his .45 and stated, "Maybe next time." He relieved the other from Gangsta's hand and then turned, walking away.

"Diamond," Gangsta called out behind him, halting him in his tracks. "Next time you may not be spared."

"Then these two guns gon' come in handy," Diamond replied

***

KA-BRRHH!

The Molotov caused an explosion once it crashed against the front of the trap house and immediately, another exploded at its rear. Flames began to hastily crawl over the house.

Carrying out Diamond's orders to rid his turf of intruders, Major and his squad had been reducing Gangsta's and Banks's foot soldiers. Major and his squadrons proved to be ruthless. Day to day intruders turned up bodied, some in more drastic ways than others.

One had even been discovered DOA from suffocation due to a bank roll being forcefully stuffed down his throat. They were letting it be known that, by any means, they were out to reclaim their territory.

The trap house was occupied by some of Banks's niggas. Major n'em had it surrounded. The flames began to engulf the trap, and rather than burn to death, the occupants rushed to the nearest door, attempting to escape the inferno.

Rrraaa! Rrraaa! Rrraaa!

Boc! Boc! Boc! Boc!

Prrraaat! Prrraaat!

At either escape, the niggas were met by a fusillade of bullets. As the house hastily burned, Major n'em fired hundreds of rounds of ammunition into it. The niggas attempted to shoot their way out, but the combination of flames and bullets they were up against proved deadly.

Hearing the sounds of sirens wailing in the distance, Major directed his squadrons to head out, and they loaded into their rides then sped away.

A moment later, miraculously, Ice, who was a top-level distributor for Banks, emerged from inside the engulfed house. Ice suffered from third degree burns and some bullet wounds. He stumbled and staggered then collapsed onto the pavement, unconscious.

\*\*\*

"Say, big fella," Little ducked his head inside the open door. "Lynch is here to see ya."

"Send 'im in, why don't ya?" Frank was annoyed with having his massage interrupted. He was lying face down on the massage bed in one of the many rooms in his mansion. The female masseuse kneaded his shoulders, her delicate hands feeling wonderful on him. Being in his line of work, he hardly ever got the chance to unwind. If it wasn't one thing, it was another.

After the futile hit taken out on Frank, Lynch dreaded having to come meet with him. He wasn't sure if Diamond had informed Frank of his little proposition, which he knew would result in the mob boss having him whacked. It was one of the reasons why he needed either Frank or Diamond out of the picture - preferably both. But he figured if Frank wanted to dead him, then he wouldn't have had to request to see him in order to do so.

Lynch stepped inside the candlelit room, finding Frank nude on the table as the masseur worked on him. Lynch shielded his eyes with a hand. "You wanted to see me, Frank?"

"Agent, I called you here because I have a problem with someone taking an attempt out on my life," Frank said, speaking through the face-hole of the table. "It's not something I take lightly."

"Any idea who?" Lynch pried.

"Could be anyone. Hmm, that feels great," he groaned as the masseuse worked on his back with massage oils. "Besides, Agent, I have you to figure out things like this for me."

"Okay, Frank, I'll look into it."

"You do that. I won't be comfortable until figuring out whomever the hell this putz is. And once you do, I want him blown to shit. Ba-da-bing, ba-da-boom!" Frank ordered and then waved Lynch away. He failed to realize the enemy was too close for comfort.

\*\*\*

"How's it been at yo' mom's?" Ashley asked, speaking with Tywanna via FaceTime on her iPhone.

"Borin' as hell, girl. Been stuck in this house all damn week," Tywanna complained. She was lying in bed in the guest room at her mother Sandra's home out in Madison, Wisconsin. "But I must admit, even though I'm missin' home, it's nice to be away from all the drama."

"I'm sure. And what about Diamond? How come he didn't go with you?"

"His ass said somethin' about not wantin' the baby and me to be around while shit goin' on in the streets. At first I was upset with Diamond for sending me to stay here, but I understand he's only lookin' out for his, so I couldn't remain upset with him for too long.

Actually, girl, I miss his ass, and hope he's bein' safe while in them streets."

"Diamond can take care of himself. You just need to take care of yo'self and my niece."

Tywanna rubbed her baby bump and replied, "Speakin' of yo' niece, she's already givin' me attitude. This li'l girl just won't stop kickin' and shit. Good thing Diamond's excited about havin' a daughter, 'cause she's obviously gonna be Daddy's li'l girl."

"I'm sure Diamond will make a good dad," Ashley added. Her words caused Tywanna to think about the twins having to grow up without Chase.

"Ash," Tywanna began tranquilly, "sorry I wasn't able to make Chase's funeral. Of course I wish I coulda been there to support you."

"Girl, yo' love is more than enough support. It's much more than what Jade offers," she said, sounding bitter.

"Don't even get me started on her ass. Still can't believe her. And Banks trippin' if he thinks he can turn a hoe into a housewife."

"Ain't that the truth," Ashley agreed. "Let's not forget she's also fuckin' Gangsta. I'm sure Banks doesn't even know about that."

Tywanna reflected back to something Lexi had mentioned pertaining to Diamond being hit up at the club that night: *It was someone he least expects, maybe one of the girls who work at the club.* She sat up on edge of the bed and inquired, "Ash, you think Jade coulda had a part in everything?"

"What'chu mean?"

"I mean think about it. She is sleepin' with Gangsta and Banks, both of whom are at the center of all the beef. Maybe she's playin' both sides. The hoe is apparently capable of it," Tywanna expounded.

"Even though Jade ain't no damn good, she doesn't have any motive, nor anything to gain from it."

"Yeah, maybe I'm just trippin'." Tywanna grabbed the remote control to the flat screen and began channel surfing. She stopped on the *Real Housewives of Atlanta*. "What about her sayin' that shit about Diamond fuckin' some bitch, think it's true?"

"Ty, Diamond's a good nigga, and clearly he loves you. I ain't sayin' it excuses him fuckin' someone else, if he is. I'm only sayin' you need to just focus on yo' relationship with him. And more than likely, Jade's ass is just hatin' 'cause she don't have what you do," Ashley voiced.

Tywanna gazed at the mute TV. "Ash?"

"Yeah, girl."

"Ever imagine life would turn out like this when we were li'l girls?"

"Life's too precious to focus on the bad."

"I just need Diamond to understand that a life lived for others is worthwhile."

***

Gangsta arrived at Yul's warehouse to pick up his supply. With seizing parts of both Diamond and Banks's turf and recruiting some of their men, Gangsta was able to push the boy Yul fronted him. Fuckin' with the Jamaicans, he was making a killing in the game - figuratively and literally. And needless to say, Yul liked having Gangsta on his side, mainly because of the threat he posed to his enemies' finances and existence.

Yul stood outside of the warehouse, and, as usual, Rasheym and Siah stood on either side of him with their artillery in hand. Gangsta stepped out of the passenger side of the candy-red M.C., and one of his top drug lieutenants, Playboy, stepped out from its driver side.

"Me wasn't aware dat you'd be bringin' along company," Yul stressed.

"He wouldn't be here if I didn't trust 'im," Gangsta assured him.

"Just like you trusted Diamond? And look how dat turned out." Yul abruptly drew his Desert Eagle from his waist and leveled it on Playboy.

Boom!

"Arrgh shit!" Playboy grunted in pain from the slug he took in the shoulder.

Gangsta looked from Playboy to Yul. "Fuck was that for?" he asked disapprovingly.

Yul stuffed the cannon back inside his waistband and casually stated, "Me expect dat from now on, you will inform me before bringin' anyone else along. Come, mon, let we go inside so he can get cleaned up while you and me discuss bidness."

Inside, Yul led Gangsta through the department where product was being manufactured and arranged by several members of his posse. The heroin was produced by boiling morphine base with acetic hydride and subjecting it to various purification steps. It was dark brown in color because of impurities left from the presence of additives. While some members were blending the dope, others were packaging it by the kilo. The operation was well organized.

Gangsta noticed the foreign substance that was being added to the product. "What's it bein' cut wit'?" he wanted to know.

"Me secret ingredient: fentanyl," Yul told him with a grin. As the two stepped up to one of the tables where dope was being mixed, Yul added, "It makes de China white extremely potent. De shit can even be fatal. But all dat matters is you'll hav' some ah de best quality dope in de streets, eh?" He scooped a small amount of the blended dope inside his long, dirty pinky fingernail, and then snorted the powder substance. "Good shit."

"If it'll bring in more money, then I'll move it," Gangsta agreed.

"Gangsta, if you really want mo' money, den you hav' to eliminate all competitors."

"I'm sure, overall, you mean Diamond."

"Me sense dat you are reluctant to kill Diamond. If you do not, den you could regret it."

"Apply enough pressure and Diamond will jus' give," Gangsta declared.

Yul placed a hand on the nape of Gangsta's neck and stared into his eyes. "Power is taken, not given."

\*\*\*

"Damn, boy, you eatin' da shit outta dis pussy. Yo' ass got a bitch goin'!" Toni leaned back on the bed with her legs agape while her boy toy, Mateo, feasted on her clit.

Mateo was Cuban, small in stature. He had a light brown hue with fluorescent green eyes and wore his hair in a man bun.

Grabbing a fist full of Mateo's long bun, Toni pushed his face deeper into her crotch as she thrust her hips forward and lifted slightly off the bed. Mateo licked and sucked on her pussy, and the way he put his entire mouth on her twat caused Toni to throw back her head. "Fuuuck!" Toni groaned. She couldn't hold it any longer and came in Mateo's mouth, and he slurped up Toni's juices.

Toni stood and strapped on her ten-inch dildo. Toni and Mateo weren't in what was considered a normal relationship. In theirs, she wore the pants. Mateo was the kind of guy who embraced his feminine side, and he was sexually fluid.

Toni bent Mateo over the bedside, spit on his ass crack for lubrication, and then inched the toy inside his ass. Toni held him by his hips while she fucked him.

"Ummm, baby. Yeees, Toni. Ahhhh!" Mateo shouted as he took the pipe.

Smacking his ass, Toni said, "Dis shit feels good, don't it?"

"Mm-kaaay, babe!" Mateo came out the ass.

Afterwards, strutting in her red-bottom stilettos towards her Benz, Toni beeped its alarm. She was supposed to have been at Red Velvet after distributing product to the trap spots nearly an hour ago, but had gotten sidetracked once Mateo had texted her to Netflix and chill.

Jumping in her whip and hitting the E-way she cut on some music. Flipping through Pandora, she stopped when she heard Dreezy's "Where Them $ @." Rapping along to the music, she was all the way turnt. Her music suddenly stopped when her Bluetooth picked up, indicating an incoming call.

"You got Toni," she answered.

"Toni, where you at right now? Been waitin' on you for nearly an hour, and Diamond's patience is growin' thin," Pelle said as his voice boomed in over the speakers.

"On the way, jus' gimme 'bout ten minutes. Major there yet?" She still felt a way about the nigga.

"You'd know if you were here, now wouldn't you?" he half-joked.

"Whatevs, nigga," she chuckled. "Jus' let Diamond know I'm comin'."

"Toni," Pelle started, sounding serious, "lemme ask you somethin'. Between me 'n you."

"I'm listenin'."

He hesitated before saying, "Don't get me wrong, I'm as loyal to Diamond as you are, but do you think he only sees us as pawns in this game?"

His question made her think twice about shit. "If so, then every pawn has the potential to become a Queen." Toni pressed the end button. *Maybe it's time that game has a Queen pin,* she contemplated.

Storming down the E-way, she checked the rearview mirror out of habit. The grey Caravan shadowing her caught her eye, and she recognized it was the very one that pulled up on her and the others outside of the club before. She grabbed the .10mm from her Chanel handbag in the middle console as the van switched lanes and began to speed up on the driver side of the Benz.

Blocka! Blocka! Blocka! Blocka!

She squeezed shots out from the window into the van, which abruptly weaved and collided into the side of the Benz causing Toni to drop her banger as she was forced to take hold of the steering wheel in order to gain control of the vehicle. The collision caused her a busted head. Once she was able to stop the car from bobbing, she desperately searched the floorboard for her banger with one hand while steering with the other and trying to keep an eye on the road.

Rrraaa! Rrraaa!

The van's side door was open and as it sped alongside of the Benz, a gunman let off his fully-automatic on Toni. Bullets decorated the driver's side of the Benz, shattering its windows and flattening the front tire, which caused sparks to fly as she rode on the rim. Miraculously, Toni wasn't hit, and she managed to get ahold of her banger.

Blocka! Blocka! Blocka! Blocka! Blocka!

Toni squeezed off a chain of shots as the van went to collide with the Benz again. She hit the driver in the neck and chest, and the Caravan jerked out of control before tumbling. She heatedly slammed her clenched fist down on the steering wheel as she continued to speed away.

***

"It's packed in this joint tonight. And the girls are rakin' it up," Pelle said as he approached Diamond, who was seated at the club's bar.

Diamond took a swig from his glass of Remy. "You reach Toni?"

"Yep. Said she'd be here in ten minutes, give or take." He ordered himself a glass of Grey Goose on rocks.

"Her ass s'posed to have been here damn near an hour ago," he retorted, glancing at his Breitling.

"What I told her." Pelle sipped his drink. "Diamond, you thought about how you'd deal wit' that fed?" he asked curiously.

"Yeah. I'ma off 'im," Diamond answered evenly.

"But don't you think he'd be more beneficial to you? As long as he's on yo' side, then you won't have to worry 'bout niggas hatin' on you to the cops."

Diamond eyed him and stated, "Fuck a hater and a cop. You jus' focus on dealin' wit' havin' the money cleaned. Tell Major I'll be awaitin' on him in my office. Send Toni whenever she gets here." He polished off his drink, set the glass on the bar with a thud, and then stepped off with Sarge close behind.

*Some niggas jus' gotta learn the hard way*, Pelle said introspectively as he observed Diamond head towards the back. He turned his glass up to his lips and focused his attention on the stripper tearing up the stage, who had her huge, fake booty swallowing the pole. *Damn! Shorty can get da pipe!*

"Yo, Sarge, I'm cool. Let me get a moment alone. Why don't you go and chill, my nigga," Diamond insisted, and Sarge headed for the front of the club. As Diamond was entering his office, someone grabbed his shoulder from behind. He hastily spun and simultaneously pulled his .45, then pressed its muzzle to the individual's stomach. He realized it was Surprise.

"Dat a gun, or are you just happy to see a bitch?" Surprise smirked. She stood before him wearing a lime green leather catsuit and white stilettos.

Diamond stuffed the weapon back into his waistband and told her, "Surprise, I'ont like that creepin' shit." Immediately afterwards, he realized he was the one doing the creeping with her.

"What up wit'chu ghostin' me lately, 'cause I ain't for all that," Surprise said.

"Jus' been busy, a'ight?" He sounded agitated.

"Then you can get busy with me." She pressed him back against the wall and stuck her tongue in his mouth. He responded by palming all that ass of hers in both hands and kissing her back.

Emerging from the dressing room on her way to take the stage, Jade caught Diamond and Surprise in the act. *Bet this pic will look nice on Snapchat*, she thought vindictively as she hurried back into the dressing room for her iPhone. Unbeknownst to either Diamond or Surprise, she snapped a photo of them in action. Satisfied, Jade went on as she heard he DJ announcing her.

Breaking their embrace, Diamond pushed Surprise back up off of him and said, "I can't keep doin' dis shit."

"What'chu doin' that's so wrong, Diamond?" she asked, grabbing his hardness through his jeans.

"Creepin' wit'chu on my girl, Surprise. That shit ain't right."

Surprise unhanded him. "Mm hmm. So now nigga's got a conscience all of a sudden. Diamond, whenever you feel the need to cut a bitch off, all you gotta do is tell me. I ain't tryna break up a 'happy home'." She said the last two words using air quotes. "Nigga, just know you can get dis pussy whenever you want." As she strutted away, Diamond grabbed his crotch and admired her bubble butt. He had to admit it was hard to deny her.

Meantime, Toni rushed into the club. She had seen Pelle standing near the bar and hurried over to him. "Where's Diamond?" she wanted to know urgently.

"In his office. Fuck happened to you?" He noticed the blood on her forehead.

Without reply, she grabbed the drink from his hand, downed it, then slammed the glass on the bar with a thud. She made a beeline for Diamond's office with Pelle in tow. Stepping inside, she came upon Diamond sitting behind his desk with Major seated across from him.

"You're late as hell, Toni," Diamond stated.

"Woulda gotten here sooner if niggas didn't try to off me," she replied, frustrated.

"Who? When?" Diamond jumped to his feet and hurried around his desk towards her.

"Some of Banks's shooters," she told him.

"Major, thought I put you in charge of wipin' out any and all enemies," Diamond shot at him.

Major stood. "I'm on it."

"Nigga, had you been on it, then I wouldn't have damn near gotten offed," Toni spat.

"Toni, he ain't to blame," Diamond spoke up.

"Know what? You right. I'ont know why you even put dis nigga in charge of shit."

"So now you blamin' me?"

"Diamond, I been by yo' damn side all these years, and you put him in charge of things over me."

Pelle piped in. "Toni, I'm sure Diamond has his reasons."

"Pelle, Major. Give us a minute, will you?" Diamond instructed, and the two stepped out, leaving them alone. "Listen Toni," he began, speaking softly, "I jus' need you to stay by my side. Already lost Gangsta and Chase to the streets. Can't stand to lose you, too."

"I can handle my own, Diamond."

"I'ont doubt that, shorty. But we all we got. And don't worry, we'll take care of Banks." Diamond pulled her in for a hug and kissed her forehead.

\*\*\*

After the concert at the Rave, Lucifer was with the salesgirl, Nina, outside in the parking lot. Vehicles moved through the lot towards the exits. Lucifer sat on the hood of his Acura with Nina standing in between his legs. The two had attended the concert VIP status and the place was lit.

Banks opted not to tag along, and after Lucifer assured him several times he'd be fine going alone with Nina, Banks reluctantly let it be. After what had happened to Ice and the others, Banks was on edge.

Lucifer had enjoyed Nina's company. He was looking forward to the rest of their night together. Nina was actually feelin' the nigga. She was interested in seeing where things with him could go.

"Shorty, how 'bout we head to a telly," Lucifer suggested.

"I'm cool with that. But first, let's hit up Michael's for a bite to eat," Nina replied.

"Thought we'd jus' order room service while we chill in bed," he smirked.

"Sounds like a plan," she smiled.

The candy red M.C. drew up before Lucifer, but he didn't think shit of it. Once the passenger's Lambo door swung upward, he peeped Gangsta aiming a Draco at him.

"Shit!" Lucifer reached for the pistol on his waist...

Boc! Boc! Boc!

Slugs ripped through Lucifer's chest and he flailed backwards onto the hood of the car, chasing his breath. Unfortunately for Nina, she became a casualty. A slug blew her brains out.

Gangsta had received a call from one of his recruits, who informed him of Lucifer's whereabouts. He made it clear not to move on Lucifer because he wanted to make him pay personally for killing Chase.

Gangsta stepped out of the whip, walked up on a helpless Lucifer, and leveled the Draco on him then stated, "The descent to hell is easy."

Boc! Boc! Boc! Boc! Boc! Boc!

## Chapter 12

Pelle stepped into the passenger side of the unmarked Dodge Durango where Lynch awaited him. Pelle hated the bind he was tied up in. After being snatched up with five bricks by Lynch during a sting, instead of going to prison for an extended amount of time, he'd decided to work for Lynch, becoming his mole. They were having a conclave in the middle of the night in a scarce Taco Bell's parking lot.

"Why do we always have to meet in strange places and shit? Thought a guy like you'd have an office," Pelle said.

"This is my office. Now update me on things inside Diamond's operation," Lynch urged.

"For starters, Diamond seems to be in over his head wit' all the beefs. It's gettin' in the way of his operation big time, although not enough to prevent him from continuin' to make money. He actually entrusted me wit' havin' some of it cleaned for him."

"When, where, and how?" Lynch wanted to know the details. He understood that money laundering is the life blood of all illegal activity.

"In a few days. He mentioned havin' a bitch who works at a check cashin' spot. Says she exchanges dirty bills for clean ones," Pelle informed him.

"Anything else I should know?"

"Matter fact, there is. The nigga Diamond ain't feelin' yo' offer, so he has it in mind to give you a dirt nap."

"So let me get this correct: Diamond plans to kill me?"

"Exactly." Pelle took a pull of the Newport he was smoking. The red cherry from its flame glowed in the dark interior of the vehicle.

"Then that means you're running out of time. Either you convince him to partner with me soon, or help me get rid of him before he decides to come after me."

"I'm doin' all I can, Lynch."

"Actually, you're not!" he snapped out of frustration.

"What more can I do, huh? Maybe you'd be better off if I helped you kill his ass," Pelle wisecracked. He noticed how Lynch narrowly eyed him. Pelle's brows knitted and he said, "Wait: you actually expect me to help you kill Diamond?"

"If need be."

"Well, that ain't part of our agreement. Besides, Diamond's become somethin' like a friend to me," he admitted.

Lynch snatched the cigarette from Pelle as he went to take a pull of it, and then Lynch flicked it out the window. "You, of all people, should be aware there's no such thing as 'friends' in the crime world. Only associates and enemies. That said, I suggest you do as I say."

"And what if I refuse? 'Cause it ain't what I agreed to."

"Then I'd just haul you in for those pounds of 'ron I busted your ass with. So you're in no position to refuse me anything, unless you wouldn't mind sharing a tiny cell with another guy for twenty years or so. Maybe even be his bitch."

Pelle shifted uncomfortably in his seat. "That bust was bogus, and you know it. Already told you several times those birds wasn't even mine."

"But unfortunately for you, you happened to be the fall-guy for your supplier. It's like I said before, there's no friends in the crime world. Besides, don't you wanna be the one in power for once in your pitiful life? All you gotta do is help me get rid of Diamond, whether it be prison or, preferably, death. Then you can replace him."

"A'ight, I'll do it," Pelle conceded. "But immediately after-wards, I expect for you to let me walk free, and provide me wit' product like we originally agreed on."

"However, only if Diamond's out of the way for certain."

"Jus' tell me whatever it is you need me to do."

"That's more like it, my friend," Lynch grinned. He began explaining the details of his plot.

\*\*\*

Whack-whack-whack!

Banks pistol whipped the hell outta the D-boy like a madman, knocking him on his side in the chair he was tied to. The D-boy was one of the few of Gangsta's men that some of Banks's boys had snatched up over the past days. They had taken the D-boy to an abandoned house, and so far neither he, nor the others, couldn't or wouldn't give up Gangsta's whereabouts.

"Tell me where da fuck I can find Gangsta, 'fore I light'cho ass up," Banks warned. He wanted Gangsta more than anything. Even more than he did Diamond.

"M-man, already told you, I'ont know shit 'bout da nigga. He jus' come through, drop off work, and pick up bread, then he ghost," the D-boy cried through swollen lips.

"Bitch-ass nigga," Banks kicked him in the stomach, "you know somethin'! So I suggest you think faster than a speedin' bullet." He aimed his .9 down on the D-boy's dome.

"Whoa, hol' up! Look, maybe you can find him at Lady's gamble spot. Seen him there a coupla times," he informed out of fear. "Dat's all I know; on my mama."

Banks peered down at the nigga repulsively and stated, "Lost my moms at a young age, and you choose to speak on yours in vain. Bet yo' mama got more heart than yo' bitch ass."

Blocka! Blocka!

First Lexi, and now Lucifer, Banks mused, as he pushed his Ashton up Center Street. He'd cried after getting the bad news about Lucifer. It was like he was crying blood. Banks was ready to paint the streets of Milwaukee red. He'd been sending hitters to wipeout any of Gangsta's men, and he had every intention to go at Gangsta with murder on his mind.

\*\*\*

In the Theater, Diamond sat at the head of the huge oak wood table, and his top-level cohorts were seated on either side of it. "I called you all here so we're on the same accord. Toni, I need you to be sure the rest of the product is moved within a week, so next week we'll be ready for the routine re-up."

"Shit has been slow motion wit' all the intruders settin' up shop. So a week could be a stretch," Toni pointed out.

Diamond looked over to Major and said, "This is where you come in at. Over the next few days, I want you to apply pressure to any mu'fucka who ain't down wit' our operation. Lay 'em down and seize all valuables."

"Done," Major assured.

"Sure 'bout that?" Toni huffed.

"Yo, what's yo' fuckin' issue wit' me, huh Toni?" he wanted to know fuming.

"Only issue I have is I'ont think you have what it takes to be in this game, 'cause it ain't based on sympathy."

"Trust, I ain't last this long in the game due to anyone's sympathies."

Diamond angrily slammed a clenched fist down on the table. "Enough! Now let's get back to the money. Speakin' of, Pelle, I still expect for you to meet wit' Keisha in order to clean the money."

Pelle only nodded his consent, as though he wasn't actually working with Lynch against Diamond to bring down his drug empire.

"As for Gangsta and Banks," Diamond continued, "after we move the rest of the product and clean the proceeds, then we give 'em the war they lookin' for."

"Diamond, that ain't good for business," Toni chimed in.

"Business..." He jumped to his feet. "I'm talkin' 'bout stayin' alive. It's me who they want offed! So if any of you ain't wit' me, then get da fuck out." Diamond stepped over to the mini bar and poured himself a shot of Patron.

Major made his way over to the bar as well. "No matter what, I'm wit' you," he pledged.

After putting back his shot, Diamond locked eyes with Major. "Do me a solid."

"Anything."

"Handle Toni wit' care. I know she's a down bitch, but she's fragile."

Toni noticed Pelle seemed off. "Everything a'ight, Pell?"

"Yeah. Jus' some personal shit on a nigga mind," he deluded. "Jus' don't let it get in the way of business."

\*\*\*

As the group exited the Theater, they headed for their rides. Diamond and Major had ridden together, as did Toni and Pelle.

Major peeped that something was off about Diamond's Bentley. "Hol' up, Diamond." He inspected the vehicle, discovering a bomb connected to its ignition, which he disengaged.

The four each shared odd expressions.

"What tipped you off?" Diamond inquired gratefully.

"When we parked the whip here earlier, the mirror was straight." He straightened the rearview mirror on the driver side, and said, "Whoever planted the bomb musta bumped it while doin' so."

*Willin' to bet my life it was none other than Lynch*, Diamond's conscience suggested. "Good lookin' out, Major. How 'bout we call an Uber instead."

\*\*\*

Playboy stepped out of his M.C. and then proceeded towards one of the few bandos Gangsta had put him in charge of. He was there to make sure shit was operating accordingly. Usually some D-boys posted out on the block catchin' plays, but since it was colder out, they were huddled inside the bando.

Before Playboy was able to enter the bando, he was ambushed by Major and some of his squadrons. *How da fuck you get caught slippin' like dis?* Playboy's conscience scorned.

Carrying out Diamond's orders, Major and his squad were making it hard for intruders to breathe. Not only had they been leaving niggas stank, but they were also robbing them of their hides. This was a major problem for Gangsta and Banks due to it affecting their pockets. It was Diamond's way of showing his enemies that even after all, he was still the nigga in power.

"Try to make a move and I'ma leave you stiff," Major warned, pressing his cannon to Playboy's back. He frisked Playboy and confiscated his pistol. "Now slowly, open the door, step inside, and lay face down."

Playboy adhered to the instructions, then once inside, Major and his squadrons held the D-boys at gunpoint and made them lay face down on the floor as well.

Major casually took a seat on the run down sofa with his cannon across his lap. "Ransack dis bitch so we can get da hell outta here," he directed one of his hitters.

"Gangsta gon' have yo' ass murked for dis shit if I'ont get the chance to do it my damn self!" Playboy threatened.

Major sharply eyed him. "Nigga, you got heart. I'll give you that much. But apparently you ain't got enough brains to register that you ain't makin' it outta here alive." From his seated position, Major leveled his cannon down on Playboy's top.

Boom! Boom!

Suddenly shots rang out in the adjacent room, Major jumped to his feet. His squadron came staggering out of the room, spilling blood all over from the two large bullet holes decorating his chest. He dropped dead. An additional D-boy emerged from the room bustin' and dropped another of the invaders, leaving just three remaining.

Boc! Boc! Boc! Boc! Boc! Boc!

Major opened up on the D-boy, putting him down with a few shots. He then turned his attention back on Playboy. "I really ain't in the mood for no more shit. Now where's da fuckin' stash?" he demanded.

"Fuck I look like tellin' you anything knowin' you gon' burn me any-damn-way," Playboy retorted.

"It's in t-the bathroom inside the b-back of the t-toilet. N-now please man, jus' lemme l-live," one of the D-boys revealed with the false hope of being spared.

Playboy couldn't do shit but shake his fuckin' head at the hopeless D-boy.

Major sent one of the squadrons to go and fetch the stash. A moment later he returned with numerous stacks of cash inside a clear plastic bag and handed it over to Major. "Body all these niggas," he instructed before turning for the door.

As Major headed for his ride, he heard multiple gunshots erupt from inside the bando, and just knew the intruders had been taken care of. Or so he thought.

Blam! Blam! Blam! Blam! Blam!

Unexpectedly shots erupted from behind Major. Bullets missed his head by some inches. Glancing back over his shoulder as he drew his weapon, Major found Playboy behind the trigger. *Dis nigga definitely got more heart than a li'l,* he thought.

Playboy had gotten the drop on Major's squadrons. He was able to reach a pistol from beneath the sofa and murked them without hesitation. He was also sure to murk the hopeless D-boy for good measure. Now he was at Major.

Boc! Boc! Boc! Boc! Boc!

Blam! Blam! Blam! Blam!

As he continued to back his way towards his ride, Major returned fire. He pulled open the driver door and then tossed the bag of cash inside, all while exchanging shots with Playboy.

Boc! Boc! Click-click-click.

"Shit." Major had emptied the clip during the gunfight. He hurried into his ride and then smashed down the street while Playboy continued to spray until Major sharply bent the corner.

One thing for sure, Playboy had happened to make it out alive. And he'd be looking to murk Major.

*** 

"I'm tired of stayin' here at my ma's, Diamond. I wanna come back home," Tywanna complained on the other end of the line.

"Not now, Tywanna," Diamond told her. He was in his office at Red Velvet, seated behind his desk taking the call via FaceTime.

"And why not?"

"'Cause bae, shit still bad in these streets. Soon as shit back good, you'll be able to return home."

"And how long's that s'posed to take? 'Cause I already been here three damn weeks."

"Can't say exactly how long it'll take, but I'm handlin' it."

"Diamond, I'm worried about you."

"Well, don't be, you know I can hold my own. Jus' focus on takin' care of yo'self and the baby."

"Guess you right."

"I do miss yo' ass bein' all up under a nigga doe," he smirked.

"Aww. And I miss you, too." Tywanna had to admit he always knew how to make her feel better. "Look, Mama just came in from work and I'm sure she'll wanna have dinner with me, so I'll let you go. Muah," she kissed him through the phone before ending the call.

Diamond sighed heavily. There was so much he was dealing with, all of the issues taking place at once was becoming a lot. However, he understood he had to continue displaying strength.

He placed his weapons in the pockets of his Ralph Lauren sports coat and then exited the office, where Sarge was posted directly outside of the door. "I'ma step outside real quick. Alone," he added once Sarge began to follow.

Stepping outside of the club a blast of frigid air made Diamond tuck his head into his sports coat's upturned collar. He peeped Surprise pull into the parking lot in her Chrysler Sebring, and he swaggered towards the whip with lust in his heart.

"Diamond, boy, what'chu on?" Surprise inquired as she alighted from the whip and shut the door. Without offering any words he kissed her, slipping his tongue in her mouth. "Nigga, I had a feelin' you'd be back for more of dis good-good."

"Don't fuck up the mood, shorty," he responded flippantly.

Though it was cold out, there was a wall of heat between them. She tossed her head back as he pecked and bit her neck, causing soft groans to escape her lips. He lifted her by her ass and pinned her back against the car, and she wrapped her arms around the nape of his neck and coiled her legs around his waist. He unfastened his Ralph Lauren pants, lowering them just enough to release his dick.

The thigh-high Prada dress she wore made it easy for his access. He pushed her thong to the side and guided his hard joint inside her wet-shot.

"Ummm…yeeesss, Diamond. You so deep in it," Surprise groaned into his ear. She sharply inhaled a breath of air as he stabbed in and out of her.

*Can't believe you fuckin' off wit' dis bitch once again*, Diamond's conscience chided. But he had to admit that he enjoyed how warm and slippery her pussy seemed to stay for him. As he pushed every inch inside of her, she buried her face into his shoulder, muffling her moans.

"Ooooh shit, baby! Jus' like that!" Her juices released and gushed all over his dick and balls.

Diamond lowered Surprise onto her feet. He then turned shorty around, bent her over the hood of the Chrysler, and dug in her from behind. His breath frosted the air as he panted while pounding away at her pussy, and she threw her head back, taking it. He fucked her so hard it caused the car to rock.

Diamond held her ass steady as he repetitively stroked. He felt a nut lingering. "Shit!" he grunted and quickly snatched his piece out of her box, then busted a nut on her phat ass. He yanked Surprise around by her arm to face him, then said, "Listen, dis don't mean a damn thang to me, shorty. It was jus' a quick fuck."

"If you say so, Diamond," she replied as she pulled down her dress.

He just needed to relieve himself, and with Ty being out of town, he had to get it from somewhere is how he looked at it. If only he looked at shit from Tywanna's point of view, then he'd surely see things differently.

As Diamond stepped away from Surprise, heading back towards the club and fixing his pants, Jade pulled into the parking lot. She wasn't surprised to witness the two together. *Either Ty's basic ass don't know how to satisfy her nigga or Surprise's sex is just bomb, 'cause dat nigga can't seem to get enough of the bitch*, she contemplated. She offed the engine, grabbed her Chanel bag, and stepped out of her Jag.

Diamond's iPhone rang. He fished it out of his pocket and checked its display. It halted him in his tracks upon seeing who the call was from. "Gangsta, I'm sure you ain't jus' callin' to say hello," he answered.

"You had a coupla spots hit where my crew hangs, and if you know what's good for you, then you'd hand over my money, Diamond."

"Fuck you mean 'your' money? Technically it's my money yo' crew ringin' in. Look, I proposed to you that we could take out Banks together, then you could run yo' operation from the turf he's holdin' down. That offer still stands."

"I'ont need no assistance wit' bodyin' Banks. Besides, how I'ont know if you won't double-cross me?"

"After all these years, and you still can't seem to trust in me."

"I'll trust in you when you're six feet deep. Let's jus' be real here, Diamond, I ain't neva seen you back down from no nigga. I'm sure I'll have to do you 'fore you do me."

"Gangsta, I never thought it'd come to some shit like this between us, definitely not over some damn money. Can't take it wit' you once you're dead."

"At least I'll die rich," Gangsta rejoined. "Diamond, jus' let me get me. I want my money, and I ain't playin' wit'chu." He killed the call.

*All money ain't good money*, Diamond thought.

"What's up, Diamond?" Jade stopped and greeted him on her way towards the club. "You here early, unlike usual."

"My club, so I come and go as I please," he replied brashly.

"True dat. Any who, how's Ty?"

"You two bein' friends and all, I figure you'd know." Due to him being tied up in his own personal issues, Daimond was oblivious to her and Tywanna having a falling out.

Surprise waved at Jade as she made her way by for the club. "Hey girl. Ready to tear up the stage tonight?"

"Don't I always," Jade responded with a feigned smile.

"I know that's right. Mm-kay, girl, I'll catch you inside. You too, Diamond."

"Fa sho'." He played it cool.

Jade peeped the two lustfully eye one another before Surprise went on her way. "Seems you and Surprise are tight," she commented coyly.

"She's jus' another employee like you. In fact, if you care to remain employed, then I advise you to take yo' ass inside to get ready for the night also." Diamond didn't need Jade all up in his business, because he knew she'd tell Ty about any dirt she could dig up on him.

Jade made her way inside the club and she told herself introspectively, *Maybe it's 'bout time someone prove to Diamond his ass ain't untouchable. And since Banks or Gangsta can't seem to do it, then I will.*

# Troublesome

## Chapter 13

The Bentley slid along the curb and parked out front of the Theater. Diamond cut the engine, descended from the whip, and then headed towards the stash house. *Hell dis nigga Pelle at?* he wondered, not understanding why he was absent all of a sudden.

He went to the Theater anticipating Pelle would eventually make an appearance. It was the day Pelle was to go and have the money cleaned, and so far, no one had seen nor heard from his ass.

Shutting the door behind himself, Diamond engaged its locks. Stepping further inside, he came upon Toni and Major. "Anything from him?" he wanted to know hopefully.

"Nothin'," Toni said dryly. She was seated at the mini bar, nursing a drink.

He looked to Major. "How 'bout you?" Major only shook his head, indicating he hadn't heard from Pelle neither. "This ain't like Pelle. I'm startin' to get a bad feelin' 'bout this shit. Toni, you hit his line again, and check all social media sites for any info. And Major, you assemble yo' squad and hit the streets in search of him, but not before you drop by Keisha's place to see if she knows anything."

While Toni got on her iPhone, Major headed out the back door for his car. With a bad feeling in the pit of his stomach, Diamond made his way to the safe, and once he opened it, he discovered it had been cleaned out.

\*\*\*

Unbeknownst to Diamond, the Theater was being surveilled from either end of the block - Gangsta and his hitters on one end, Banks and his on the other. And yet the two of them weren't even aware of one another's perspective presence. They were both there for the same objective: to murder Diamond.

Once they each had observed Diamond pull up to the stash house, both niggas were anxious to move on him. Gangsta understood Yul had made a solid point about him needing to whack Diamond, especially after he'd recently caused him to lose out on loads of cash. And Banks found all the reason to off Diamond following the death of Lucifer, because for the most part, Diamond was the cause and effect of his problems. Yet and still, even with Diamond out of their way, the streets weren't big enough for both Gangsta and Banks.

"Let's do this," Gangsta roused his hitters.

"Let's ride out," Banks prompted his hitters.

Unknowingly, the two spoke simultaneously and cocked back the slides of their pistols.

\*\*\*

Tywanna was submerged neck deep in a bubble bath. The setting was relaxing, candles were lit all around the bathroom, and the silence was gold. She didn't mind staying with her mother for the time being, although she'd prefer to be home with Diamond. Being away from him for a period of time was hard for her, especially while she was pregnant with his child. Her love for Diamond was unconditional, and she knew the feeling was mutual.

Subsequent to the bath, she looked at her pregnant, naked self in the mirror. "Girl, you still lookin' good," she complimented herself.

Her iPhone chimed, alerting her of social media activity. Checking the phone, she was stunned by what she was viewing. She received a photo from Jade on Snapchat of Diamond being intimate with some bitch at the club. She didn't know what to think, and more than anything, she despised to think that Jade was right.

Angry tears rolled down her cheeks as she tried calling Diamond, only to receive his voicemail. She thought better against leaving a voicemail or sending a text, because she wanted to tell his ass all about himself personally.

Tywanna threw on her robe, then steamed out of the bathroom, and Sandra could see something was a matter with her. "Why are you crying, baby?" She stopped Tywanna in the hallway.

"Diamond's cheatin' on me. Now I know why he really doesn't want me back home," she cried.

"And how do you figure that?" she asked, and Tywanna answered by holding out her phone for Sandra see the photo. "Darling, I'm sorry." She pulled Tywanna close in an embrace.

"How could he do this to me, when all I've ever done is love him faithfully? Don't he care that we have a child on the way?" she said through sobs.

"It's okay, Mama's here for you."

"That's the thing, Ma, I need Diamond to be here. But apparently me and his baby don't even matter to his ass. Look, I just need some time to be alone. So tonight I'll pass on dinner."

"Alright, baby. Take all the time you need." It was tough for Sandra to see her child heartbroken. She felt that due to Diamond's infidelity. Ty could do without him.

Tywanna went into the guest room to be alone where she laid across the bed sobbing uncontrollably. She couldn't believe Diamond would actually sleep around on her. Who was the bitch? How long had be been fuckin' her? Were things between him and the bitch serious? Countless questions ran through her mind. As much as she loved Diamond, she didn't know how to feel about him in that moment.

\*\*\*

"What'chu mean Pelle betrayed us?" Toni questioned, perplexed.

Needing to take some of the edge off, Diamond grabbed a bottle of Ciroc from the mini bar and turned it up to his lips. He wiped away liquor trekking down his chin with the backside of his hand. "I mean he cleaned out the entire fuckin' safe, Toni!" He'd immediately realized Pelle had betrayed them, but he didn't yet realize to what extent.

The safe had contained $1.3 million, which Pelle had apparently ripped off. This was a huge problem for Diamond since he was in debt with Balistrieri, and now he had no means to keep his part of their agreement. His loyalty to Balistrieri made it hard for him to accept Pelle's betrayal.

Neither Diamond nor Toni could believe he'd been plotting on them the entire time. Diamond had trusted Toni's judgement of Pelle, and within their crew, the consequence of breaking ones trust is murder.

"Diamond, I never expected Pelle would pull some shit like this," Toni said distastefully. "Trust, I'ma find him and body his ass."

Diamond hit the bottle once more before sitting it atop the bar. "Trustin' you is what got me into this shit, Toni," he stated firmly. Pulling his .45 he aimed it at her forehead. "I warned you if Pelle turned out to be foul then I'd kill you." As much as he didn't want to kill her, he just had to.

"Thought you said 'we all we got', Diamond." She drained the remains of her drink. "Go ahead. Do what you have to," she budged him boldly, staring into his eyes.

"I'm sorry. I find it hard to do this myself. But it has to be done." He pressed the muzzle to her forehead.

Kaboom!

"Shit!" Diamond exclaimed frantically once the front door was kicked in.

Boom! Boom! Boom! Boom! Boom! Boom!

Instinctively Diamond turned his weapon on the intruders and relentlessly squeezed off a succession of shots, and Toni dove behind the bar for cover. The bulletproof vests depicting DEA stopped the bullets. Noticing their raid gear, it became apparent it was unanticipated authorities he was shooting at.

"DEA! Hold your fire and drop your weapon!" Lynch ordered and then opened fire as Diamond disobeyed.

"Arrgh!" Once Diamond was struck by a bullet, he instantly dropped his .45 and grabbed his wounded arm.

"On the floor now!" Lynch shouted as he rushed towards Diamond with his weapon aimed, palm over his forearm. "Give me a reason." He was more than willing to pump more bullets into Diamond's ass. After holstering his weapon, he removed his cuffs and slapped them on Diamond's wrists behind his back.

There were numerous cops with M-16s swarming all throughout the place. One of them cuffed up Toni and led her out to a squad car, and others ransacked the place.

"I warned you the next time I show up at your place it'd be with a warrant." Lynch held out the paper for Diamond to see as a cop pulled him up onto his feet.

Diamond smirked. "And I warned you I'd shoot first, ask questions later."

"Well fortunately for me, your aim ain't very good. I'm not the one standing here shot." Lynch really preferred to kill his ass. He looked to the cop and said, "Take him away."

After leaving Diamond waiting in the interrogation room for nearly three hours, Lynch entered and closed the door behind himself. He made sure to cut off the intercom because he preferred their interview to be officially off the record for his own sake.

Stepping over to the table in the center of the dimly lit room, Lynch took a seat directly across from Diamond. Diamond sat there cuffed in front, hands resting atop the table with a bloodstained gauze wrapped around his right forearm covering the bullet wound Lynch had caused him. The two exchanged glares.

"I want my mouthpiece," Diamond opened with, exhausting his rights.

"No need for that just yet. I assure you this discussion will be off the record."

"Ain't shit to discuss, Lynch. Or should I call you Agent?"

"How 'bout we discuss your freedom. Give up Frank, and I'll make sure you walk," he offered.

Diamond scoffed and shook his head. "Shoulda known dis shit bigga than me."

"Diamond, I tried to offer you the opportunity to side with me. It was you who chose not to."

Diamond chuckled. "It's clear to me that you've been after Balistrieri all along. And you figure that whether wit' me on yo' side or outta yo' way, then it'll be easier for you to get to him. Is that why you took out attempts on both our lives, 'cause you're afraid I'll enlighten Balistrieri on the offer you made me under the table?"

"You don't know what the hell you're talking about." Suddenly his mood changed.

"I know that apparently you need Balistrieri outta the way for some reason. And unlike you, I choose to remain loyal to Balistrieri."

"Think Frank genuinely gives a damn about you? He'd have your ass whacked without remorse!" Lynch retorted. He forcefully scooted his chair back away from the table, its feet scraping over the floor. He stood and said, "You know, maybe I'd be better off discussing terms with that pretty little friend of yours instead."

"Toni's not one to snitch. Damn sure not on me."

"Don't be so sure of yourself, Diamond. She just may feel the need to have your ass put away for her own good. 'Cause from the looks of things, had we not barged in when we did, you were gonna kill her in cold blood."

Diamond casually sat back in the chair and eyed him narrowly. "Yeah, well, Toni would rather kill or be killed than snitch."

Lynch began to pace back and forth and said, "At least I have Pelle to thank. His testimony alone will be more than enough to put you away for the rest of your natural life."

"I'm sure you used yo' dirty li'l tactics on Pelle to force him to work for you. It's dirty cops like you that ain't to be trusted. The type that'll take a hustler's dope and sell it to the next hustler, plant shit on him if you can't catch him in any other way, and beat the shit outta him or shoot him if nobody's filmin'. To hell wit' you dirty cops."

Abruptly, Lynch halted his pace. "Without dirty cops like me, you all wouldn't be able to make so much damn money and afford all those luxuries. So you're welcome!"

"We take that same money right back to the white man, coppin' all the flashy shit a hustler have to have. And if we're knocked, the

DEA takes all of our shit and sell it back at auction. So it ain't like you're doin' us any damn favor," Diamond explained. "Now take me to my cell. I'm done here."

# Troublesome

## Chapter 14

Tywanna had immediately made her way back into town after receiving a collect call via the Milwaukee County Jail from Diamond, who informed her that he'd been arrested.

She knew better than to ask him a bunch of questions. "What do you want me to do?" was all she had asked.

"Contact my attorney," he had instructed.

Tywanna figured that he'd been snatched up due to his street affairs. It made things very stressful on her. Not to mention she was still upset about the photo of Diamond with some other bitch. But she'd hold down her man for better or worse.

At his arraignment, the judge had denied his bail because of the extremities of the charges. He'd be detained at the county jail momentarily. She needed to go visit him.

Diamond stepped into the visitation booth and took a seat in front of the monitor that Ty showed on. His body was tight and face was serious. He continued to hold his powerful presence. Tywanna thought he had a way of looking good even in the county orange uniform that fit baggy on him. She smiled when she seen him on the monitor, he smiled back. "How you doin', bae?" he asked.

"Fine." She had told herself the ride to the county she'd maintain her composure.

"And my daughter?" he smiled.

"Her ass been kickin' a lot lately."

"Jus' means she's the mixture of fight and fortitude the streets breeds."

"I'm sure." She wanted to move on to the matter at hand. "Diamond, tomorrow I'm goin' to see yo' lawyer. What do you want me to tell him?"

"I spoke wit' him over the phone. He'll wanna discuss fees. He don't have to trip over that though. I got paper."

"What about me, Diamond? I only have so much money put away. Soon I'll be in need of more."

He put his forefinger to his lips to keep her from saying more. "Jus' get up wit' Major. He'll have a hunnid for you. Jus' let him know I said it's yours. Also, tell him I'd like to see him."

"Alright. Diamond, I hate to see you in there."

"I know. I'll be out soon, though. But I'm wit' AB, Finesse, T-Money, O, Greazy, Juvie, Humpty, Spook, and Lil G n'em in here. It's like bein' in the streets." He smirked, more for her benefit. "Damn crackers jus' tryna press a nigga, get me to rat. Feel me? I'm a'ight, Ty, don't stress about me. I need you to look after the baby. Love, you gotta be tough. Remember everything I taught you."

"I will." Tywanna understood he needed her to be down for him.

He could read that something was bothering her. "What is it, Ty? Tol' you I'll be good."

"That's not it," Tywanna interrupted. She adjusted in her seat, folded her arms over her bulging belly. "When do you plan on tellin' me about the li'l stripper bitch you been fuckin' with, Diamond?" she asked resentfully. "And don't even lie about the shit, 'cause Jade sent me a photo of you all over the bitch in the club."

*Da hoe Jade don't know how to mind her own fuckin' business*, he contemplated. "Ty, I ain't even gon' lie, yeah, I fucked da bitch. But she don't mean shit to a nigga, a'ight."

"How could you make me look like a damn fool? I do everything for you, Diamond. I cater to yo' ass. And you still don't have the decency to consider how fuckin' some bitch would affect me." For the first time since knowing him, she was mad as hell at Diamond. "You don't care 'bout no one but yo' damn self. Do you know what you doin', whose feelings you hurtin'?" She cried softly.

In that moment, Diamond realized how selfish it'd been of him to satisfy his lust for Surprise. He understood that since he chose Tywanna as his and gave the impression that she was his only woman, bringing another woman into their relationship violated the trust he established in the beginning. "I never meant to hurt you, girl. You the only one a nigga love," he professed.

"Diamond, love is when the other persons happiness is more important than yo' own," she expressed.

"Tywanna, jus' know that nothin' is more important to me than you 'n my daughter bein' happy. Believe me, I love y'all more than myself. Can you forgive me?"

She could feel he meant every word. "When someone hurts you they take power over you. And when you don't forgive them, they keep power over you. So I will forgive you, Diamond, but I won't forget."

*\*\**

At the Sybaris Pool Suites, Banks and Jade were in the Jacuzzi tub. Banks was blazing a blunt while Jade was under water moving her lips up and down slowly on Banks's dick as she deep-throated him.

With all the shit taking place in the streets, Banks felt the need to duck off for a moment. He couldn't believe the very night he had the perfect opportunity to off Diamond, the fuckin' DEA had raided him. And he noticed Lynch at the center of it all. Fortunately for Diamond, twelve got to his ass before he could, although he didn't wish prison on even his worst enemy; and that being Diamond, Banks would rather murk him. Now that Diamond was currently on the inside, Banks was left to focus on Gangsta.

He was still feeling the impact of Lucifer's death. He felt guilty for not being there to have Lucifer's back. Bad enough he already blamed himself for the death of Lexi. One thing for certain, Gangsta had his coming. He was eager to splatter his fuckin' brains, but until he had the opportunity, there was money to be made. In the end, however, power over the streets will be his.

*You'll never love Jade the way you do Lex*, his conscience suggested as he peered down at Jade slurping and sucking on his love tool.

Jade just cared to please Banks and make him love her. His anger towards her was his view that she was beautiful while being treacherous. Although his attempt to discipline himself in regards to her became useless. He knew that fuckin' Jade was a breach of confidence. And he knew not to trust her, yet he still allowed himself to keep her close despite it.

"Damn, bitch, you suckin' da shit outta dis dick," Banks groaned as she ran her pierced tongue over the tip of his joint, and the shit had him in a trance. Feeling the pressure mount in his dick, he palmed the back of her dome encouraging her. He took a pull of the blunt, let his head fall back, then exhaled smoke. "Uh!" He released inside her mouth and she swallowed every drop.

***

Tywanna took a seat in the chair that was reserved for clients and positioned directly in front of Levin's ornate desk. The attorney office was opulent. The chairs were soft leather, the walls pecan, and the windows looked out onto the outline of the city. Tywanna wasn't surprised. It was Diamond's style to be affiliated with the heavy hitters.

"So you're Diamond's woman? Absolutely stunning," Levin smiled courteously. He was a slender man with peppered hair carefully combed back and he had the confidence of a well-paid, seasoned gentleman. "Let's get down to business, shall we. First off, I'm working with a cap of twenty-five grand. This is what Diamond paid in advance. I'll need a retainer of seventy-five grand just to get involved. That's a discount.

"As far as Diamond's concerned, this is a huge case. He's staring at decades, maybe even life in prison. It's a little premature to discuss. However, it all depends on the amount of evidence against Diamond."

"So what exactly is he being charged with?" she interrupted.

"Diamond's being accused of several things: conspiracy, tax evasion, money laundering, weapons, murder, attempted murder of an police officer."

Tywanna didn't know what to think. Of course she understood the life Diamond chose to live came with consequences. She hated the possibility of him ending up imprisoned for a very long period time. Especially now that they had the baby on the way. She had to do whatever she could to help Diamond out of his predicament.

\*\*\*

After a few rings, Major answered. "You reached Major."

"This is Tywanna. I'm callin' about Diamond, he - "

"Check it, meet me at the Denny's out on Good Hope Road," he interrupted. "I can be there in an hour. We can grab somethin' to eat."

An hour later, Tywanna blended in with the lunch crowd at Denny's. She sat in a booth awaiting Major. Knowing she had the money on the way, she felt a little more relaxed. Her plan was to bring the rest of the payment to the lawyer for Diamond. Seventy-five bands had to go to Levin upfront, and he already had a portion of it. After paying up the fifty large to the lawyer, the remaining half of the money would be enough to hold her over for a little while. She had to plan like Diamond wasn't there.

"Never talk money over the line." Major slid inside the booth across from her. He didn't even say what's up. "You called 'bout da paper, right? Well, I'll have it for you tonight. Where do you want me to drop it?"

"Thought we were gonna have somethin' to eat," she said, confused.

"That was jus' somethin' I said to prevent you from talkin' too much on the line. The DEA are listenin' in, recordin' and shit. Half of the shit they got on niggas is because niggas don't know how to shut da fuck up over the line. I was aware of what you wanted, and I got'chu on it."

"My bad for the phone thing."

"It's cool," he replied with little emotion.

Ty sat quietly a moment while she studied Major. She got the notion he represented a departure from the characteristics typically assigned to and associated with young Black men. In some ways, he reminded her of Diamond.

Major was dark-skinned with a low cut, and good-looking. He was a paper chasin' and pistol toting nigga. He was gentle, and somehow threatening.

"Lemme ask you somethin'. How come Diamond trusts you, and enough to have you hold money for him?" Tywanna was curious to know.

Major sat with his hands folded in front of him. "'Cause I'm sharp. You can't be in this game runnin' around cashin' out on too much shit, jackin', and makin' a scene. You know, dull shit. And on top of that, he put me on. When a man puts you on and creates an opportunity for you that you otherwise would not have had, the law of nature dictates that you be grateful and loyal. I'ont hate on him for bein' in power and havin' more money than me. Unlike most, I'ont compete wit' him as a man. He gamed me a lot. Dat nigga like a big brotha to me."

"Well it's good to know he can trust someone. I can tell that you respect Diamond and feel the need to be loyal to him."

"That's jus' the way it is," he told her. "Look, I gotta get goin'. How 'bout you text me wit' the address to the location you want me to drop the bread, and I'll be sure to get it to you."

"That's fine by me. Oh, I almost forgot. Diamond said he'd like to see you."

"A'ight then, cool." He slid out from the booth and then headed out.

***

Diamond lay back on the uncomfortable bunk bed in the small jail cell. He was housed on the federal pod since he was facing fed charges. After his bail had been denied, he had to rely on the work of his lawyer to get him off, and he was confident in Levin.

Following his visit with Tywanna. it was comforting for him to know that she'd dropped Levin the cash as he requested. Despite Ty still being heated about the photo of him with Surprise, Diamond was sure she wouldn't just turn her back on him. He hated he'd hurt her because she didn't deserve it. She'd been through the thick of it with him, and meant a lot to him. Not to mention she was carrying his baby.

And he knew that he could trust Major to give her the money. Diamond had been grooming Major since he was a short. He'd seen the potential Major possessed. He understood that since Major was left in charge, he'd be left with dealing with Gangsta and Banks, and with him being on the inside, Diamond realized they'd take the opportunity to seize power over the streets. His streets. He was confident in Major holding his own, although he was well aware that Gangsta and Banks were capable of ruthless murder. Little did he know, they'd each plotted to murder him the night of the raid.

His thoughts shifted to Toni. Had she not invited a fuckin' rat into their circle, then he wouldn't be sitting in damn cage. But he had to admit that he, too, was played by Pelle, and for that, Diamond wanted to kill his ass. Of course the thought to kill Toni was difficult for him, but it had to be done, and had Lynch not bombarded the Theater when he did, then she'd be nothing more than a memory.

And Lynch had another-fuckin'-thing coming if he thought he'd get off with double crossing him. First thing first, he needed to get back to the streets. And whenever he did, he realized what must be done about Lynch.

"Yo, Diamond." T-Money stepped in the doorway of the cell, breaking Diamond's thoughts. He was a slim, tall, light-skinned nigga with dreads. "You been in here all day, you a'ight?"

Diamond sat up in the bed. "Jus' in here thinkin' 'bout shit. You realize the game's cold?"

"Yeah, and life's a bitch. But a real nigga stay down for the come up."

"T-Money, much respect to you for not snitchin' on me. Wish I could say the same 'bout Savage," he added bitterly.

"No problem, dawg. That fool-ass nigga Sav jus' wasn't built for this shit. At least he's one less nigga we gotta worry 'bout turnin' states evidence against us, feel me?"

"Now I gotta figure out how to shut up the nigga Pelle. He knows too fuckin' much," Diamond stressed. "Maybe I can pay him off."

"Bad idea. Niggas like that tend to get greedy. Next thing you know, he'll be blackmailin' you for more. Diamond, there's only one way to deal wit' a rat: exterminate his ass," T-Money told him.

"You right. I'll put Major on him."

"Now that you have shit all figured out, get'cho ass offa that bunk, and come kick it wit' me and the guys. Let's go and show them fool-ass niggas how to play some dominoes."

Diamond hopped down from the bunkbed. "I'm wit' that."

As they made their way over to the others, Diamond failed to peep the small crew of niggas mugging from across the day-room.

"Look at dis nigga," one of the niggas scoffed, whose name was Spade. Spade was black as ever with a Philly-fro and gold teeth. He made his way over and blocked Diamond's path.

"We got a problem?" Diamond questioned.

"Recognize me?"

"Should I?"

"Nigga, you smoked my brotha!" Spade spat. He was one of the shooters that had hopped out of the gray Caravan on Diamond and the others outside of Red Velvet, and his brother was the other shooter who Diamond had killed.

"Then my condolences," Diamond told him.

Spade took a swing at Diamond, who avoided the punch, then he rushed Diamond and they tussled. Before any of their crews could get involved and it became an all-out brawl, C.O.s hurried over and broke the two apart and gave them a direct order to lock in their cells.

"Dis ain't over," Spade warned before he turned on his way.

Diamond knew he'd have to watch his back, or Spade might stab him in it.

\*\*\*

"I just can't believe Diamond would cheat on me," Tywanna was saying. "And with some stripper, at that." She pulled the Lexus to a stop at the stoplight.

"Girl, you have all the reason to be mad at him right now," Ashley responded from the passenger seat.

"And I hate the fact that Jade was right all along. I'm sure she only sent me the photo to hurt me. Ugh, I can't stand her ass!"

"She ain't no better, fuckin' Gangsta and Banks at the same damn time. Trust, what goes around comes around."

As Tywanna pushed the Lexus towards the condominium complex, she was met with police. She noticed they had both Diamond's vehicles on the flatbed of two police tow trucks.

Once she pulled to the curb, a lawman wearing an ill-fitting suit immediately approached the car with a purpose. "Turn off the ignition. Step out of the car and move away from it," he ordered.

"And who are you?" Tywanna asked.

He pulled out his badge. "DEA. Agent Vincent Lynch. We are authorized to seize this vehicle, which is now government property."

"Uh uh, this is my muthafuckin' car!" she protested.

"According to this document, it isn't," he said, and held out the paper for her to see. "Also the apartment and all of the belongings inside are the property of the government."

Tywanna pushed open the door, then stormed over to Lynch. "Explain to me how you people can just take our things," she demanded as angry tears shot out of her eyes.

"Calm down, Miss. All material items purchased with illegal gains from criminal activity and transactions are subject to seizure. If you can verify the source of your income and prove that these items are within the boundaries of your earnings, you can get them back."

"That's bullshit," Ashley piped in. She used her iPhone to film the incident in case there was any police brutality.

"Also," Lynch went on, "I have a warrant to run you down for questioning. It'll be best for you to be cooperative under these circumstances."

Unwilling to cooperate with Lynch, Tywanna handed Ashley her Prada bag and stuck out her wrists. Lynch cuffed her as he read her her rights. He placed her in the back of his vehicle and then hauled her away.

\*\*\*

"Shit. The fuckin' Rasta said this shit fatal," Gangsta said while standing over the corpse of a junky with a syringe protruding from his frail, track marked arm slumped to the side.

The junky had OD'ed on the Fentanyl-infused dope. In fact, he was the eighth one to OD on the shit, although junkies continued to demand the supply. And as a result, two of Gangsta's distributors had already been arrested and charged for the death of junkies.

"Get rid of the body," Gangsta ordered. "And make sure you dump it over on the east side of town." It was what he'd done with the others also, causing twelve to focus their war on drugs in Banks's territory and slow down his operation.

Two men rolled up the corpse in a rug, and they carried it away.

Gangsta, followed by Playboy, made his way upstairs of the apartment complex. He'd seized control over the complex, and he turned it into a one-stop trap spot with junkies coming and going by the drove. Armed men secured each of the complexes three levels. Not to mention the security cameras. The complex was impenetrable and well operated.

"I ain't feelin' this dope cut wit' Fentanyl. Next re-up I'ma let Yul know the shit too risky for business," Gangsta said.

"Think he'll give a damn?" Playboy responded, knowing how relentless Yul was.

"He will if he cares to keep my business," he replied. His cell rang and he and he answered. "You on."

"He took Tywanna!" Ashley said frantically on the other end.

Gangsta stopped in his tracks. "Who took Tywanna where?"

"The DEA. Said his name's Vincent Lynch. He and papers talkin' about he had a warrant to take her in for questionin'."

"How 'bout you, are you good? And where are the twins?"

"Yeah, I'm good. The twins are with Chase's mom. I'm just worried about what's goin' on with Ty," she stressed.

"Listen, Tywanna's a soulja. She can handle herself. Diamond groomed her that way. For now you go with the twins, and I'll check on you later."

Gangsta had never trusted Lynch, not even a little. He'd tried getting Diamond to understand that a crooked cop would never do straight business. After witnessing the raid, he was sure that eventually Lynch would come after him, and before allowing Lynch the satisfaction of slapping bracelets on his wrists, he'd go out in a hail of bullets.

*** 

During the interrogation, Tywanna didn't say a word. Diamond had taught her never to say shit without a lawyer present. Lynch tried hard pressing her and told her under the RICO Act, she could also be charged if she was aware of or in any way linked to distribution of narcotics. He had to hand it to her, unlike most niggas that would have folded, she remained stiff.

"I'll make it so your baby's father can never raise his own damn child," Lynch had threatened her, and that's when Tywanna flew off the handle cursing the muthafucka out.

Subsequent to the interrogation, Ty stepped into the women's pod of the county jail wearing the bulky orange uniform. Most of the women there had drug related charges stemming from their own situations. But, like Tywanna, they weren't nothing more than the girlfriends to niggas moving weight. They were conspirators because they wouldn't snitch on their niggas. Most of their problems were their interest in their niggas paper, adornments, and lifestyles.

She found her way to her cell, and since the bottom bunkbed was apparently already claimed, Tywanna tossed her bedroll on the top bunkbed. Her pregnant ass didn't like the idea of having to climb in and out of the bunk.

A big, burly bitch appeared in the cell's doorway, Tywanna figured she must be her cellmate. "Hey, I'm Ty," she introduced herself.

"Listen here, bitch, I'ont give a fuck about who you is. Let's get one thing straight: stay the hell outta my way." Her voice was masculine.

*Oh, hell nah! This bitch done tried it,* Tywanna contemplated. She damn sure wasn't afraid. Fighting didn't mean shit to her. She grew up in the hood doing that. Her only concern was to protect her baby.

"I'ont know what type of bitches you used to, but I ain't the one. Win, lose, or draw, bitch, we can get it in, right here, right now." Tywanna stood her ground.

The bitch balled her fists but before she could budge, Tywanna witnessed an arm swiftly wrap around her thick neck from behind as someone held a razor to her throat.

"Bitch, don't make me cut you from ear to ear," the person warned. "I hate bitches like you. While I have to be here, I'ont wanna see yo' damn face."

Tywanna couldn't see who was behind the big body, but her voice was familiar. She slashed the razor across the big bitch's face, and the bitch screamed as blood poured from her gashed cheek. The bitch broke free of the chokehold, then rushed over to the sink to clean herself up.

Tywanna got a look at the person standing there wearing a smirk. "Toni! I'm so happy to see you, girl," she exclaimed.

"Yeah, me too, given the circumstances. Now grab yo' shit, you movin' into the cell wit' me."

Toni and Tywanna made their way to the cell they'd be sharing. After moving Tywanna's things into Toni's cell, they went to inform the guards of the cell change to make it official.

## Chapter 15

While awaiting Diamond to show up for a visit, Major decided it was best they discuss business first. He didn't really know just how Diamond would take the news that Tywanna had been arrested. And to add insult to injury, all of his possessions had been seized, including the club. Major knew Diamond wanted to see him in order to take care of some business for him, which is why he needed Diamond to have a clear head.

Diamond took a seat before the visitation monitor and said, "Thanks for comin'."

"Glad to be here."

"How you?"

"Look big homie, all due respect, let's get down to business. Then afterwards we can rap," Major insisted.

Diamond didn't mind that he'd come there on business. "A'ight, here's the deal. I asked you here 'cause I know I can trust in you, Major. I need you to get in touch wit' Balistrieri. I owe him some paper and, however, I'm countin' on you to straighten it out. You're a sharp nigga so I'm sure you'll figure somethin' out. More than likely he'll be skeptical, given the circumstances. So it's vital that you make him understand I'm no duck."

"I'll be sure to do this ASAP."

"That brings me to Pelle. I need you to locate him, and whenever you do..." Diamond finished his words with a nod of the head.

"Say less," Major spoke up.

"And most likely Gangsta and Banks will come at you hard, so keep yours on you. Listen, wit' me currently on the inside I'll need you to hold down the streets. And try to stay alive while doin' so."

"Fa sho'."

"One more thing: have the bitch Surprise come see a nigga. Need to holla at her ass 'bout some shit."

"No worries, I got'chu." Major moved along. "How you holdin' up in there?"

"As best as I can. Lookin' forward to gettin' back to the streets."

"What's Levin talkin' 'bout?"

"Now that Ty lined his pockets, said he's lookin' closely into each charge. They're all some bullshit charges anyway, so I'm sure he'll find somethin' to get me off."

The mentioning of Tywanna brought Major to the topic he resented. "Diamond. Ty was taken into police custody."

Diamond sat still. Anger consumed him. It was one thing for Lynch to fuck with him, but fuckin' with his pregnant girl was another. "Police custody?" he parroted in a low voice, calmer than Major expected he'd be.

"It happened yesterday, and as far as I know, she was taken in to be questioned. 'Bout you. Now she's bein' held for resisting arrest and assault on an officer."

"And how come her bond hasn't been posted?" he wanted know heatedly.

"Trust, I tried. They wouldn't allow me. And get this, the feds seized all of yo' possessions: whips, crib, everything. Includin' the club. Sarge called me sayin' the muthafuckas raided Red Velvet last night, and he told me they searched through all of the club's belongings and tore the place up."

"Fuck the club and shit for now. Most importantly, I gotta get Tywanna outta jail," Diamond told him.

"I'll keep tryna post her bond."

"Do that. And I'll get in touch wit' Levin to see what he can do."

Back on the pod, Diamond made his way to the tree of phones. He snatched up a phone and dialed Levin's office. A moment later, the lawyer was on the other end.

"How's it going, champ?" Levin answered.

"Listen, the fuckin' feds done snatched up my girl, and apparently they seized all of my shit," Diamond stressed.

"Yes, I'm aware of this," he said casually. "And I'm working on it as we speak."

"Levin, I'ont give a damn what you gotta do, but I'll pay you double if you can get me and my girl outta this hellhole sooner rather than later." Diamond knew he was talking the lawyer's language.

"I'll keep that in mind. You just try not to worry yourself, and I'll try to have you both out soon enough." He was hard at work on the case.

*** 

"Diamond's more than likely goin' through it, if he knows I'm in jail right now," Tywanna said.

She and Toni were in the cell after lockdown. The days they'd spent with one another brought them closer than before. Tywanna was grateful that Toni provided her with protection, for being pregnant made her fragile. On the other hand, Toni merely protected her out of the loyalty she still held for Diamond.

"And I'm sure Ash ain't takin' it well that I'm in here," Tywanna went on. "She's probably stressin' more than me. I just don't want her to stress more than she already has after losin' Chase. He genuinely made her happy."

"Fucked up how he had to go," Toni expressed.

"It really is." She hesitated before adding, "I just get the feelin' that Jade's tied into a lot of the mess."

"What'chu mean?" Toni was curious to know.

"Think about it; she seemed to be on the scene of every place drama went down. Also she's fuckin' with Banks, and from what I gathered, he has it out for Diamond and anyone close to him," she expounded.

Jade definitely knew every place Diamond would be whenever shit popped off, and she was never in harm's way during' any of it, Toni thoughtfully considered. "Let's say Jade is playin' both sides. Then that type of shit gon' fuck around and get her ass murked. And if Diamond believes she had anything to do wit' him nearly losin' his life, he'll definitely be the one to murk her himself," she told her.

"Toni, I know this may sound naïve of me, but Diamond's so gentle. I just can't imagine him actually killin' someone."

Toni reflected back to Diamond being prepared to pull the trigger on her. She knew he'd rather not have to, but the rules in the game were strict. Finally she responded. "Well, he damn sure ain't against it. Believe me."

In such a way the feds had spared Toni's life, and Lynch was sure to throw it in her face during the interrogation in his attempt to get her to roll over on Diamond. Although she remained steadfast, willing to accept whatever consequences she faced.

\*\*\*

"So, how much is there?" Tate asked Banks, who sat across the table from him in the backroom of Magic Clippers.

Banks unzipped the Louis Vuitton tote bag, which sat atop the table. "Three hunnid bands, all blue-faces," he answered.

"A'ight. You take that and bring me back a half mill in a week tops." He changed the subject. "Listen, Lynch is still expectin' us to do Balistrieri. And 'til it's done, the forty percent he's peelin' for the product will continue to affect our pockets. So I'm countin' on you to get the job done, Banks."

"Balistrieri's not an easy target, ridin' in bulletproof whips and shit. And he's rarely ever seen out on the town. I'll need an advantage."

"I'll talk with Lynch, I'm sure he'll be able to assist with that. Stay in touch."

Banks stood and signaled his boys. Nowadays he barely went anyplace solo. He grabbed up the tote bag and they all headed out. In the parking lot as he stepped towards his Ashton, Banks noticed a crew of niggas approaching the barbershop. "Shop's closed for the night, fellas," Banks told them.

"We're here for a 'cut', a'ight?" Playboy quipped and drew his banger, and his boys followed suit. "Now nigga, run that bag, and then take us inside where the real paper is."

Banks had to think fast. He couldn't allow the crew to walk them in, because he was sure the crew wouldn't allow them to walk out. Going with his first mind, Banks tossed the tote bag towards Playboy and simultaneously pulled his own burner.

Blam! Blam! Blam! Blam! Blam!

Boc! Boc! Boc! Boc!

Both crews engaged in a big shootout. Banks and his boys took cover beside parked vehicles as they let off, and Playboy and his backed away towards their rides as they aired out the parking lot. Niggas on each end took it in slugs.

Rising from behind the vehicle, Ice dumped down Playboy n'em as they loaded into their rides. He decorated the cars with numerous bullet holes as they sped away.

Banks picked up the tote bag from the ground and stepped up beside Ice. "Good lookin' for havin' a nigga's back. I respect ya gangsta."

"I ain't backin' down from nothin'. I'm 'bout bustin'," Ice stated malevolently.

Banks figured the niggas had to be part of Gangsta's crew, because since Diamond was on the inside, he had no reason to send hitters. He knew that he'd have to go after Gangsta relentlessly.

\*\*\*

Yul and Gangsta occupied a table in the shabby Jamaican Inn bar near the back, where the lighting was dim and they were secluded from the rest.

Gangsta was there to explain his position requesting a change to their agreement. However, he was prepared and understood that Yul had a right to decline his request and hold him to the agreement they made in the first place.

Yul put back a shot of Jamaican rum like it was water. "Only a real mon enjoys de taste of rum." He slid a shot glass across the table towards Gangsta, who reluctantly picked it up and then downed the drink. Yul grinned inwardly at the scowl the rum caused Gangsta to make.

"Shit's like drinkin' fire," Gangsta coughed.

"Perhaps next time you'll want a chaser," Yul chuckled.

"Good idea."

"So me take it dat bidness has been goin' well, seein' dat you seem to be movin' de product widout a prollem."

"The product is boomin' and money is comin' in faster than I expected. There's only one problem."

"An' dat tis?"

"It's like this." Gangsta leaned forward, folded his arms atop the table and said," If we're gonna continue makin' paper together, then I no longer wanna push any dope cut wit' Fentanyl. The shit's too damn risky."

Yul eyed him for a brief moment. "Are you sayin' you wanna betray and change de agreement?"

"More like amend it," Gangsta clarified. "Listen, the shit is killin' muthafuckas left and right, and that ain't good for business. I can't have some dead junky bringin' heat from twelve to my operation. A coupla my men are already down facin' charges 'cause of the shit. So how 'bout you front me off wit' some raw 'n uncut product, and I'll kick you back an additional fifteen percent on each key."

Cutting the heroin with Fentanyl was Yul's way of stretching the product and increasing its value for cheap. Therefore, he wasn't willing to compromise. "Me don't give a fuck 'bout no blood-clot junkies dyin'. All dat matters to me is money. Me dought you felt de same, Gangsta."

"And I do."

"Booie!" Yul shot back. "If so, den you wouldn't give a damn 'bout killin' some fuckin' junkies. Not to mention Diamond."

"Believe me, Yul, I'ont give a damn about killin' no muthafucka. Not even Diamond," he stated, riled.

Yul took a drink of the rum. He eyed Gangsta and stated, "You will continue to accept de product as is. Understood?"

Gangsta understood he was obligated to handle and take responsibility for his agreement. But not without hatred or revenge.

***

Tywanna had been released from the county after Levin had leaned on the Milwaukee prosecutor to get the charges against her dropped, and it wasn't easy, although she didn't resist arrest or assault any officer.

Her freedom meant that she could help Diamond out. She hated having to leave Toni behind, but she knew Toni would be able to hold her own. And she was sure Diamond and Toni would both be out soon enough.

Ashley had picked her up and taken her to Applebee's for a bite to eat. Ty ordered enough food to feed a family, and it tasted like heaven compared to the jail food. Ash watched as Tywanna devoured the meal. She was just happy to have her bestie back after five long days she'd been on lock up.

"I was so worried about you and the baby," Ashley said.

"We were fine. Toni made sure of that." She sank her teeth into a piece of chicken.

"Ty, where are you gonna live? Since yo' home was seized you can't live there. At least not for now," Ashley said concerned.

"I'll just have to stay at my mama's place for the time bein'."

"She gon' be pissed at Diamond gettin' you involved in everything."

Tywanna waved her hand in the air as if it didn't matter. "Diamond's a good man, and she knows it." Bringing him up put her in another frame of mind. "I wanna talk to Diamond. Make sure he's alright."

"I'm sure he wants you to come down and see him. But first we gotta get you a glammed up for him, 'cause you lookin' like a hot mess." Ashley noticed Tywanna was dressed in the same, wrinkled attire she went in wearing and her hair in plaits. "Right about now, bitch, you are in need of a fashion rescue mission." She smiled.

They processed Tywanna at the county jail, checked her identification, and pointed her to the visitation waiting area. The waiting area was filled with all kinds of women, all ages, and some children.

She was told Diamond momentarily had a visitor, so she'd be next. *Who the hell could be visiting' him?* she wondered.

After her makeover, Ty was on fleek. She had her hair in soft baby doll curls with her brows freshly arched. She rocked a form-fitting pink and grey True Religion sweat suit that showed off her baby bump, and matching Air Jordans.

When the guard finally called out "Miller", Tywanna stood up. She noticed the bitch from the photo Jade had sent her exiting the visitation booths. *Can't believe he has this hoe comin' to see him*, she thought angrily.

Tywanna jumped in Surprise's face and said, "Who were you hear to see?"

"Um, s'cuse you?" Surprise wasn't aware of who the pregnant girl was addressing her.

"S'cuse you, hell. Don't tell me you were here to see my baby's daddy, Diamond!" she yelled.

Ashley jumped in between the two. "Tywanna, what's yo' problem?"

"She's the hoe whose been fuckin' Diamond!"

"Hoe?" Surprise tried keeping her composure. "Look, I ain't here for all that, so back the fuck up off me. Maybe you need to talk with Diamond."

"Don't act all cute and snotty like I won't beat yo' ass in here," Tywanna threatened her.

"Ty," Ashley intervened, "you go and see Diamond and leave her alone. 'Cause she ain't the one you should be heated at." She ushered Tywanna down the corridor for her visit with Diamond.

Surprise made her way out. She hoped Diamond would be able to square things away with his wifey.

The visit with Surprise wasn't what it seemed on Diamond's behalf. He permanently felt the need to put a stop to their fling all because he didn't want anybody but Tywanna, and she deserved his commitment. He understood that just because a bitch could fuck him good, it didn't mean she was good for him.

The C.O. halted Diamond as he was headed for his cell. "You have another visitor. Booth two. Must be your lucky day," he scoffed.

*Must be Major wit' some news*, Diamond considered. He returned to the visitation booths and was both delighted and surprised upon seeing Tywanna on the monitor. "Damn, bae, wasn't expectin' to see you. Good thing you're out," he smiled.

"Don't even sit here and act like that hoe ain't just come see you. How could you have her here while I had to sit in jail for yo' ass, Diamond?" Tears fell down her cheeks.

"It wasn't even what it look like."

"You lyin'-ass nigga!" she yelled.

"Calm da hell down, Tywanna."

"Fuck was she doin' here then, huh?"

"'Cause I wanted to tell her ass you're the only one for me!" he shouted, fuming. She fell silent and just eyed him. "Ty, I wanna marry you and establish a strong family. The only things that matters to me are you and our treasure. Treasure…that's her name."

Tywanna felt foolish for mouthing off to him. In close to a whisper she said, "Diamond, I'm sorry."

"It's cool. Jus' don't ever again use yo' sexy lips to accuse me. I know I cheated before, and believe me, I regret it. And when I come home, you won't have to worry about that anymore."

"And when do you think that'll be? And what about all our possessions they seized?" she asked desperately.

"Levin's on top of both. He's tryna figure it all out."

"Well, what am I s'posed to do?" Her voice trembled. She was using all of the strength in her to keep from breaking down.

"Jus' use the bread you have left over to take care of yo'self for now. I'm sure Ash will help 'til I'm home. And trust, I'm comin' home so wait for me."

During the ride, Tywanna explained that the whole thing was just a misunderstanding. "Can't believe I acted like that."

"From the looks of shit, you had a right to be upset," Ashley commented. "Well, now at least you know, and obviously the nigga loves you."

And Tywanna loved him, too. She felt his strength, craved his love and affection, felt safe tucked at his side, and was confident that everyday he'd make the right moves for his family. Although she understood that if he was to remain part of the drug empire he built he had to acknowledge that he should be unattached. Or, who-ever he loved will be inevitable targets.

\*\*\*

"Agent, how the hell is it that I have you on my payroll to pro-tect my distributors and Diamond ends up pinched?" Frank was en-raged about Diamond's arrest because not only was he Frank's most profitable distributor, but he also was out of the money Diamond owed.

"Frank, I can't see everything coming, don't have eyes in the back of my head, you know," Lynch responded hesitantly.

"Then I suggest you grow a pair. Look, I don't give a shit what it takes, I want Diamond out."

"It's not that simple, Frank. Diamond's charged with some things not even I can help him out with. We'll just have to see if the charges stick," Lynch deceived.

Unbeknownst to the mob boss, Lynch was actually the reason Diamond was on lock. As long as Diamond was out of the equation, Lynch figured it'd be easier to succeed in seizing power over the drug trade.

"Either you find a way to get Diamond off, or you find a way to get me the money he owes me, Agent."

## Chapter 16

Banks and some of his crew were at the seedy Diamond Inn hotel. They were there having a hotel party.

"Damn, what's takin' shorty so long to come bounce dat ass," Big Man griped while he and the others impatiently awaited the stripper to entertain them.

Jade stepped into the bedroom, where Surprise was getting prepared, and she closed the door behind herself. "Bitch, yo' ass need to get out there 'cause them niggas waitin' to cash you out."

"I won't be long," Surprise told her. Since Red Velvet was momentarily shutdown Surprise could use the extra cash. And the best part about it is she was able to keep all of her tips. "What about you, ain't you dancin', too?"

"Girl, my nigga out there, what I look like dancin' for his crew?" She grabbed her pocketbook, pulled out a baggy of coke, and laid out a line on her pocket mirror. "Besides, more coins for you. 'Cause if I danced wit'chu, then yo' ass would hardly make a penny," Jade jeered. She snorted a line of the coke.

"Jade, you tried it!" She slipped into red lingerie. Her figure was looking good, ass and titties juicy. Her body was snatched.

*Bitch, you ain't all that*, Jade wanted to say, but instead said, "You doin' the hell outta that look."

"Good. 'Cause I ain't bring shit else to wear."

"Shid, it really don't matter what you wearin' 'cause them niggas payin' to see a bitch get naked anyway. Okerrrt!" Jade sounded off, mimicking Cardi B, and they both laughed.

"True dat." Surprise couldn't agree more. She looked in the mirror at herself.

Jade took a seat on the bed. "Surprise, I see you really liked workin' for Diamond, huh?" she solicited.

Surprise applied some lipstick and then said, "Long as a bitch gettin' paid."

"Girl, I see y'all be eyein' each other and shit. What's up with that?" she asked coolly.

"He and I are just cool, that's all." Nonchalant.

"Bitch, bye! Spill the tea, is his dick good?"

Surprise looked back over her shoulder at Jade. "No lie, the nigga do got some good-ass dick," she grinned.

"I'm sure you hopin' he gets outta jail sometime soon."

"Well, when I visited him, he told me he'd be gettin' out sooner than people think," she divulged.

Jade wasn't expecting to hear she had gone to visit the nigga. "And durin' these visits, what do y'all talk about now?" she probed.

"Jade, wouldn't you like to know? And for the record, it was only once. Strangely enough, his baby's mama happened to show up, and the bitch started screamin' at me and shit, like she knew me and Diamond had fucked around. I can only imagine how her visit went with Diamond."

It satisfied Jade to know Tywanna crossed paths with Surprise the way she did. "Baby's mama drama is the worst. Bitches all mad at you 'cause their baby's daddy choosin'. Well, bitch, maybe if you was fuckin' and suckin' the nigga right, then he'd bring his ass home," Jade commented.

"Preach, bitch!" Surprise agreed.

Jade tooted another line of coke. "Look, girl, hurry up and get out there and make that schmoney." She put her drug paraphernalia away before heading out.

Meanwhile, Banks grabbed a bottle of Ciroc from the bucket of ice cubes, then handed it to Ice. "Real shit, I got love for the rest but, you and I are cut the same," Banks was saying. "Jus' look at them niggas." He gestured towards the rest of his crew, who were anxiously awaiting the stripper. "None of 'em have any self-control. Fuck can I trust 'em wit' my life? But you, I trust."

"I feel you, dawg. Jus' lemme know what it is you need me to do," Ice replied, down for whatever. He turned the bottle up to his lips.

"For now, jus' stay ready. I'm on somethin' major..." Banks let his words trail off, hoping Ice didn't take offense to his word choice. "My bad. I know how you feel 'bout that nigga," he sympathized.

"Ain't shit. I'ma ice his ass the first chance I get," Ice swore. He had it out for Major, and the only thing that would satisfy him was taking Major's life.

Shaped by the streets, all Ice knew was hustlin' and staying strapped. Twenty-one years old, he was a tan complexion with long dreads and a smaller build. His demeanor was chilling because he had ice in his veins.

Big Man stepped over by Banks and Ice. "Dawg, this party lame." He grabbed the bottle from Ice and took a gulp. "Aye Jade, come pop dat pussy for a real nigga," he said as she walked up. Banks shot him a death stare, making it clear to everyone that Jade was off limits, and Big Man shut the fuck up and fell back.

"You a'ight? What is it?" Banks asked Jade, noticing she seemed bothered.

"Thought you'd like to know what the bitch just told me 'bout Diamond," she answered.

The mere mentioning of Diamond caused Banks to become tense. "Fuck would she know anything 'bout the nigga?"

"Told me she visits him."

"Then she has to have some useful info, and I'm gon' find out."

Just as Banks began to step away, Big Man put a hand on his shoulder halting him and said, "Yo, lemme deal wit' this bitch. Time to get the party started." He made his way to the room, entered, and then locked the door behind himself.

Surprise turned around, startled at the sight of the tall, wide, black-skinned man. "This ain't that," she stated firmly.

"Damn, boo, you bad." Big Man licked his chops, then hit the bottle. He held out the bottle offering her a drink.

"I'd rather not. Where's Jade? I need to holla at her." He grabbed her by the arm stopping her as she went to bypass him, and she snatched her arm away. "I'd 'preciate if you not put yo' damn hands on me," she told him, displaying attitude.

"Chill, baby, I jus' wanna know 'bout da nigga Diamond. I know you visited him. What did he tell you?"

*I know Jade did not run her dick suckers to this nigga 'bout me and Diamond*, she said to herself resentfully. "What Diamond tells me is between him and me. Now would you please get the hell out?"

"Oh, I see. You loyal to dat nigga." He used his fingers to comb hair out of her face, then he clamped her by the throat with one of his bear paw-like hands and raged, "Well, bitch, fuck Diamond!"

Wop-wop-wop-wop!

Big Man struck Surprise over the head several times with the Ciroc bottle, splitting her dome. She fell onto the bed, screaming in agony and horror as blood gushed from her laceration, and she faded in and out of consciousness.

"Nothin'-ass bitch, got somethin' for yo' ass. And you better like it!" Big Man shouted, sounding like a madman. He ripped off her thong, yanked down his jeans and boxers to his knees, and forced his hard dick inside her pussy. He violently rammed himself in and out of her while she faintly begged him "no" repeatedly.

"Hoe, shut the hell up, and take all dis dick!" Big Man demanded and slapped the shit out of Surprise. He flipped her over onto her stomach and then forced his dick into her tight asshole. He grunted as he raped her ass, and blood was everywhere.

The commotion could be heard coming from inside the room. No one attending the party expected shit to go down like this.

"I ain't wit' this shit," Ice stated in condemnation. "I'm out." He, followed by others, filed out of the hotel room.

A moment later, Big Man emerged from the room holding up his jeans in one hand and the blood spattered bottle in the other, breathing heavily. He turned up the bottle and then said, "Bitch ain't wanna give up no info."

"Nigga, what the hell did you do?" Jade asked hysterically as she hurried into the room. She found Surprise raped and beaten to a bloody pulp. Surprise was sprawled across the blood-drenched bed and her pretty face was unrecognizable. "Oh, my God!"

"Let's get the fuck up outta here," Banks urged as he pushed Big Man towards the exit. "Bring yo' ass on, Jade!" he shouted from the adjacent room. After Jade collected her pocketbook, they all fled the hotel, leaving Surprise for dead.

\*\*\*

"Little, leave the kid and I be," Frank directed, and his goon pulled the huge double doors to the den closed and then posted right outside for security purposes. Major took a step towards the chair positioned before the massive oak wood desk Frank remained seated behind. "Hold it right there. Lift your shirt and turn around," he ordered Major.

"All due respect, Mr. Balistrieri, I was cased on my way in," Major protested.

Frank came up gripping a nickel-plated .44 Magnum that was covertly strapped beneath the tabletop of his desk, and he leveled it on Major's chest. "Do as I say. If you have nothing to hide, then it shouldn't matter," Frank spoke evenly. Major obliged, and once Frank saw for himself he was clean, he set the gun atop the desk.

"Please, have a seat," Frank directed, and Major sat in the plush chair opposite of him. "So you're here on behalf of Diamond. How is he?"

"Fine for the most part. He asked me to meet wit' you in order to straighten a coupla things out," Major said reservedly.

Frank sat back in his chair. "I'm listening."

"First and foremost, Diamond wants to ease any doubt or concern you more than likely have of him, given the circumstance. Mr. Balistrieri, I assure you Diamond's loyalty continues to stand wit' you."

"Wonderful. But that doesn't make up for the money Diamond owes me."

"Which is what I wanna get to next."

"Are you gonna tell me you have my money?"

"Not exactly. Although I plan to get every penny of it to you as soon as possible. Thing is, you'll have to provide me wit' the product."

Frank chuckled lightly. "And how will I get the money Diamond owes me out of that?" Curious.

"Well, until Diamond's debt is paid off, I'll move product for you free of charge," Major expounded.

"Doesn't sound bad at all." Frank sat up in his chair. "And what's your angle?"

"After the debt is squared away, I'm willin' to adopt the contract you have established wit' Diamond. The difference is, I won't buy any more product on consignment, only outright."

"Let's say I'm willing to agree to your offer." Frank rose to his feet. "I want you to understand that every payment must be on time and not a penny short." His eyes glinted like a sword edge-up in the sun as he came around the desk. "Or else…"

"Understood."

Frank lit himself a cigar. "Diamond should be proud of you, kid. You're very sharp. I'm sure he wouldn't have sent you if he didn't trust in you. Well, now his debt is officially yours."

\*\*\*

Diamond slammed down his final bone on the table. "Dominoes!" He was in the day-room kickin' it with his homeboys. They bet a friendly wager: loser owes a thousand pushups. And Diamond and Spook, who was his partner, were a house shy of winning.

"Yeah, that's right, wash them mu'fuckas," Spook trash-talked while Lil G shuffled the dominoes.

"Spook, yo' game's trash. You lucky Diamond's carryin' yo' ass. If anybody, yo' bird-chest-ass could use some pushups right about now," Lil G's partner, O cracked, and caused others around to laugh.

While watching the Fox6 news, Juvie recognized the victim plastered on the screen. "Say, Diamond, didn't ol' girl work at yo' strip joint?" he asked, pointing at the TV.

Looking over at the screen, it hit Diamond like a ton of bricks when he saw the photo of Surprise. He jumped to his feet, then hurried over to the TV area. "Everyone shut da hell up so I can hear!" he shouted over the crowd around, and then listened close as the news anchor made her report.

"The body of twenty-three-year old Mary Rice was discovered at the Diamond Inn hotel yesterday evening. Authorities report that the victim was raped, and had been beaten to death with a blunt object. The room she was discovered in had been checked out under a false name. At this time during the investigation, authorities report there are no leads to any suspects..."

"Turn it off," Diamond ordered, not caring to hear anymore. *Who the hell woulda done this shit to her?* he asked himself introspectively. If only he knew.

"Hoe prolly got raped and bodied for bein' stuck-up," Spade commented unremorsefully to his boys and dapped one of them.

Diamond stepped to Spade and spat, "Nigga, have some fuckin' respect!"

"Nigga, only thing I respect is the game." He stared daggers at Diamond before stepping off.

\*\*\*

Upon entering the small venue, Tywanna and Ashley were met with an audience singing along with the singer's tune.

The woman on stage, Spirit, was bald with her brows on fleek, and the burgundy lipstick she wore popped off of her light skin. She rocked a black tight Norma Kamali dress and a banging pair of burgundy 6-inch Balenciaga sling backs. Spirit's voice was soulful while she sang with conviction about love.

Tywanna and Ashley found a small table for two near the stage. A busboy approached and took their orders. Tywanna opted for a glass of ice water with a fresh lemon slice, and Ashley a Dolce La Pierre cocktail. A moment later the busboy returned with their drinks.

"Ty, since when are you into the music scene?" Ashley inquired.

"Actually, I was invited here. Besides, I've always thought of musicians as poets."

"So, who exactly invited you here?" Ashley sipped at her drink.

"A friend of Diamond's and mine."

"And what friend of yours I'ont already know?"

"One I'd like you to meet," Tywanna smiled.

Ashley sat her drink on the table. "Uh uh, Ty."

"What?" she feigned ignorance.

"I know yo' ass did not drag me here to meet some nigga."

"Trust, girl, you'll like him," Tywanna assured.

"And what makes you so sure?"

"See for yo'self, 'cause there he is now."

Major stepped onto the stage, his dominant and alluring presence commanding attention from the audience before him. He wore some Balmain blue distressed jeans, a white button-down Tom Ford shirt with the sleeves rolled up, and some brown leather Balmain Taiga boots. He easily had on five racks worth of gear, not including the Audemers Piquet he wore on his arm. He looked like money.

*Damn, the nigga is lookin' like a snack*, Ashley admitted to herself.

As Major grabbed the microphone for a mic check, he took notice to Tywanna sitting among the crowd with her absolutely gorgeous homegirl, who he briefly held eyes with. He looked over the sea of faces before him. The trap/soul beat dropped and he spit his rhymes.

♪As far as I can see, I done seen it all/
half the things I've seen, most ain't seen at all/
y'all ain't seein' me, but I be seein' y'all/
you hate to see me stand, you'll love to see me fall/
but you gon' see me ball, like I was on the court/
I seen more than I shoulda seen when I was on the porch/
I seen niggas get rich, seen niggas get jacked/
seen niggas get indicted, and seen niggas get whacked/
then I jumped off the porch and seen all that shit up close/
niggas tried to dead me, now I'm like seein' a ghost/
when I look into their faces all I see is fear/
they'll love to see me gone 'cause they hate to see me hear/
my mama ain't gotta cry but I can still see her tears/
I was once blind to the facts but now I see 'em clear/

and I can see my future, I can see years ahead/
I see myself rich, doin' life, or either dead/
and I'ma see to it that my family get fed/
I don't see nobody, I'm aimin' for the head/
I done seen poor, I done seen rich/
I done seen the realest niggas turn into a snitch/
I done seen the truth, I done seen the lies/
I done seen my life flash right before my eyes.../♪

Following Major's performance, Ashley found herself applauding along with the rest. "Now that was dope!"

"That it was," Tywanna agreed.

After exiting the stage, Major dapped a couple of cats and hugged Spirit as he made his way over to Tywanna and her friend. "Glad you could make it," he addressed Tywanna.

"Thanks for invitin' me. Major, this here is my girl Ashley," she acquainted the couple.

"Pleasure to meet you, Ashley," Major smiled and embraced her petite hand in his gentle grasp. *Shorty even finer up close*, he mentally noted.

"Likewise," she blushed.

Ty peeped her girl drooling all over Major. "Why don't you pull up a chair and join us?" she requested.

"Sounds good." Major grabbed a chair from the vacant table beside them and positioned it between both the girls. He waved over the busboy. "I'll take a glass of Hennessey on the rocks. And get the ladies another of whatever they're havin'." After the girls gave their orders the busboy went on his way.

"So who's yo' friend-girl?" Ty questioned.

"Oh, you mean Spirit. She's jus' an artist I work wit' on my record label, Major League Records," Major answered.

"Well, homegirl can blow!"

"I enjoyed yo' performance. It was real, to say the least," Ashley complimented Major.

"Thanks. I only rap what I live, it's easier for me to express myself that way."

"Yeah, you rocked the mic up there," Tywanna piped in.

"Glad you liked it, 'cause the shit I've seen wit' Diamond was the inspiration behind it. Have you spoken wit' him lately?"

"He called earlier today."

"And?"

"Said his attorney doesn't think the charges against him will stand."

"More than likely they're trumped-up charges anyway. If there's anything I can do to assist in him wit' gettin' back to the streets then jus' let me know."

"You bein' loyal to him is all I can ask for. He's just ready to come home, and I can't wait to have my baby back. Me and Treasure."

"Who?" Ashley asked perplexed.

"Treasure is our daughter's name. Diamond picked it out, said it's because she's his treasure," Tywanna divulged.

"And a man will protect his treasure wit' his life," Major added.

"Any man that'd do so is worth lovin'." Ashley thought about Chase.

Major looked to Ashley. "Sounds to me like you know somethin' about it. I take it yo' man is overprotective of you," he probed coolly.

Ashley fell silent for a brief moment. "Well...he used to be," she said barely audible.

He understood. "My condolences."

In order to shift the mood, Tywanna stood and said, "It's gettin' late and I need to rest up for the baby."

"Then I'll take you home," Ashley responded.

"It's okay, girl. You stay and chill with Major. I can take an Uber."

"Nuh uh, I won't stand for you takin' an Uber this late in yo' condition," Ashley protested.

"Then I'll just take yo' car, and Major will give you a ride." Tywanna grabbed Ashley's keys off the table before Ashley could respond.

"Ashley, if you don't mind, I'm cool wit' that idea," Major piped in.

"She don't mind," Tywanna answered for her.

"Guess I'ont have a choice." Ashley peered through slit eyes at Tywanna, who wore a smirk.

"Major, you just make sure my girl gets home safe."

"Without even a scratch," he promised.

"And Ash, I'll see you first thing tomorrow mornin'. You two enjoy the rest of the night." Tywanna bounced leaving the couple alone.

As the night prevailed, Major showed Ashley the undivided attention she was in need of. He listened closely to her and seemed to know all the right things to say. Their conversation was mutually enticing and intriguing. He had a way of making her feel comfortable and secure in his presence, so much so that she opened up about her twins and relationship she had shared with Chase and how losing him affected her. He had been familiar with Chase, but didn't have much of a bond with him.

Major wiped away the tears that rolled down Ashley's cheeks. There was something about her that he adored, even admired. He took her as a woman he could respect. Major took a swig of his Hennessey and then said, "Tell me, Ashley, where do you see yo'self in the future?"

"I hardly think about the future. It comes soon enough."

Major sat his drink on the table. "Seems to me it's not the future you're afraid of, it's repeatin' the past that makes you anxious." He combed Ashley's hair out of her pretty face using his hand and said, "Listen, I ain't no saint, but every sinner has a future."

Before they knew it, Major's and Ashley's lips locked as they shared a passionate kiss. Their chemistry was undeniable. The entire night they were lost in each other's presence, as though no one else existed. He made her feel a way she hadn't felt since losing Chase.

Abruptly, Ashley pulled away and said, "Sorry, Major, I can't." Thoughts of Chase caused her to feel guilty, for she was still grieving him.

"It's cool," Major replied smoothly. "How 'bout I get you to the crib for the night?" He stood and then helped her into her jacket before they headed towards the door.

*Here I am with a good nigga and can't seem to keep Chase off my damn mind. Hope Major can forgive me,* Ashley contemplated.

Major held the door open for Ashley, and all of a sudden he pulled her back inside.

Blocka! Blocka! Blocka! Blocka! Blocka!

\*\*\*

Urrrkkk!

Tires squealed as the Cadillac Escalade peeled off. Big Man applied pressure to the accelerator once Ice had jumped inside the whip after bustin' at Major.

While they had been moving through traffic, Ice had taken notice of Major's silver Audi Quattro parked before the building. Once Ice had stuck his head inside the place, he found Major standing on stage in the spotlight, and Ice wanted to shoot his ass dead on the spot. But he figured it'd be better to ambush the nigga as he was stepping out.

Big Man bent a sharp right at the corner. "You downed his ass?" he wanted to know.

"Can't say. Fuckin' gun jammed on me," Ice replied disapprovingly. He snatched back the slide of his .40 and released the shell wedged inside its chamber.

"Nigga, tol' yo' fool ass to grab da K from the backseat."

"Big Man, shut da fuck up wit' all that 'I-told-you' shit," Ice fumed. "That nigga good as dead, if he ain't already."

\*\*\*

"Ashley."
"Tywanna."

In the waiting area of St. Joseph's Hospital, the two hurried to one another. Tywanna wrapped Ashley into her embrace, she could feel Ash trembling uncontrollably, and Tywanna pressed her head to her chest.

Judging by the sound of Ashley's voice over the phone, Ty could hear that she was in distress and in need of comfort. So Tywanna had sped all the way to the hospital to be at her friend's side.

"I came as fast as I could. Girl, what happened?" Tywanna asked concerned.

"Major was shot," Ashley sobbed while in Tywanna's arms. "We were havin' a perfect time, and then once we decided to call it a night, as we were headed out the place and someone shot at us."

"That's horrible."

"If it wasn't for Major, I coulda been killed. He saved my life, Ty," she expressed gratefully.

Tywanna dreaded the answer to her follow up question: "Is Major alright?"

"Yeah, I'm a'ight," Major piped in as he stepped up. "Are you fine, Ashley?"

"She's not the one who was shot," Tywanna said.

"It's nothin'. Jus' a shot in the hand. I've gotten worse goin' for a layup at the park," he replied casually. His left hand was wrapped in a cast. "Ash, my fault the night had to end so damn dramatically. Didn't mean to put you in harm's way."

"Don't fault yo'self, Major. You didn't know any of this would happen," Ashley told him.

"Besides, you did keep yo' word and made sure my girl here was safe. And she don't even have a scratch on her," Tywanna added with a smile to lighten the mood.

"She can always feel safe wit' me," he vowed.

Ashley met Major's eyes and said, "Thank you for the nice time tonight. Maybe we can do it again - I mean, without the dramatics and all." Despite how the night turned out, she genuinely liked Major and cared to give him a chance.

"How 'bout we discuss it while you let me give you that lift to the crib like we had planned?"

All in their mix, Tywanna piped in, "Go ahead, girl. I'll meet you at yo' place and stay by for the remainin' of the night. Unless…?" She raised a brow.

"Tywanna, you need to stop," Ashley replied sheepishly.

"I'm just sayin'. You need some."

Major lightly chuckled and shook his head at the two friends. "Let's get outta here." He took Ashley's hand as they headed out, and he wouldn't mind taking her hand in marriage.

***

Miraculously, the charges against Toni were dismissed with prejudice, so she was being released back into the streets and was more than ready to make her presence felt. While on the inside for the past few weeks, she had a lot of time to think. One thing she thought about most was what the streets would be like with her in power.

Outside of the county jail, Toni stepped into the passenger side of her Benz, and Mateo was pushing the whip. "I missed you while you were gone, baby," Mateo cooed. He leaned over and kissed Toni, and their tongues swirled around in one another's mouth.

Toni slid her hand inside Mateo's skinny jeans. She pulled out his dick and caused him to purr as she flicked her tongue over its tip. She withdrew his dick from her mouth, licked her lips, then said, "Tastes better than I remember. We'll finish this up later. Right now, I got some shit to deal wit'. You bring what I told you?"

"Yes, baby, it's in the back seat."

Toni reached into the back beneath the blanket and came out with a Mini-14 submachine-gun. "Good boy," she praised Mateo. Toni activated the tracking app on her iPhone, reached out, and input the address into the car's GPS. "Let's ride."

Mateo pulled off into traffic. Following the directions on the GPS, it brought them to a compact studio-apartment above a shabby dry cleaning spot. Toni recognized the navy blue Yukon Denali parked out front and knew they had the correct place.

"Park right there," Toni directed, pointing towards the dark side street. "I'll be right back. Keep the ride runnin'." She hopped out with the artillery in hand and approached the apartment.

Boom! Boom! Boom! Boom!

As Toni was finna pull a kick-door, she was unexpectedly met with gunfire from the opposite side. Slugs tore through the timber door, blowing out wood fragments, and before Toni could get out of the way, one hit her in the thigh.

Rrraaa! Rrraaa!

Toni opened up the submachine-gun, returning fire into the apartment.

"Look, Toni, shit don't have to end this way," Pelle shouted from inside the apartment once the shots subsided.

"Pelle, I took you in 'cause I trusted you. And you betrayed me. This the only way shit gon' end!" she snapped and fired more shots.

"It ain't like I wanted to. I had no choice."

"Miss me wit' that shit. Everyone has choices, and we have to live wit' 'em. But in yo' case, you have to die wit' yours." Toni barged inside the apartment, lettin' off. Pelle's handgun was no match for her submachine-gun. She popped him in the chest, rib-cage, and both legs, and he collapsed onto the floor. While Pelle lay on his back bleeding profusely and trying to crawl away, Toni stood abroad him leveling the gun on his top.

"J-jus' hear…me out," Pelle begged as he gasped for air. "It w-wasn't easy for…me to betr-tray you, or D-Diamond. But I was in a t-tight spot, a'ight? Lynch popped me wit' s-some…w-work a while back then he threatened to throw m-my ass in prison if I d-didn't cooperate. Told me if I-I helped him get…rid of Diamond he'd make me the man in the s-streets, and front me wit' as many keys as I w-want."

Toni didn't realize how bad Lynch had it out for Diamond. "And you took the offer," she scoffed. "And why does Lynch need Diamond out the way?"

"Don't k-know…" He coughed up blood that filled his lungs. If he didn't get to a hospital soon he'd bleed out.

"More than likely it has to do wit' greed. Wit' Diamond gone then Lynch could use power-grabbin' muthafuckas like you to make his ass rich. So I'm guessin' you the one who helped him plant that bomb on Diamond's ride. And set us up to get raided at the Theater. But what neither of you planned for was the probability of Diamond or I still standin' when the smoke clears. Well unfortunately for you both, here I stand."

"Think about it, T-Toni. You could r-run the streets wit' me. All y-you gotta do is make s-sure we never again...have to worry 'bout Diamond. And you have that p-power," Pelle tried to reason.

"Can't believe you have the fuckin' audacity to try encouragin' me to turn on Diamond!" she barked.

"Toni, can't y-you see that as long as Diamond's around then..." He grunted in pain. "Then you have n-no chance at levelin' up. He's gonna c-continue to keep you r-right where he wants you, which is b-beneath him. Jus' look at how he g-gave Major the opportunity to run his own cr-crew over you. Diamond knows...y-you have it in you to dethrone him and he'll do anything t-to prevent it. Even if h-he has to sm-smoke you."

"You wrong, Diamond wouldn't. He knows I'm loyal to him. Pelle, you coulda had a good thing, but instead you chose to be disloyal."

"It ain't s-somethin' that's easy f-for me to live wit'!" Pelle raved.

Toni looked him dead in the eyes. "And you won't have to."

Rrraaa!

Pelle's body jerked with every shot, and he died instantly. Before leaving, Toni collected the stash that Pelle had ripped off. She stepped over the corpse on her way out.

"You're bleeding." Mateo noticed Toni's leg was covered in blood once Toni was back in the ride. Mateo dispelled down the side street.

"I'll live," Toni winced.

Mateo could tell that something really bothered Toni. "You fine?"

"I'ont know." Toni wondered if any of what Pelle said was even remotely true about Diamond.

# Troublesome

## Chapter 17

Entering the compact conference room, Diamond found Levin seated behind a table wearing an expensive-looking suit. He gestured for Diamond take a seat in the uncomfortable chair across from him.

"How's it going. Diamond?"

"It'd be better if I was back in my natural habitat."

"About that." Levin leaned forward and folded his arms atop the table. "It took some doing, but I managed to get your conspiracy charges dismissed. Turns out there was no substantial evidence to corroborate the allegations against you to begin with. Since there were no drugs, firearms, or cash found on the scene, the prosecutor saw things my way. Not to mention the only witness against you was discovered murdered a few days ago. Authorities believe it was a drug deal gone bad, so you're in the clear on that."

"Good riddance. Nigga tried to help the fuckin' alphabet-boys railroad me," Diamond stated with resentment. He figured that Major had a part in Pelle's timely murder. "Now that the charges are dismissed, I can get back to my life..."

"Not so fast," Levin rejoined. "There's still the attempted murder of an officer charge which needs to be sorted out."

"It's like I told you, I was under the impression that they were robbers instead of DEA," he replied angrily.

"And since the authorities failed to announce themselves when kicking in the door, you had every right to fire your weapon. You just need at least one of them to admit to it. Because it won't be easy putting your word against federal agents'."

Diamond knew exactly how to get Lynch to do as he needed. He leaned back in his chair. "Levin, I need you to get in touch wit' Agent Lynch. You tell him to either help me outta here, or I'll be sure to have a talk wit' Frank Balistrieri."

\*\*\*

Jade had been having morning sickness lately. In her bathroom, she took out a Clear Blue pregnancy test, pissed on it. then awaited its results. "Pregnant".

*Can't believe this shit*, Jade said introspectively. She took a seat on the closed lid toilet, her head spinning from the news. It wasn't that she didn't want to have a child, her biggest issue was that she couldn't exactly say who the father was, Gangsta or Banks. How was she going to tell either of them that she didn't know which of them was the father of her child?

Hearing a knock at the front door brought her back to reality. Jade hurried and hid the test in the medicine cabinet, knowing it was Banks at the door. He had no idea she was pregnant, and for now, she preferred to keep it that way.

"I'm comin'," she announced at the second round of knocks as she approached the door.

"Damn, shorty, what took yo' ass so damn long? Lemme find out you hidin' another nigga in here," Banks cracked as he stepped inside of the apartment then locked the door behind himself. He stepped to Jade and pecked her on the forehead.

"Boy, stop. I was in the bathroom," was all she offered. Jade took a seat on the sofa like everything was normal. She noticed how sharply Banks was dressed and asked, "Where do you plan on goin' tonight?" while flipping through channels on the TV, stopping on *Basketball Wives*.

"My usual spot around eight tonight." He placed his iPhone and .9 on the end-table then took a seat beside her. "Actually, you're goin' wit' me. Need you to be there to bust a move for me."

She looked over to him curiously. "What kinda move?"

"I'll fill you in on the details on the way," he replied. "Besides, all you have to do is look fly and play yo' role. Somethin' Lexi had no problem doin' for me." He noticed her change of expression and asked, "What's that face for?"

"It's just...whenever you mention Lex, I can't help but feel like you're comparin' she and I," Jade admitted.

Banks pulled her closer to him. "Listen, Lexi can never be replaced in a nigga's heart. But it doesn't mean I'ont have enough room in my heart for you. Honestly, I never expected things would turn out this way between us. But I'm startin' not to regret it. Lexi meant somethin' to both of us, and I'm sure if she was still here, neither of us would do anything to purposely hurt her."

What Banks said had actually made Jade feel worse. Because, quiet as kept, she was partly the reason Lexi wasn't here anymore. A tear slid down her cheek and Banks wiped it away. He kissed her, allowing their tongues to dance. His feelings towards Jade was more than he anticipated.

After the two unrobed, Banks bent Jade over the armrest of the sofa, and she reached back and grabbed his hard dick, then guided it inside her tight asshole. Banks smacked Jade's ass while he dug in her.

"Fuck, Banks! Yesss…hit this ass!" Jade panted as Banks lunged deep inside her. She looked back over her shoulder at Banks enjoying the feeling of his long, fat joint filling her asshole.

"Shit, girl, you comin' out the ass." How wet and tight her ass was encouraged Banks to fuck her harder. He pulled out of her ass then turned her around and sat her on the armrest of the sofa, spreading her legs wide as he slipped inside her twat.

Jade wrapped her arms around Banks, digging her long designer nails into his back. "Ohh… Fuck this pussy, nigga! Put all of that dick deep in it." She began to quiver as orgasm took over her body.

"Damn," Banks groaned. He was on the verge of bustin' a nut. "Dis shit feel so good, boo!"

Jade pushed him back, then dropped down to her knees and swallowed his dick whole. She sucked its tip and slowly massaged it with her warm mouth and soft lips. She looked up into Banks's eyes while sucking on his balls and ejaculating his dick. Banks's toes curled as he busted all over Jade's pretty face.

"I love you, Banks," Jade admitted.

Banks held her chin and replied, "I'd rather you trust me than to love me."

\*\*\*

Ashley did a twirl in the mirror, admiring the person staring back at her. She wore a Donna Karan dress and a pair of Jason Wu stilettos. Her accessories were diamond hoop earrings and matching tennis bracelet. Her hair was wavy falling down her back with a bang swooped to the right, and her beat was light.

"Yaaas!" Tywanna exclaimed. "Girl, you slayin'. So where's Major takin' you anyway?" She was seated on Ashley's bed.

"He didn't say. Just told me to dress fly so he can show me off."

Tywanna watched as Ashley applied finishing touches to her makeup in the mirror. "You really feelin' him, huh girl?"

"Who, Major?"

"No, bitch. The Boogie Man. Yes, Major!" Ty laughed.

Ashley took a seat on edge of the bed. "Tywanna, he's everything a woman could want in a man: fine, respectful, kind, mature, strong, smart, funny, humble. And did I mention fine?" She smiled. "Not only that, but we also have a lot in common. And he and the twins get along well. My only problem is I just can't seem to get over Chase."

"Ash, Chase was the love of yo' life, and the father of yo' children. You'll never get over him. As long as Major can respect that, then he's worthy of givin' a fair chance."

Ashley knew in heart that Tywanna was right. Major seemed understanding, and he never made her feel uncomfortable or forced. She pulled Tywanna in for a hug and said, "Thank you for bein' a friend."

"Best friend. Get it right," Tywanna corrected. "Now make sure you got on yo' good panties."

"Panties. For what?" Ashley grinned.

"Get it, girl, aoow!" Tywanna chimed and they shared a laugh.

There was a knock at the front door. "Ty, you mind gettin' that while I finish up here?" Ashley requested.

Tywanna wrestled her pregnant-self out of bed and made her way to the door. She pulled the door open finding Major. He was rockin' a navy blue and pinstriped Yves Saint Laurent three-piece suit with Mauri gators. Tywanna let him in then closed the door, and he took a seat on the sofa.

"How are you and Treasure?" Major asked.

"Fine. She's already stubborn like her daddy. How's that hand of yours?"

"Doc said I'll be able to have the cast removed in about a week or so. Then I'll…" Major's words trailed off once Ashley entered the front room, and he rose to his feet. She was beautiful to him from head to toe, and Ashley thought he was every bit of fine. They took a moment to drink each other in.

"You two should get goin'," Tywanna said, breaking their trance. "Twins, come say goodbye to Mommy."

The twins came scurrying in from the adjacent bedroom, where they were watching *The Lion King*. Ashely squatted and gave them each a hug and kiss. The twins both ran over to Major and he scooped them up in his arms.

"Girl, you sure you'll be able to handle them alone?" Ashley asked Tywanna.

"Would you stop worryin' and shit? Besides, it'll give me some practice for my own baby. Now you just go with Major, and try to have a nice time."

"Alright. Just call me if you need me to come home."

"Girl, bye. Major, will you please hurry and take her ass," Tywanna said.

Major planted the twins on their feet. "C'mon, Ash, before we're late for our reservations." He helped Ashley into her coat and then led her out by her hand.

***

Fox & Hounds was alive. Glasses were clinking, and silverware in action as the diners flowed in and out. Banks and Jade fit right in with the well-dressed crowd; Banks in a Versace button-down, slacks and loafers, and Jade in a super-tight Chanel dress with Vera Wang heels and handbag. Together they were the perfect-looking couple.

To ease her nerves, Jade took a drink of the bubbly. She felt eerie being with Banks in the exact place where he'd last seen Lexi before she'd been killed. She was just ready to do her part in Banks's deal and get the hell out of there.

"Jus' relax. Everything will go smoothly," Banks comforted Jade, seeing that she was a nervous wreck.

"That's not it, Banks."

"Then what is it?"

"Don't you feel strange bein' here? I mean, thinkin' of Lexi…" Her words trailed off.

Banks leaned back in his chair. "Can't think about that right now. I'm here on business." He grabbed her hand and told her, "Relax and focus on doin' yo' part. And we'll be outta here soon enough."

Banks was there to meet with one of his out of town clientele. He had Jade along to make the transaction. Her part was to look good and act natural so the deal could go undetected. Making eye contact with his client, who was seated across the room, Banks gave him the signal by casually glancing at the Rolex on his arm. The client leaned over toward the gorgeous mahogany-skinned chick accompanying him and whispered something into her ear, then she raised from her seat, grabbed her Kate Spade purse, and casually headed for the ladies room.

"Baby, go do yo' part," Banks told Jade. She collected her bag and stood, then Banks pulled her lips down onto his. As she made her way towards the ladies room he checked out Jade's ass. He grabbed his glass of bubbly and then took a drink of the Moet.

Jade entered the ladies room then stepped up to the sink beside the mahogany-skinned chick, who was applying some lipstick. Jade set her Vera Wang bag on the sink beside the Kate Spade purse. Never making as much as any eye contact, they made the transaction and then the chick turned for the door.

Jade pulled a .25 handgun from her bosom. "Nuh uh, bitch, where you think you goin'?" she said, stopping the chick in her tracks.

"S'cuse you?" The chick seemed throwed.

"Lemme check the shit before you decide to go any-damn-where." Jade looked inside the bag, and once she made sure all the cash was there, she concealed the gun in the bag before she made her way out.

***

Major pulled the Audi to the curbside and parked outside of Fox & Hounds. He observed how Ashley seemed disturbed. "Some-thin' the matter?" he cared to know.

"Well, I'm sure you don't know this, but this is the place where my homegirl, Lexi, was murdered," Ashley divulged. "It just brings back memories."

"My bad. Had I known, then I wouldn't have even considered bringin' you here. How 'bout we go someplace else instead? Let's just go someplace we can talk."

"I'd like that," Ashley told him. Major brought the engine to life, and just as he was about to pull out into traffic Ashley noticed Jade and Banks emerge from the restaurant walking arm-in-arm. "OMG!" she exclaimed in surprise.

"What is it?"

"Can't believe Jade's here, and with him of all people."

"You mean Jade from Diamond's club?"

"Yep. Hoe used to be a close friend of mine, until she started fuckin' Lexi's man. And from the looks of it, I would swear they're boo'ed up. I can't stand for this shit." Abruptly, Ashley pushed open the passenger door and jumped out into the cold weather.

"Ash, what the hell are you doin'?" Major hurried out of the whip after Ashley as she stormed towards Jade. She was furious that Jade had the fuckin' nerve to bring her ass to the very place Lexi had been killed, and with Banks, as though it didn't matter.

Smack!

Ashley open-handed Jade right in the face. "Hoe, you ain't shit! I should whoop yo' ass right now!" Major rushed over and grabbed her.

Caught off-guard, Jade was at a loss for words. Tears welled in her eyes.

"Yo, my nigga, calm yo' damn girl down," Banks told the man whom he failed to notice was Major - that was, until their eyes met.

"Lexi was our friend, and you disrespect her like this. And Banks, you ain't no better," Ashley stated heatedly. "Both of y'all can go to hell." She broke free of Major's hold and ran back to the ride.

Jade stood there with her guilty conscience screaming at her. She was in a daze.

Banks planted a hand on the small of Jade's back, causing her to startle a bit. "Baby, go on get in the whip and I'll be there in a sec," he told her. Once she stepped off, Banks turned his attention to Major. "I hear you the nigga holdin' shit down now."

"You heard right." Major was assertive.

"Sure you can handle that kinda pressure?" He stuck his hands inside the pockets of his Versace slacks. "I mean, pressure busts pipes or makes diamonds. There's already a Diamond. And you could never be him."

Major scoffed lightly. "All due respect to Diamond, I'm my own man."

Banks turned for his whip, and over his shoulder he said, "Then I hope you're man enough to take a bullet."

*Not if I put a bullet in yo' head first*, Major thought. Returning to his Audi, Major entered and found Ashley crying. It did something to him to witness her cry because he adored her smile so much. "You a'ight?" he asked gingerly.

"Just can't believe Jade's ass. I could kill her right now."

"Remind me never to get on yo' bad side."

"Boy, whatever!" She smiled.

"Now there's the smile I adore so much," he complimented. "Listen. Once again, my fault that our night had to end filled wit' so much drama."

"Who says this is how our night has to end? I'm still up for goin' someplace to be alone and talk."

"I know the perfect place." He push-started the Audi and then dipped into traffic down the street.

\*\*\*

Major and Ashley sat parked overlooking the lakefront. The scene was blanketed with snow due to the snowfall. And the night sky was adorned with stars that sprinkled light down onto the frozen lake making the ice glisten.

"This is so beautiful," Ashley commented.

"Not as beautiful as you." Major smiled. He wrapped his arm around Ashley then pulled her close, and she molded into his hold. "Ash, I been wit' my fair share of girls, but none in comparison to you. All the shit they're in love wit' is my style and looks, all window dressing. Guess what I'm tryna say is you're the best that a nigga ever had," he divulged.

"Aww. That's so sweet of you," Ashley cooed.

"And I'm willin' to make you mine and accept the responsibility of bein' a father figure to those bad-ass twins of yours."

She playfully nudged him and chuckled, "Uh uh, don't do my babies."

"Fa real though, jus' know I ain't hopin' to replace Chase. I'm jus' hopin' to love you 'n the twins half as much as he did." He kissed her on the forehead.

In that moment, Ashley knew that Major had captured her heart. She never imagined she'd gain feelings for another, but Major had a way of making her feel good. I'll always love Chase but I won't allow it to prevent me from lovin' again, she contemplated.

Ashley gazed into his eyes. "Major, tell me yo' feelings are real and mean it," she spoke softly.

"My feelings for you are nothin' but real, Ashley."

"Mine too." She pulled his lips onto hers, their tongues were like two dolphins swimming in sync. Major's hands roamed slowly over her body, his touch made her pussy moist. She unbuckled his belt followed by undoing his slacks, and then she pulled out his hard, long dick admiring its size. She climbed on his lap straddling him, and wearing a dress with no panties made it easy for her to slide down on his pole. She moaned as she rocked her hips back and forth, feeling him deep inside her.

Major kissed and bit her neck. "Boo, dis pussy slippery," he grunted into her ear. He palmed Ashley's ass and began to slam her up and down on his joint.

"Ooohh, Major. Ummm... Just like that, baby!" She grasped his shoulders and threw her head back while she rode him like a bull. "I'm finna cum. Make me cum, Major." She released her juices all over him. Her pussy gripped his dick as she wounded her hips.

"Oh, shit." He lifted her up off him as he busted a nut. Breathing heavily, he said, "Damn, girl. You did that."

Ashley sat back in the passenger seat and pulled down her dress. "Now ain't this a better way to end the night?"

\*\*\*

In his apartment, Banks was seated on the sofa, and Jade was beside him with her heels kicked off in front of her. He counted up the stacks of cash. "Baby, you did good tonight," Banks said. "Jus' didn't anticipate yo' homegirl showin' up. And she really felt a way about us bein' there together. I get that Lexi was her friend, but what we do is none of her damn business."

"I know, right?" Jade's guilty conscience weighed heavy on her. For some time she had the mind to tell Banks about the part she had in Lexi being killed but couldn't seem to bring herself to, partly because she didn't know how he'd react. She knew just how much he'd been in love with Lexi. Shit, she could tell that he still was. She felt that she had to tell him the truth, even if it hurt him.

Jade interlaced her arm with Banks's.

"What, you ain't get enough earlier? 'Cause I got another round in me," he smirked.

"Banks," she spoke hesitantly, "it wasn't my fault."

"Hell are you talkin' 'bout?"

"I'm talkin' about Lexi."

"What about her, Jade?" he eagerly wanted to know.

She burst out in tears. "I was afraid for my life, Banks. I didn't know what to do. He and I were together and he threatened to kill me if I didn't tell him where y'all were that night."

He forcefully pushed Jade off him, and she fell onto the floor. "Bitch, you mean to tell me that if it wasn't for you helpin' Gangsta, then Lexi wouldn't be dead?" He jumped to his feet, enraged. "Knew you was no good from the fuckin' start. Can't believe I betrayed Lexi for yo' ass. I'm stupid for ever even fallin' in love wit' you."

It was the first time she'd heard him profess his love, but it wasn't the way she imagined. "Banks, baby, please. I love you."

"You don't know what the hell love is, Jade! Love is what Lexi had for me," he retorted angrily. "And 'cause of you, I'ont have her love anymore!" Banks grabbed his .9 from the coffee-table and pressed its muzzle to Jade's temple.

"Banks, no! I'm pregnant!" she cried.

He let the pistol fall down at his side. "What?"

"I'm pregnant," she parroted in close to a whisper as tears slid down her cheeks.

The one thing he wanted most with Lexi was a child, and now Jade was giving him one instead. He didn't know exactly how to feel. As badly as he wanted to kill Jade in that moment, he didn't have the heart to. She'd managed to find a place in his heart, making it difficult for him to hate her. "Bitch, get the fuck out. Now!"

Jade hurried to her feet and headed towards the door, leaving behind her belongings. Sobbing hysterically, she looked back over her shoulder at Banks, who'd sat back down on the sofa, and he didn't even bother to look at her. She left barefoot without her coat and pulled the door closed behind herself.

Banks sat there with his head all fucked up. *How the hell could I fall for her ass? And now she's tellin' a nigga she's pregnant. Maybe the baby's Gangsta's. Not only was the bitch fuckin' Gangsta, but she helped him kill Lex. It's time I get rid of that nigga*, he thought with malice.

\*\*\*

Major walked Ashley up to her house, where they stood on the front porch. He didn't want the night to end. Grabbing Ash at the waist he pulled her close to him. "A nigga jus' can't get enough of yo' ass," he crooned thuggishly.

"There's more than enough to offer." She draped her arms around his neck, raised on her tiptoes and they engaged in a kiss. While the couple shared their affection, the front door was pulled open, interrupting their moment.

Standing in the doorway, Gangsta said, "It's time you say goodnight, Ash."

"What are you doin' here right now?" Ashley inquired, sounding annoyed.

"What, I ain't welcomed at you and Chase's crib?"

"That's not what I meant." She turned to Major and said, "Look, thanks for the wonderful night." She pecked Major's cheek before sliding by Gangsta into the house.

"Yo, Major," Gangsta called after him as he turned for his ride. Gangsta pulled the door shut then stepped off the porch and approached Major. "You couldn't even be half the man Chase was to my li'l sista, so don't think for a second you're gonna take his place."

"If it makes you feel any better, I ain't tryna replace him."

"Good," he scoffed. "I'ont know what Ash sees in you, or Diamond, for the matter, but don't make me have to take a look at you."

"Tell me somethin': what's it about Diamond that gets to you?" Major wanted to know.

Gangsta smirked. "Diamond ain't shit. Don't let yo' loyalty for him get'chu smoked." He turned for the house.

Major was beginning to understand that inheriting Diamond's power came with enemies.

Ashley came out from the twins' room, they were sound asleep. "Where's Ty?" she asked Gangsta, who was closing the front door.

"Had to take care of some shit. So she called me to look after the li'l ones." He sat on the sofa.

"Told her to call me if anything came up."

"It's cool. I'ont mind watchin' 'em. Besides, said she ain't wanna bother you and that nigga Major," he said distastefully.

"He's a good nigga, Gangsta." She went into her bedroom in order to slip into something more comfortable.

"Well, he ain't good enough for you," he replied loud enough for her to hear.

"I'ont see any problem with him. And I'ont say shit about you fuckin' Jade's hoe ass," she responded from her bedroom.

"Jade and I ain't up for discussion."

"Mmm. But me and Major is?"

"Rather you not see him anymore," he told her.

Ashley reappeared into the front room wearing silk pajamas. "And exactly why you don't want me to see Major?"

Gangsta couldn't even seem to look at her when he said, "'Cause he ain't Chase, that's why."

Ashley had never really thought about how losing Chase affected Gangsta. Because he hardly allowed his emotions to show, so much so that he didn't even shed a single tear during Chase's funeral. She took a seat beside him. "I know Chase was close to you, so I get why you feel that way. Trust, in the beginnin' it was the same with me also. Then I realized I'll love Chase no matter who comes into my life. And Major respects that."

"Look, I ain't feelin' the idea of you seein' Major. But as long as he treats you wit' respect, then so be it. If he ever hurts you, then I'ma smoke his ass." He stood and then pecked her on the forehead. "Gotta get back to the trap."

"Gangsta, wait." Ashley halted him in his tracks as he was headed for the door. She thought about mentioning to him seeing Jade out with Banks, but instead she said, "I love you, big bro."

"Luh you too, li'l sis." He bounced. If only Ashley knew how lifesaving the info would have been to him.

# Troublesome

## Chapter 18

"Hell's takin' this nigga so damn long?" Banks wanted to know, growing impatient.

"Jus' chill, dawg, he'll get at us when it's time," Ice told him.

Outside of the gambling spot, Banks and Ice were sitting in a black SUV, both strapped. They were awaiting Big Man to let them know when Gangsta was finna leave the spot.

The gamble spot was in full swing. Niggas from all throughout the streets came there to make large wagers. There was all kinds of gambling. The host, Lady was a short, frail older woman with long white hair from aging. She ran a respectable and orderly spot.

Meanwhile, inside the spot, Gangsta lined up his pool cue and sent a striped pool ball to a corner pocket on the table. He bet ten large on the game.

"Easy money," the opponent said once Gangsta missed the shot.

"Would you shut the fuck up and jus' play," Gangsta responded frustrated. He looked over to Playboy, who stood off to the side, and said, "Grab me a shot of Henn."

Lady used her cane to make her way over towards Gangsta. "Now Gangsta, I'ont want none of ya goddam shit in my spot tonight, ya hear? Lucky I let ya black ass back in after what happened the last time," she told him, referring to the brawl he'd been involved in.

"Don't worry, Ms. Lady, I'm cool. And that fight wasn't even my fault, Nigga tried to cheat me. Besides, you know I spend good money here, that's why you let my black ass back in."

From across the room, while blended in with a crowd of craps shooters, Big Man inconspicuously observed Gangsta. He'd been on Gangsta all night. But the nigga had been there for over two hours, and didn't seem to be prepared to leave anytime soon. Fuck it, now or never, Big Man thought as he whipped out his iPhone to send a text.

Big Man // 1:38 a.m.
Change of plan. He ain't comin'

out no time soon, so let's do him
right here.

Banks // 1:40 a.m.
Bet. Jus' cause a distraction.

Playboy handed Gangsta the shot of Hennessey, and Gangsta
drained it one gulp. It was Gangsta's turn on the table, he lined up
his pool cue and did a trick shot, knocking two balls into the side
pocket. He was down to his final ball before being left with the eight
ball. He moved around the table in order to find a good shot, finding
his spot he set up his pool cue.

"Aye. nigga, get'cho damn hands off my cash!" Big Man
shouted, causing commotion. While everyone's attention was
drawn to Big Man, Banks and Ice made their way towards Gangsta
with guns in hand. Banks and Gangsta locked eyes as Banks aimed
his .9 on him.

Blocka! Blocka! Blocka! Blocka!

The impact of the slugs Gangsta took knocked him backwards
onto the pool table. Playboy upped his strap and exchanged shots
with Ice. The spot went into a frenzy. Some bystanders hit the deck
while others stampeded towards any exit. Banks n'em continued
lettin' off as they backpedaled out of the spot. Their bullets left casualties - including Lady, whose white hair was now painted crimson
red from a bullet to her head.

"Shit," Playboy winced once realizing he'd been hit in the side.
He stepped over to Gangsta, who was sprawled over the pool table,
out of it.

***

The cell door was systematically opened, interrupting Diamond while on his bunk reading *Gangster's Code* by J. Blunt. *Hell
these flashlight cops on?* he wondered. He marked his book, and
then went out to see what was up.

At the C.O.'s desk, Diamond was informed that he had a visitor. *Ty ain't s'posed to come 'til tomorrow, so who the hell could this be?* Diamond pondered. He entered the visitation booth, and to his dismay, it was Toni.

"Fuck are you doin' here?" Diamond asked, angered by the sight of Toni.

"Thought I'd come see how you holdin' up in there."

"Toni, it's 'cause of you I'm even in here right now. Had you not brought along Pelle, then none of this would be."

"Pelle's not a factor anymore," Toni told him.

Diamond studied her for a brief moment before realizing exactly what she meant. "But I thought Major..."

"Major?" She scoffed. "Sorry to disappoint you."

"Yeah, well, however, it doesn't make shit right between you and I," he stated.

"I even got the money and shit back for you," she said desperately.

Without even thinking twice about it, he replied, "Keep it."

"All I've ever been is loyal to you, Diamond. I've never used yo' personal weaknesses or confidences against you. I've never even told anyone about our past." Tears formed in her eye wells.

"What happened in the past is jus' that, in the past."

"I been down for you longer than anyone. Can't believe you willin' to turn yo' back on me," she cried.

It'd been a long time since Diamond witnessed Toni shed tears. He knew she was tough, so the fact that she cried made him understand how deeply hurt she was. Of course he had love for Toni and would still even kill for her, and evidently she held mutual feelings. But Diamond wasn't willing to compromise his beliefs.

Diamond stood and said, "Take care of yo'self. Now leave. And don't ever come back here again, Tonisha." He walked out on her, even though it was painful for him to do so.

\*\*\*

"Mind if I come in?" Sandra entered the guestroom, where Tywanna was in bed on her iPhone scrolling through her Instagram page checking out throwback photos of she and Diamond.

Tywanna sat up in bed and said, "Hey Ma. Didn't think you'd be off from work 'til later."

"Well, I decided to take off early to be here with you."

"That's sweet of you, but you didn't have to. I was just waitin' on Diamond's call. He normally calls around this time."

"Baby listen." Sandra stepped over to the bed and sat on the edge beside Tywanna. "I'm concerned about you. With everything going on pertaining to Diamond, I think it's best you move in with me."

"So you expect for me to just leave Diamond? He's the father of my child," she protested.

"If anyone, he's the one who left you to be a single mother."

Tywanna jumped to her feet. "How can you say that? He didn't leave me, unlike when Dad left you!"

"Don't you get fresh with me, little girl," Sandra retorted.

"Well, it's true. Dad left you, and now you have it in mind that every man is like him. Have you ever stopped to think that maybe it was just you?"

Smack!

Sandra suddenly slapped Tywanna, and Tywanna stood there in shock holding her cheek. Her mother had never laid a finger on her in such a manner, but never before had she insulted her mother. On the other hand, Sandra instantly felt horrible about how she reacted. She only cared to help her daughter.

"Baby, I'm so sorry," Sandra uttered.

Tywanna rushed over to the closet and grabbed her luggage, tossed it on the bed then began packing her belongings inside.

"Tywanna, wait, what are you doing?"

"I'm leavin'."

"Where are you gonna go?"

"I'll go stay with Ashley for the time bein', 'til I figure things out."

"You don't have to go anywhere. You can stay here for as long as you need."

Ty yielded her packing. "Ma, I love you and all, but it's best I go somewhere away from you for now."

"Tywanna, I insist that you stay. It's a snowstorm out there, and you don't need to be driving in those conditions," Sandra said in hopes of convincing Tywanna not to go.

"Don't worry about me. I'll be fine." Tywanna grabbed her luggage and stormed out.

"Tywanna, baby…"

Tywanna tossed the luggage into the trunk of her rental car, then she entered the car and put on her seatbelt and was on her way. While on the snow blanketed expressway she phoned Ashley via Bluetooth.

"Hey girl, what's good?" Ashley answered. Major and the twins could be heard playing in the background.

"Ash, I'm on my way to yo' place as we speak." She was trying to maintain control of the vehicle on the icy road.

Ash detected dejection in her friend's voice. "What's the matter, girl?"

"Just had a fight with Mama over Diamond. She actually had the nerve to say I should leave him." Heated.

"You shouldn't be heated at her. I'm sure she only want what's best for you," Ashley reasoned.

"Well, what's best for me is makin' sure my baby has a mother and father. Just 'cause Diamond's locked up doesn't mean he ain't a good man," Tywanna expressed. The car's wipers thudded against the accumulating snow.

"Ty, you ain't wrong for lovin' yo' man unconditionally. Diamond deserves a chance to be in his child's life no matter what."

Tywanna's phone chimed indicating she had an incoming call on the other end. She peeped down in the cup holder at the phone's display, seeing the call was from Diamond. "Ash, that's Diamond callin' now. I'm gonna let you go. Smooches."

"Alright, girl, I'll see you in a sec. And Major says to tell Diamond what's up."

"I will. Ahhhh!"

"Tywanna! You okay?" Ashley heard tires squeal.

Tywanna drove over a patch of black ice, and it caused her to lose control of the vehicle. As the car aggressively fishtailed, she attempted to gain command. The car began to spinout, then lifted off the ground and went tumbling several times before it came to a stop on its side. Fortunately, she'd worn her seatbelt, or she could have been tossed from the vehicle. Tywanna was left with lacerations, contused and unconscious.

\*\*\*

Diamond heatedly slammed the phone receiver on its base. "Damn," he cursed in frustration. He'd called Tywanna three times already with no answer, and he knew she was aware this was around the time he normally called. *Hell's goin' on, why she ain't answerin'?* he wondered. He hated having to be away from his girl and baby, wished he could be there with them.

"Everything a'ight?" T-Money asked, noticing Diamond seemed frustrated. He stood there on security for Diamond.

"Yeah. Ty ain't answerin' and it got a nigga trippin', that's all." Diamond decided to call once more in the hopes that Ty would finally answer. If only he knew why she wasn't able to pick up for him.

"Phone check, nigga!" a familiar voice barked from behind.

Diamond looked back over his shoulder, finding himself staring down a long, sharp shank. With a sick feeling, he saw it was Spade, and his boys were standing there with shanks also. Where had they come from?

"Y'all niggas better kill us," T-Money warned.

"We intend to," Spade retorted. And quickly one of the niggas ran up on T-Money and they began struggling over the weapon. – that was, until others joined in, taking T-Money down.

Diamond never took his eyes off Spade.

"That's right, nigga, look me in the eyes before I dead you," Spade stated menacingly. He lunged at Diamond and rapidly stabbed him several times in the torso, and Diamond doubled-over and dropped onto his knees.

After putting in their work, Spade and his boys scattered, undetected. Diamond touched his stomach then raised his hand seeing it was covered in blood. Right beside him on the floor lay T-Money in a pool of blood with a shank protruding from the side of his neck.

Diamond's weak body collapsed to the floor as he faded in and out of consciousness. So many thoughts crossed his mind in that moment. Thoughts of Major formed. Would he be able to survive what Gangsta and Banks would come at him with? And Toni. He hated to leave her believing he didn't care about her anymore. He thought of not ever being able to see his child. He couldn't leave Tywanna alone. He'd promised her that he'd live every day for her and his daughter.

*Deliver me from my enemies*, was his final thought before everything went black...

To Be Continued...
Trap God 2
Coming Soon

## Submission Guideline

Submit the first three chapters of your completed manuscript to ldpsubmissions@gmail.com, subject line: Your book's title. The manuscript must be in a .doc file and sent as an attachment. Document should be in Times New Roman, double spaced and in size 12 font. Also, provide your synopsis and full contact information. If sending multiple submissions, they must each be in a separate email.

Have a story but no way to send it electronically? You can still submit to LDP/Ca$h Presents. Send in the first three chapters, written or typed, of your completed manuscript to:

**LDP: Submissions Dept**
**Po Box 870494**
**Mesquite, Tx 75187**

*DO NOT send original manuscript. Must be a duplicate.*

Provide your synopsis and a cover letter containing your full contact information.

Thanks for considering LDP and Ca$h Presents.

# Trap God

# Troublesome

KILL ZONE **II**

BAE BELONGS TO ME III

SOUL OF A MONSTER III

By **Aryanna**

THE COST OF LOYALTY **III**

By **Kweli**

A GANGSTER'S SYN III

THE SAVAGE LIFE II

By **J-Blunt**

KING OF NEW YORK V

RISE TO POWER III

COKE KINGS IV

BORN HEARTLESS II

By **T.J. Edwards**

GORILLAZ IN THE BAY IV

**De'Kari**

THE STREETS ARE CALLING II

**Duquie Wilson**

KINGPIN KILLAZ IV

STREET KINGS III

PAID IN BLOOD II

**Hood Rich**

SINS OF A HUSTLA II

**ASAD**

TRIGGADALE III

**Elijah R. Freeman**

KINGZ OF THE GAME IV

**Playa Ray**

SLAUGHTER GANG IV

RUTHLESS HEART

# Trap God

**By Willie Slaughter**

THE HEART OF A SAVAGE II

**By Jibril Williams**

FUK SHYT II

**By Blakk Diamond**

THE DOPEMAN'S BODYGAURD II

**By Tranay Adams**

TRAP GOD II

**By Troublesome**

YAYO II

**By S. Allen**

GHOST MOB

**Stilloan Robinson**

KINGPIN DREAMS

**By Paper Boi Rari**

CREAM

**By Yolanda Moore**


<u>**Available Now**</u>

<u>RESTRAINING ORDER **I & II**</u>

By **CA$H & Coffee**

<u>LOVE KNOWS NO BOUNDARIES **I II & III**</u>

By **Coffee**

<u>RAISED AS A GOON I, II,  III & IV</u>

<u>BRED BY THE SLUMS I, II, III</u>

<u>BLAST FOR ME I & II</u>

<u>ROTTEN TO THE CORE I II III</u>

225

# Troublesome

A BRONX TALE I, II, III

DUFFEL BAG CARTEL I II III

HEARTLESS GOON

A SAVAGE DOPEBOY

HEARTLESS GOON

By **Ghost**

LAY IT DOWN **I & II**

LAST OF A DYING BREED

BLOOD STAINS OF A SHOTTA I & II

By **Jamaica**

LOYAL TO THE GAME

LOYAL TO THE GAME II

LOYAL TO THE GAME III

LIFE OF SIN I, II

By **TJ & Jelissa**

BLOODY COMMAS I & II

SKI MASK CARTEL I  II & III

KING OF NEW YORK I II,III IV

RISE TO POWER I II

COKE KINGS I II III

BORN HEARTLESS

By **T.J. Edwards**

IF LOVING HIM IS WRONG…I & II

LOVE ME EVEN WHEN IT HURTS I II III

By **Jelissa**

WHEN THE STREETS CLAP BACK I & II III

By **Jibril Williams**

A DISTINGUISHED THUG STOLE MY HEART I II & III

LOVE SHOULDN'T HURT I II III IV

RENEGADE BOYS I II III

# Trap God

By **Meesha**

A GANGSTER'S CODE I &, II III

A GANGSTER'S SYN I II

THE SAVAGE LIFE

**By J-Blunt**

PUSH IT TO THE LIMIT

By **Bre' Hayes**

BLOOD OF A BOSS **I, II, III, IV, V**

SHADOWS OF THE GAME

By **Askari**

THE STREETS BLEED MURDER **I, II & III**

THE HEART OF A GANGSTA I II& III

By **Jerry Jackson**

CUM FOR ME

CUM FOR ME 2

CUM FOR ME 3

CUM FOR ME 4

CUM FOR ME 5

An **LDP Erotica Collaboration**

BRIDE OF A HUSTLA **I  II & II**

THE FETTI GIRLS **I, II& III**

CORRUPTED BY A GANGSTA I, II III, IV

BLINDED BY HIS LOVE

By **Destiny Skai**

WHEN A GOOD GIRL GOES BAD

By **Adrienne**

THE COST OF LOYALTY I II

**By Kweli**

A GANGSTER'S REVENGE **I II III & IV**

THE BOSS MAN'S DAUGHTERS

# Troublesome

THE BOSS MAN'S DAUGHTERS II

THE BOSSMAN'S DAUGHTERS III

THE BOSSMAN'S DAUGHTERS IV

THE BOSS MAN'S DAUGHTERS **V**

A SAVAGE LOVE **I & II**

BAE BELONGS TO ME I II

A HUSTLER'S DECEIT I, II, III

WHAT BAD BITCHES DO I, II, III

SOUL OF A MONSTER I II

KILL ZONE

By **Aryanna**

A KINGPIN'S AMBITON

A KINGPIN'S AMBITION **II**

I MURDER FOR THE DOUGH

By **Ambitious**

TRUE SAVAGE

TRUE SAVAGE II

TRUE SAVAGE **III**

TRUE SAVAGE **IV**

TRUE SAVAGE **V**

TRUE SAVAGE **VI**

By **Chris Green**

A DOPEBOY'S PRAYER

By **Eddie "Wolf" Lee**

THE KING CARTEL **I, II & III**

By **Frank Gresham**

THESE NIGGAS AIN'T LOYAL **I, II & III**

By **Nikki Tee**

GANGSTA SHYT **I II &III**

By **CATO**

# Trap God

THE ULTIMATE BETRAYAL

By **Phoenix**

BOSS'N UP **I , II & III**

By **Royal Nicole**

I LOVE YOU TO DEATH

**By Destiny J**

I RIDE FOR MY HITTA

I STILL RIDE FOR MY HITTA

By **Misty Holt**

LOVE & CHASIN' PAPER

By **Qay Crockett**

TO DIE IN VAIN

SINS OF A HUSTLA

By **ASAD**

BROOKLYN HUSTLAZ

By **Boogsy Morina**

BROOKLYN ON LOCK I & II

By **Sonovia**

GANGSTA CITY

By **Teddy Duke**

A DRUG KING AND HIS DIAMOND I & II III

A DOPEMAN'S RICHES

HER MAN, MINE'S TOO I, II

CASH MONEY HO'S

**By Nicole Goosby**

TRAPHOUSE KING **I II & III**

KINGPIN KILLAZ I II III

STREET KINGS I II

PAID IN BLOOD

By **Hood Rich**

# Troublesome

LIPSTICK KILLAH **I, II, III**

CRIME OF PASSION I & II

By **Mimi**

STEADY MOBBN' **I, II, III**

By **Marcellus Allen**

WHO SHOT YA **I, II, III**

**Renta**

GORILLAZ IN THE BAY **I II III**

**DE'KARI**

TRIGGADALE I II

**Elijah R. Freeman**

GOD BLESS THE TRAPPERS I, II, III

THESE SCANDALOUS STREETS I, II, III

FEAR MY GANGSTA I, II, III

THESE STREETS DON'T LOVE NOBODY I, II

BURY ME A G I, II, III, IV, V

A GANGSTA'S EMPIRE I, II, III, IV

THE DOPEMAN'S BODYGAURD

**Tranay Adams**

THE STREETS ARE CALLING

**Duquie Wilson**

MARRIED TO A BOSS… I II III

By **Destiny Skai & Chris Green**

KINGZ OF THE GAME I  II III

**Playa Ray**

SLAUGHTER GANG I II III

By **Willie Slaughter**

THE HEART OF A SAVAGE

By **Jibril Williams**

FUK SHYT

# Trap God

**By Blakk Diamond**

<u>DON'T F#CK WITH MY HEART I II</u>

**By Linnea**

**<u>ADDICTED TO THE DRAMA I II III</u>**

**By Jamila**

**<u>YAYO</u>**

**By S. Allen**

<u>TRAP GOD</u>

**By Troublesome**

**<u>BOOKS BY LDP'S CEO, CA$H</u>**

<u>TRUST IN NO MAN</u>

<u>TRUST IN NO MAN 2</u>

<u>TRUST IN NO MAN 3</u>

<u>BONDED BY BLOOD</u>

<u>SHORTY GOT A THUG</u>

<u>THUGS CRY</u>

<u>THUGS CRY 2</u>

<u>THUGS CRY 3</u>

<u>TRUST NO BITCH</u>

<u>TRUST NO BITCH 2</u>

<u>TRUST NO BITCH 3</u>

<u>TIL MY CASKET DROPS</u>

<u>RESTRAINING ORDER</u>

<u>RESTRAINING ORDER 2</u>

<u>IN LOVE WITH A CONVICT</u>

**<u>Coming Soon</u>**

BONDED BY BLOOD 2

BOW DOWN TO MY GANGSTA

Trap God

www.ingramcontent.com/pod-product-compliance
Lightning Source LLC
Chambersburg PA
CBHW070447260626
47161CB00004B/1227